D0897384

THE LIBRARY, THE WITCH, AND THE WARDER

WASHINGTON WARDERS SERIES (MAGICAL WASHINGTON) - BOOK 1

MINDY KLASKY

ALSO BY MINDY KLASKY

You can always find a complete, up-to-date list of Mindy's books (including books in other genres) on her website.

~

The Washington Warders Series (Magical Washington)

The Library, the Witch, and the Warder

~

The Washington Witches Series (Magical Washington)

Girl's Guide to Witchcraft

Sorcery and the Single Girl

Magic and the Modern Girl

The Washington Witches Series, Volumes 1-3 (a boxed set containing *Girl's Guide to Witchcraft, Sorcery and the Single Girl*, and *Magic and the Modern Girl*)

Capitol Magic (a cross-over with the Washington Vampires Series)

Single Witch's Survival Guide

Joy of Witchcraft

"Dreaming of a Witch Christmas" (a Yule short story)

Nice Witches Don't Swear (a crossover with the Magic and Mayhem Kindle World, available only on Amazon in the US)

~

The Washington Vampires Series (Magical Washington)

Fright Court

Law and Murder

Capitol Magic (a cross-over with the Washington Witches Series)

"Stake Me Out to the Ball Game" (a short story published as part of the
Uncollected Anthology)

Magic Times Two (*Fright Court* released in a two-for-one book duo with a
novel by Deborah Blake)

The As You Wish Series

"Wishful Thinking"

Act One, Wish One

Wishing in the Wings

Wish Upon a Star

The As You Wish Series (a boxed set containing *Act One, Wish One,
Wishing in the Wings*, and *Wish Upon a Star*)

Copyright © 2018 by Mindy Klasky

All rights reserved.

No part of this book may be reproduced in any form or by any electronic or mechanical means, including information storage and retrieval systems, without written permission from the author, except for the use of brief quotations in a book review.

This is a work of fiction. Any references to historical events, real people, or real locales are used fictitiously. Other names, characters, places, and incidents are products of the author's imagination, and any resemblance to actual events or locales or persons, living or dead, is entirely coincidental.

Cover design by Dreams2Media.

Published by Book View Café Publishing Cooperative
P.O. Box 1624, Cedar Crest, NM 87008-1624
www.bookviewcafe.com

ISBN 978-1-61138-724-7

Discover other titles by Mindy Klasky at www.mindyklasky.com

031318mkm

To John H. Johnson III,
who could teach David a thing or two
about grappa-ing up!

1

David Montrose swore as his computer screen faded to black. His keyboard locked and ornate letters bloomed across the dark screen, swirling over an image of Hecate's Torch: *You're doing an excellent job! Take five minutes to stretch!*

It was bad to come into the office on a Sunday.

It was worse to find a foot-high stack of Request for Protection forms in his inbox, all labeled "Urgent."

But it was worst of all to be snared by the computerized web of his employer's latest ergonomic consultant. Whoever had convinced Hecate's Court to implement the automatic lock-out should be shot. No—drawn and quartered. At dawn. After a night spent completing Requests for Protection until their eyes bled.

"Ah, ah, ah!"

The chiding sound came from directly behind him. This time, David managed to bite off the curses that flooded his tongue. It was one thing to swear at a computer. It was another to vent to the one man who could—and would—fire him in seven seconds flat if offered the slightest justification.

Norville Pitt had been applying the fine-toothed comb of

over-zealous management for three years now—ever since David made the rookie mistake of pointing out an error in an invoice his boss had prepared for the court. It was such a minor thing, an accidental double billing for a centerstone purchased by the Atlanta Coven.

It wasn't David's fault that three senior judges of Hecate's Court had been passing by Pitt's office at the precise moment David pointed out the mistake. Or that one of those judges lived in Atlanta and paid particular attention when she heard the name of her home coven. Or that the resulting review of Pitt's work held up the processing of an entire batch of invoices, disqualifying Pitt for a performance bonus at the end of the quarter.

Norville Pitt had despised David from that day forward.

David forced himself to meet his supervisor's gaze above the locked computer screen.

"Slacking off?" Pitt asked, pushing his thoroughly smudged glasses back up the bridge of his nose and peering at his ever-present clipboard.

David bristled. "Just taking the court's mandatory ergonomic break."

Pitt sniffed, the sound reverberating in the back of his fat-padded throat. For just a heartbeat, David fantasized about closing his hands around the man's neck, making those already bulging eyes pop like the rubber stress toys the court had distributed last week—another workplace satisfaction tool mandated by another clueless consultant.

But Pitt couldn't be gotten rid of as easily as a latex squeeze toy, not without a banishing spell. And warders didn't have that type of magical power. So David forced himself to ask, "What can I do for you, Norville?"

"I was monitoring your data entry upstairs."

Yet another indignity David should be used to after three years of banishment to the records division. Every keystroke of his work could be viewed on his supervisor's screen. He waited, knowing Pitt wouldn't be able to resist citing mistakes—real, imagined, or trumped up on the spot.

As expected, Pitt caved first, licking his fleshy lips before he pounced. "On line 27a, you're entering your own name."

"I'm the primary monitor for each artifact," David said with pretended patience.

He certainly didn't *want* to be the primary monitor for the relics he recorded. Most clerks who completed a Request got the dubious satisfaction of seeing their name in the court's records. As far as David could tell, he was unique for the way his warders' powers registered a form. Every time he completed a document, he felt a distinct sensory jangle.

The magical athame he'd cataloged first thing that morning sounded like a burbling stream. The silver goblet on the second Request smelled like fresh-cut grass. The rowan wand he'd been cataloging when the computer froze him out tasted like spearmint. He had a headache from the jumble of sensory input.

But someone had to be responsible for arcane tools not under the direct control of a specific witch. And he was busted back to a file clerk until Hecate herself deemed him worthy of warding a witch directly.

As Pitt never tired of reminding him, David had graduated from the warders' Academy first in his class. He even had the silver ring to show for that superior achievement, a plain band glinting on the middle finger of his left hand.

But he'd been bonded to the Washington Coven's young phenom of a witch, Haylee James. And after more rocky years than he ever should have wasted, she'd come to despise his brand of rules-following protection. She'd cut him loose, making up enough stories that no sane witch would touch him, not with a six-foot wand.

The court had restricted him to file clerk duties, insisting that was the only way they could keep an eye on him, make sure he didn't ruin another witch's career. And now, Norville Pitt wanted to take that from him too.

Pitt's oily smile grew wider as he proclaimed, "According to the September 1 update to section nine-slash-J of Filing Manual 706X, we're taking a different approach to line 27a for all files going forward."

I don't have access to the September 1 update. The changes had become effective almost three weeks ago, but the court would never trust a mere clerk with an actual manual. David wasn't expected to think, to study, to actually read the rules. He only did what Hecate commanded, through the dubious medium of the court's bureaucracy.

And the court would tell him about the September 1 update some time in the new year. It took that long to have training materials drafted and revised and certified by the Central Bureau Administration's Task Force Training Committee. Which Norville Pitt certainly knew. Because he would be the last person to sign off on the materials in question.

David bit back a sigh and managed to keep his voice even. "What's the different approach?"

"Line 27a should now list the direct supervisor of the clerk completing the data entry. Upon review, the supervisor will allocate clerk responsibility for each file going forward. The assigned clerk will then update each individual file."

"But I'm the only clerk in your line of command."

Pitt's frog-like eyes gleamed as he rubbed his hands together. "Yes."

"Then you're going to assign the files to me."

The overhead light gleamed off Pitt's sweating pate as he nodded. "Yes."

David knew there was nothing to gain by complaining. Hecate had set him this test, and he must calmly accept her will. But he couldn't keep from saying, "Then it's an absolute waste of your time and mine, for me to follow the new rule."

Pitt set his hands on his hips, using the motion to hulk over David. For the first time since his enforced break, David wished he'd stood for his mandatory ergonomic adjustment. He would have towered over Pitt by nearly a foot—much-needed distance from the fetid body odor emanating from the yellow-stained underarms of the man's short-sleeve dress shirt.

Pitt grinned. "I took the liberty of zeroing out all the forms you entered today. In fact, all the forms dating back to the first of the month."

Zeroing out. David said hotly, "I could have changed the one field."

"Oops." Pitt eyed him levelly.

David's fingers folded into a fist, but the bell on his computer chimed before he could take any irrevocable action. He glanced at the screen to see the court's decorative script once again rippling over its streamlined image of a torch. *Thank you for taking a break! Now you can return to excellence!*

"David!" A bright voice cut through the crimson fog in his brain. "I'm so glad I caught you here. Norville, I don't think you realize what a treasure you have in this one!"

David stood in automatic deference to the witch who'd entered the room. At the same time, Pitt oiled up his most ingratiating smile. "Linda!" he oozed. "What brings you to the processing center? And on a Sunday night, no less?"

As always, Linda Hudson held herself with the easy grace of a retired ballerina. Raindrops only enhanced her appearance, shimmering on her silver hair and the shoulders of her blazer.

The long-threatened autumn storm must have finally started outside. Not that anyone could tell inside this tomb of an office.

The witch answered Pitt's question, but she kept her eyes on David. "I'm trying to locate an illustrated copy of Rocher's *Scrying with Still Water*, one with the original watercolors tipped in. The Imperial Library has a notation that it's under the control of Hecate's Court."

The instant Linda named the book, David felt a scrape against his consciousness, the prickle of a sycamore burr rasping against his palm. The Rocher book was part of the Adams collection, a carefully compiled set of books that covered all aspects of the Guardians of Water.

The twitch in his arcane memory meant he'd cataloged the volume some time during his tenure as a clerk. He tugged on the bond, and the date rang clear: He'd added it to the court's records almost three years earlier. Two years, eleven months, and four days ago, to be precise.

The first time Linda had visited him in this hellhole of an office.

Then, she'd brought the Rocher as an excuse, as a ruse for getting past Pitt's watchful eyes. She *owned* the Rocher herself. She owned the entire Adams collection. It wasn't actually an orphaned artifact at all.

By asking for it now, she was sending him a secret message.

David's heart rate rocketed as he realized the witch was conspiring against his most unwelcome boss. Linda Hudson needed to talk to David *now*. And she didn't want Norville Pitt knowing what she had to say.

2

Pitt drew himself to his full height, which put his eyes at the approximate level of Linda's chest. Preening, he said, "I'd be happy to search our—"

"I couldn't possibly trouble you for something so routine. I'll let you get back to work now."

Linda was a witch, and she stood in the heart of Hecate's Court. There was no way any warder could dream of protesting her direct dismissal. Pitt cast David a poisonous glance and sidled to the door. "Don't be too long, Montrose," he said, getting in one last shot as his squat finger jabbed his clipboard. "This latest setback will *destroy* your productivity ratio." He stalked out of the room.

David considered slamming the door closed behind the toad. Instead, he reached into his pocket and closed his fingers around a silver device on his keychain, a Hecate's Torch that matched the emblem that had twisted on his computer screen. *Blessed Hecate,* he thought, the words coming fast by force of habit. *Let me always serve you with honor.*

The silver charm marked him as a warder, sworn body and mind and soul to the goddess of witchcraft. He'd received his

Torch the day he graduated from the Academy; he could still remember tasting a splash of brandy when his fingers first closed over the symbol. He carried it with him always, a constant reminder of the oath he'd sworn to uphold Hecate's law, to protect the defenseless, to preserve order throughout the Eastern Empire.

As always, the whorls of metal calmed his pointless rage against Pitt. Sighing, David gestured toward his desk chair, offering Linda the sole seat in his cramped quarters. "I suppose I should thank you for getting him out of here before I did something I'd regret."

Linda's laugh was a refined descant as she accepted the chair. "Then I arrived not a moment too soon."

He gestured toward the pile of forms he'd wasted his day on. "I don't know how much more of this I can take."

Linda's eyes were serious. "The court can't keep you here forever. It's not like you killed someone."

He glared at his silver ring, picturing Haylee's feral grin in its wan reflection. "Maybe I should have."

"Don't even joke about that," Linda warned sharply. "Not even to me."

He sighed. "I'm sorry." He ran his hand down his face, trying to banish the fatigue of nine hours lost in front of his computer. Of three lost *years*, Hecate's will be done... Lifting his chin, he said, "You weren't really looking for a copy of Rocher. What brings you down here on a Sunday night?" He nodded toward her damp shoulders and glistening hair. "It must be important, if you came out in the rain."

She met his eyes steadily. "George's birthday is tomorrow. His sixtieth."

He forced his voice to stay even. "I know how old my father is."

"Come see him, David. That's the best gift you could give him. Give both of us."

He thrust his hands into his pockets and wished the tiny office was large enough to pace. "That's not true." She started to protest, but he cut her off. "I know you mean well. He's your warder, and you only want what's best for him."

"For both of you," she insisted.

He shook his head. "My visiting isn't 'best'—for either of us."

"He loves you—"

David's harsh laugh stopped her from telling more lies. He'd seen the fire in his father's eyes when a three-judge panel broke David's bond with Haylee. "Exhibiting character unbecoming to a bonded warder," they'd intoned. "Unfit to serve. Unsuitable to meet the needs, mundane and magic, of registered witch Haylee James."

David had been ashamed. But George had been furious. Seventeen generations of warding, and no Montrose man had ever been dismissed by a witch.

It didn't matter that Haylee had bent the rules until they shrieked. It didn't matter that David had agonized over breaking ranks, had skipped meals, skipped sleep, had appeared in court as little more than a jangling, desperate shadow of himself.

George despised him for failing.

"I'm sorry," David said, and he was, because he respected Linda. She was a good witch, a strong woman, living outside the petty politics of the Washington Coven even as she worked within its powerful circle. "You shouldn't be caught in the middle here."

"I'm not caught," she said. "I've put myself here voluntarily. Trust me."

He *did* trust her. She'd known him all his life. She'd waded into the Montrose household after his mother died, voluntarily submerging herself in the testosterone-soaked pool of mourning. As his father's witch, she'd reined in George's fury against fate. She'd insisted that David continue his Academy classes even when he wanted to walk away, when he threatened to become a lawyer and end the family's warding history. She'd even finessed James's and Tommy's questions, preserving the Washington Coven's secrets from the boys who were as mundane as the mother they still cried for in their sleep.

Now, as if she hadn't paused for him to say something polite, Linda said, "If you aren't bound to a witch by Samhain, you'll have to work for the court another year."

He laughed in frustration. He'd known the rules since his first week as a cadet. Any warder not bound to a witch by the start of the arcane year was bound to serve Hecate's Court for the next twelve months. "Six weeks," he said bitterly, counting the time till Samhain, till Halloween. "Plenty of time to convince a registered witch to accept a disgraced warder."

Linda shrugged and said, "There are older ways." He couldn't completely silence his snort of disbelief. Nevertheless, she continued. "Hecate held sway long before we witches worked in covens. Make a direct pact with the goddess. Offer yourself to her service on Samhain."

"You're serious," David said.

"I'd never joke about Hecate." When he didn't respond, Linda's lips twisted in sorrow, or maybe something uglier. Pity. She sighed. "I'll ask around some more. Maybe some crone has lost her long-time warder. Your father might have some ideas. Come to dinner tomorrow, and we can all talk together."

"I'll try," he lied.

This time her frown was far more clear. She knew he wouldn't be there. But she stood up, letting her jacket drape gracefully around her slim body. "Offer yourself to Hecate by Samhain, David. Make things right by then."

Right with George, she meant. Or right with some mystical witch who would accept his service outside of the Washington Coven, outside of Haylee's sphere of influence. Or right with Hecate herself.

He shivered at the notion of baring his soul to the goddess. At least Linda left before he had to lie again.

Turning back to his computer and the stack of Request for Protection forms, he tried to convince himself things would go faster as he entered them the second time. He'd already built his warder's bond with each item, storing the unique links in his astral memory. With luck, he could boost his statistics back to where they should be and still get home by dawn.

Five hours and three court-enforced ergonomics breaks later, he reached for the last file. A ball-peen hammer tapped inside his forehead; he couldn't say when its rhythm had started to match his breathing. His senses were muddied, filled with the scents and sounds and sensations of the court's orphaned artifacts.

But he'd proven his point to himself—to himself and to Norville Pitt. He wouldn't be defeated by a random, unannounced change in the rules. Tapping his keyboard, he opened the final electronic form.

Before he could make the last entry, a drumroll flooded his senses. He heard it—the thunder of kettledrums—but he *felt* it too, a simultaneous tug on his body and his mind, sudden and unexpected, like a sonic boom shattering his bones.

He was being called by one of the artifacts he'd cataloged. Not one of the recent ones. Not part of the stack that blurred on the desk in front of him.

This relic was older.

More valuable.

And its call was more urgent than anything he'd felt before.

3

David followed the fading echo of kettledrums onto the astral plane. A steel-grey thread drew him, shimmering in his second sight.

As he yielded to the call, more information sparked along his connection to the summoning relic. The drumbeat was linked to wooden boards bound in leather, covering parchment pages that rippled with age. Without conscious effort, he realized the volume was the medieval *Compendium Magicarum.*

He'd set the bond years ago, in one of his earliest studies as a cadet. Now the amplified drums resonated inside his head, repeating and radiating with the urgency of a Beethoven symphony.

But the kettledrums weren't alone. They were linked to two other entities: The heavy scent of night jasmine and a pure bar of emerald light. The *Compendium* had just been used by a witch— the jasmine—to awaken her familiar—the green light.

Impossible!

Even as David tested the triple bonds jangling inside his skull, he checked the inner calendar that every witch and warder held close. The moon was full that night.

No familiar should ever be awakened on the night of a full moon. Any witch knew that.

Nevertheless, tendrils of jasmine unfurled within his powers, wrapping closer around the shimmering green light. The witch was reaching out, grounding herself in the solid strength of her familiar. Beneath the twining vine of her perfume, the emerald light pulsed, growing stronger as it stretched to full awareness and locked onto the network of all other nearby familiars.

The *Compendium* was the bond that joined them all together —David and the unknown witch and her just-revived familiar. The book drummed through his warder senses because it was being used to shred ancient rules.

On the astral plane, he started to reel in the steely thread that connected him to the misused book. The guide wire pulled him to the edge of the physical world. He braced himself and emerged in a wreath of shadows, reflexively using warder's magic to obscure himself from accidental human observation.

But such caution was unnecessary at a quarter past three in the morning. A quick magical calibration confirmed he was still in DC, in Georgetown, not five miles from the court's offices. His human senses told him he was in a garden, an immaculately maintained one, despite the storm winds that had ripped through earlier that night. Remnants of rain dripped from a tree limb, and he dashed water out of his eyes.

A large stone mansion hulked at his back, its rippled glass windows dark for the night. *Peabridge Library Colonial Garden* read a sign beside the footpath.

In front of him, a cottage glowed like a jack o'lantern, golden light spilling out of every window. He could sense the *Compendium* inside—along with the witch and her impossibly awakened familiar.

Clutching his Hecate's Torch inside his right pocket, David stalked to the cottage's front door and pounded with his left fist. Nothing.

What sort of rogue witch ignored one of Hecate's Warders on her very doorstep?

He knew the answer even as he asked the question. This was exactly the type of rule-breaking Haylee would have loved. He might as well summon the Washington Coven. Let them rein in their own wayward witch—get her under control or face Hecate's Court in the morning.

But who knew which Coven member was on call that night? It might actually *be* Haylee, and she was the last person he wanted to see. The last witch who should be in charge of disciplining a rebel like the woman inside the cottage.

He repeated his pounding on the door.

"I'm coming!" The woman's voice was sharp. But her anger was nothing compared to the rage chewing away beneath his ribs.

A deadbolt shot back. The door swung open.

The witch looked like a refugee from a Girl Scout slumber party—if Girl Scouts accepted members in their mid-twenties. She wore flannel pajamas, a deep cobalt blue sprinkled with white sheep. Her bare feet stuck out of the cuffs, looking cold on her hardwood floor. A Polarfleece blanket draped across her shoulders.

She stared at him as if he were the first warder she'd ever seen. That fake innocence might work on some of Hecate's Warders, but it wouldn't make headway with him.

Glancing over the witch's shoulder, he spotted the familiar. The creature presented as male, with wary hazel eyes peering above strong cheekbones. His hair was jet black and cut short enough to stand on end. David could sense enough of his aura to know he was a cat. A fitted black T-shirt emphasized the feline presence, along with dark jeans that were tight enough to be obscene. He wore sleek leather shoes.

And he was poised to flee into the kitchen. At least one person inside the cottage understood the gravity of the situation.

David swept over the threshold before the witch could mount

a defense. "What the devil do you think you're doing? Awakening a familiar on the night of a full moon?"

She laughed.

Here, in the middle of the night, with a moon-born familiar standing ten feet away, she laughed.

David's rage seared his throat like a habanero pepper. This witch should be falling to her knees, cowering in terror, trembling before the power he represented—all of Hecate's Court in its arcane glory. He might be a disgraced warder, but he was a disgraced warder bound to her *Compendium*, the book she'd just abused.

"What the devil?" she repeated, closing the door behind him.

All right. That probably wasn't the type of curse she usually heard. But he wasn't about to take Hecate's name in vain. The last thing he needed was a witch running to Pitt, reporting him for violating one of his warders' oaths. His pride pricked, he demanded, "What is your name?"

"You're the one pushing your way into my house," she shot back, shifting her feet on the hardwood floor. "Don't you think you should tell me your name first?"

He glanced past the witch to her familiar, hoping to gain the most basic information he needed. The former cat, though, merely gave a shrug.

Now David knew three things about the familiar: He'd just been awakened on the night of a full moon. His native form was a cat. And he'd never met the witch who'd summoned him back to life. Because any familiar with the slightest hint of self-preservation would have had the common sense to answer an obviously enraged warder, if he possibly could.

Tightening his jaw, David returned his attention to the witch. He summoned every ounce of his hard-won warder's dignity to say, "I am David Montrose."

"Jane Madison," the witch said, extending her hand. No sane witch would offer her surname to a stranger—not without a little

pressure. At least she winced after she spoke, as if she'd just realized her mistake.

By force of habit, he shook the hand she offered.

She seemed to gain a little confidence from completing the
social exercise, and her shoulders stiffened beneath that ridiculous blanket. She pushed her glasses back up the bridge of her
nose and demanded, "What are you doing here at three thirty in
the morning?"

Was she actually mad? She had to know someone would
respond to her awakening a familiar on the night of a full moon.

He answered very carefully, delivering each syllable as if she
were certifiably insane. "I'm one of Hecate's Warders." She
stared at him blankly. He would have questioned her understanding of English, if he hadn't already heard her speak. He
went on: "I was summoned by your unlicensed working
tonight."

"My unlicensed working... You mean reading from that book
downstairs?"

"The *Compendium*," he clarified. She truly didn't seem to
understand the magnitude of her offense. Trying to mask his own
growing onfusion, he stuck with basic facts. "You worked a spell
within the territory of the Washington Coven without first regis-
tering with the Coven Mother."

"Look," she said. "I don't know what this is all about." As if to
prove her innocence, she glanced at the familiar.

Obligingly, the creature nodded. "She really doesn't. The poor
thing doesn't know much of anything at all. Just look at those
glasses—can you believe how wrong they are for her face?"

A witch was in violation of the most basic Covenants. David
—a summoned warder—was doing his best to restore a little
sorely needed law and order. And this rogue familiar was offering
fashion advice?

At least the witch seemed dissatisfied with her familiar's criti-
cism. She scowled as she said, "Thanks."

The familiar exposed both palms, shrugging as if to convey, *What else do you want from me?*

David interrupted their little act. "You expect me to believe that?"

He was almost distracted by the buzzing of his phone in his pocket. He had no idea who was calling at this time of night, but he wasn't about to interrupt his interrogation to find out. This witch wasn't trying to skirt the rules. She didn't seem to know there were any rules at all. And that made her very, very dangerous.

She sighed in exasperation. "I don't *expect* you to believe anything! Look. I'll tell you what happened, but I'm not going to get down on my knees and beg your forgiveness. I didn't do anything wrong."

He took a breath, ready to recite the Covenant on Familiar Activation, but she interrupted him before he could begin. "Go on," she said, waving toward the doorway where the familiar still huddled. "Go sit in the kitchen. I'm putting on some real clothes, and I'll meet you in there."

He was shocked. No witch should be *this* brazen. In all the years he'd served the court—as a cadet, as a warder, even as a clerk—no one had ever dismissed him with such an air of casual disregard.

David glanced at the familiar, to see if he was in on whatever game she played. The creature merely gaped at his witch, a look of true horror widening his eyes.

"Neko?" she prompted, as if the familiar were a somewhat stupid child. "Do you know how to put on the tea kettle?" He nodded, apparently unable to find his voice. "Good. The tea is in the pantry. Top right shelf."

She turned toward the bedroom that was barely visible at the back of the cottage. The blanket across her shoulders could have been an ermine cape and her flannel pajamas a coronation gown. She was absolutely in control of her domain.

But then she whirled back toward her familiar. "No," she said. "Not right. Left." She turned back to her bedroom. Took one more step. Spun again to face her accomplice. "Wait! Second shelf from the top."

"I'll find the tea," the familiar said, as if he were more afraid to deal with a crazed homeowner who had lost her teabags than he was to confront a nearly speechless Hecate's Warder.

The witch shut her bedroom door carefully. David waited until he heard hangers slide on the closet rod before he followed the familiar into the spartan kitchen.

"Neko," David said, putting a stop to a tea-based search and destroy mission that would put most ground troops to shame.

The familiar froze in his tracks. "Yes?"

David nodded toward the witch's refuge. "What's her game?"

Neko shook his head. "I don't think it's a game. I'm pretty sure she didn't have the first idea what she was doing down there in the basement."

"There's you and the *Compendium*. What else?"

Neko's eyebrows rose. "You don't know?"

David resisted the urge to sigh. The familiar led the way across the living room and opened a door on the far wall. He gestured for David to descend, apparently to a basement. "There's a light switch at the bottom," Neko said helpfully. "On the left."

David frowned and stalked down the stairs, relying on the light that shone behind him. He palmed the switch at the bottom, wondering what idiot had designed the electrical system in this godforsaken cottage.

The room at the bottom of the stairs leaped into focus.

There were books—a lot of them. They were stacked on shelves, on the floor, on every available flat surface. But there was more than a library, a lot more. His warder senses immediately identified a cache of runes, a jumble of wood and clay and jade tiles. Dozens of wands broadcast their magical potential. Crystals, active and inactive, were scattered around the collection, with a massive reservoir sheltered inside a single wooden box. An iron cauldron, fashioned out of a meteorite, crouched in one corner. In the center of the room stood a carved bookstand. It looked like mahogany, a perfect match for the shelves lining the walls. One volume—the *Compendium*, he knew from the rumble of kettledrums across his senses—was displayed on the stand, its creamy pages glowing in the overhead light. David immediately recognized the spell to awaken and bind a familiar.

"What the hell?" he finally asked.

Neko said matter-of-factly, "The Osgood collection."

"The Osgood—" David started to ask, but the words caught in his throat as his phone rang again.

He didn't consider answering.

Every warder in the Eastern Empire knew the story of the Osgood collection. It had been brought together by Hannah Osgood, one of the most powerful Coven Mothers Washington had ever known. There'd been tragedy in her family—lost children, no heir. She'd hidden her hoard to keep it from enemy hands. Witches had sought the collection for years, ransacking every known safehold, zeroing in on every centerstone ever set. But the books had been missing for generations.

Until tonight.

Until David Montrose found them in the care and keeping of a most unsuitable witch.

4

Stunned, David forced himself to ask, "How—"

The familiar had the temerity to interrupt him. "The last keeper of the collection had a key made. It was hidden where only a witch would find it."

"Which your Jane Madison did tonight."

"Not *my* Jane Madison. She woke me, and I'll serve her for now. But the Collection's last keeper bound me to the hoard itself. I go where it goes."

"You're a familiar, but you're not bound to a witch?" David had never heard of that arrangement before.

Neko shrugged. "I don't make the rules." His lips twisted into a wry grin. "Look, you can stand here and gape all you want. But my witch ordered me to make tea, and I'm not about to fall short on my first assignment."

David nodded, still bemused as he followed Neko up the stairs. His fingers brushed against his Torch, as if that would be enough to bring order and sanity back into his life. Even with his calming little mantra, the kitchen lights seemed too bright. The sound of water filling a teakettle was deafening.

That "last keeper" Neko mentioned... She must have submitted a Request for Protection Form on the *Compendium*. She clearly hadn't trusted the court, hadn't been willing to offer up her riches to their control. Nevertheless, she'd wanted a warder on the case if the collection was rediscovered. Now it was up to him to make the best of things, to manage the greatest collection of arcane wealth he'd ever imagined.

When Jane Madison reappeared, she'd shed her blanket and flannel pajamas in favor of some knit black dress. It managed to reveal what her earlier outfit had not. Behind the off-kilter eyeglasses and the unbrushed brown hair, she had a decent figure. Good hips, anyway. A little flat in the chest, but not enough to matter.

Not that he had time to think about that.

Her still-bare toes curled on the wooden floor. Neko jumped to attention. "Would you like me to get your slippers?"

David automatically followed the familiar's gaze to the back of the couch. He could just make out the curve of plush bunny ears flopping over abandoned footwear.

"No. Thank you," the witch replied, her voice was frosty as her feet looked.

Neko barely noticed. Instead, he said, "You don't have any cream." He managed to make the oversight sound like a mortal sin.

"I drink mine black," the witch said tersely.

At least the water was finally coming to a boil. David watched Jane Madison make the tea, obviously trying to use routine to mask her apprehension. She lined up three mugs from the shelf above the sink, crowing with victory when she found a teaspoon and a saucer to hold the used teabags.

He glanced at the slightly battered box of tea. Oolong wasn't his first choice. That would be gin—sharp and clear, the bite of juniper slicing through the bemused fog that threatened to over-whelm his brain. But his job was to make sure the Osgood collection remained safe and secure, so no gin tonight. Just tea brewed strong enough to hold a spoon upright.

Following the witch's vague gesture, he collected his mug and stalked to the metal table against the far wall. His fingers closed tightly over the cup's ceramic handle as he waited for her to meet his eyes. With a conscious effort, he forced his voice to be civil. "Thank you, Miss Madison," he said.

"My pleasure." She bit off her own words, sounding as stiff as he did. Her formality gave way to nerves again as she took a quick sip of tea. He winced as he imagined her tongue burning on the near-boiling liquid. She mastered any visible response before she set her cup on the table. Taking a deep breath, she said, "All right, then. You're a Hecate's Warder. What is that? Some sort of cop?"

He started to protest the casual language but settled for a tight-jawed nod. "I enforce the Covenants."

"The Covenants?" She sounded as if she'd never heard the word before. "Let me guess. The witches form a Coven? And their laws are the Covenants?"

He gave another nod, still trying to measure how much of her innocence was an act. If he believed Neko, she truly had no idea what she'd done. As if to prove the familiar right, she asked, "You do realize I'm not a witch, right?"

"You worked a spell." His steady voice left her no room to argue. "You have the power. You found the key, and you opened the book. You read from the page."

"Anyone could have done that."

"If you didn't have the power, the key would have stayed hidden."

The simple logic of that statement smothered her reply—for less than a minute. "Even *if* I have some power, I'm not a witch." She counted off her explanations on her fingers. "One: I don't wear a pointy hat. Two: I only use a broom for sweeping. Three: I've never even owned a cauldron."

She thought this was a joke. Some sort of game. A story she'd no doubt share with her girlfriends over sweet pink drinks, complete with ironic paper umbrellas.

He barely suppressed his fury. Sure, witchcraft sounded like fun and games to most mundanes. But one fact remained: Jane Madison had unveiled the Osgood collection. And now the entire hoard was his responsibility, thanks to his bond to the *Compendium.*

He could already imagine Norville Pitt's jealousy, writhing like the steam above his cup of oolong.

Even as he pictured his enraged boss, he heard Linda Hudson's earnest command, repeated just that evening: *Offer yourself to Hecate by Samhain.*

He had to prove to the goddess he was worthy of her service. He was trained to help the needy, to guide the lost. But the woman hunched over her tea in this out-of-the-way Georgetown cottage was the furthest thing from a daughter of Hecate he could imagine. He was wasting his time here, with only six weeks left to save his career.

Yielding to a sudden surge of frustrated anger, he spat out: "You lit the pure beeswax taper, didn't you?"

"Yes, but I didn't—"

"And you touched your brow, your throat, and your heart?"

"Yes, but I—"

"And you traced the words in the spellbook with your finger?"

"Yes, but—"

"And you read the spell aloud?"

"Yes—"

"And you awakened a familiar." He pointed to Neko. "*That* familiar. On the night of a full moon."

Neko froze, halfway through testing his tea with the tip of his tongue. He obviously had no problem reading a warder's temper.

But Jane Madison only shifted on her chair before she asked, "So what's the deal with the full moon? How does it change things?"

David sighed. He tried not to sound as if he were responding to the class idiot.

He failed.

Completely.

"Any familiar awakened on the night of a full moon has freedom to roam." The witch merely stared at him. Giving up on quoting the Covenants, he said, "Neko can go anywhere. He isn't tethered to your physical space. He isn't bound the way a normal familiar is bound."

She whirled on Neko. "Were you going to say anything about that?"

The familiar shrugged. "Probably not." He might have wanted to please his witch by making tea, but he definitely wasn't cowed by her inherent power.

She turned back to David, looking chagrined. "Why don't we cut to the chase? Just for the sake of argument, I'll say I worked a spell. You're the police, and I broke the rules. Do I pay a fine? Show up at witch court?"

"You have to stop using your powers. Until you've trained with someone who knows the consequences of working magic."

"Well, that's easy enough." She relaxed into her chair as if a weight had suddenly evaporated from her shoulders. "I can promise you I'm not working any more magic. Ever. This is all too weird. It's not like I *planned* any of this, you know."

He felt his own cool balm of relief. He wouldn't be bound forever to this unpredictable woman. He didn't have to pretend she was his ticket back to the court's good graces. "No spells, then."

She nodded fervently. "No spells."

"I'll be monitoring you," he warned.

He should do a hell of a lot more than that. A good warder would report the find to the court.

But if David told Pitt about the collection, that toad would take over every last artifact. The *Compendium*. Neko. Jane Madison. And he'd use an impressionable witch—and every relic in the basement—to advance his own glory.

That impressionable witch's chin jutted with defiance. "You go ahead and do whatever you have to do."

She wasn't as brave as she sounded. He saw the bobble in her throat as she swallowed. He could read nerves in the quick glance she cast toward Neko. She had questions, a lot of them.

But before she could decide to trust David, her throat tensed. She barely swallowed a yawn. He resisted the urge to glance toward his watch. It had to be four in the morning. Maybe later.

Late enough, anyway, that she wouldn't try to work more magic that night. In fact, she might be intimidated enough to avoid the basement altogether. He could take some time, maybe talk to Linda. He could figure out what to do with the treasures downstairs, how to protect them. How to keep Pitt from getting anywhere near them.

With a faint twist to his warder's powers, he expanded his link to the *Compendium*. There were the kettledrums again, crashing against his powers. And beside them was an entire orchestra—woodwinds and strings and brass, all woven together in a single intricate whole. With one strong bond to the *Compendium*, it was terrifyingly easy to bond to the rest of the collection.

Now he'd know if the witch did anything with the tools in her basement—if she shifted a single rowan wand.

He set his mug on the table with a decisive gesture and rose to his feet. Wanting to put a little fear of Hecate in her, he said, "Of course, you're responsible for whatever your familiar does—for *all* actions he takes."

"Of course," she said, making a valiant attempt at sounding like she faced down warders every day of her life.

If she'd been a trained witch, she would have known she could simply order David off her property. A simple, direct command would sever his drumbeat link to the *Compendium*—and the rest of the Osgood collection—forever.

Instead, she glared at Neko and said, "I won't be working any magic, so he'll have nothing to do."

The familiar responded with a perfectly arched *who, me?* eyebrow.

Which reminded David... He pointed to the kitchen counter and said, "And one more thing, Miss Madison. That."

"The aquarium?"

"The fish."

"What about Stupid Fish?"

"Keep an eye on it." He looked at Neko, who became utterly obsessed with picking a bit of lint from his spotless sleeve. "You never know what bad things might happen when you're not paying attention."

It took her a moment to catch on. She shook her her head and vowed, "I'll pay attention."

"Just make sure that you do," he said before he stalked across the living room and out the front door.

He'd barely turned his collar up against the steady breeze, sole remnant of the night's storms, when his phone buzzed again in his pocket. The vibration made him remember the two calls he'd missed while he was teaching Witchcraft 101.

He swore when he saw the name splashed across the glass screen: Connor Hold.

A nightingale twittered inside his skull, the sound that he'd associated with Connor forever. No wolf-shifter should be calling tonight, though, not with the full moon risen four hours earlier.

His pulse echoed in his ears as he answered the still-buzzing phone. "Montrose."

"Help..." The word was stretched, somewhere between a growl and a whine, full of pain and something else. "Me..." David barely made out the last word, drowned as it was by fear.

No.

Terror.

He shoved his phone into his pocket and *reached* toward Seymour House.

5

T*hirty years earlier.*

"Hurry!" Con shouted. "Last one there's a mangy hound pup."

Davey wasn't about to be a mangy hound pup. He pushed past his best friend, slamming a sharp elbow into Con's ribs to make sure he won the race. Con's fingers closed around his ankle, but Davey shook free, taking the steps to the attic two at a time. He automatically ducked behind the junk stored up there—Con's old crib and a bunch of boxes marked "Baby Clothes—Boy" and "Baby Clothes—Girl."

"Come on," he whined, as Con dove into the blanket fort. "Let me see!" When Con didn't move fast enough, Davey pounded him on the back. "I helped take it! Let me see the Collar!"

Davey *had* helped. He'd raided his father's emergency supplies for matches, the wooden kind you scraped against a zipper to light. Together, they'd built a tepee fire, just like they'd learned in Webelos. They'd torn up a circle of grass at the end of the backyard farthest from the house. In the center, they'd piled a bunch of dead leaves and pine cones and some cotton balls Con had stolen from his mother's drawer in the bathroom.

After that, Con chickened out, so Davey lit the match. The first one broke. The second one blew out before he could kneel beside the kindling. But the third one caught the cotton balls, and the fire spread to the leaves and pine cones. Both boys had added kindling then, and Davey put three big branches on top.

They'd run into the garage and waited for the shifters' guards to notice the fire. It hadn't taken long before a bunch of men were shouting and swearing, using words Davey had never heard before.

Looking through the garage window, Davey could see the big branches had caught. So had the fence. At least, the boards closest to the tepee had, six or seven of them, sending up huge clouds of black smoke as paint bubbled from the bottom to the top.

With all the guards fighting the fire, the boys ran into the house, just like they'd planned all along. Con had ordered Davey to stand watch outside Mr. Hold's study. Only shifters were allowed in there. The whole time Davey stood in the hallway, he wondered if he could really smell smoke inside the house. What if the fence burned all the way up to the back door? What if the roof caught on fire?

But he'd been imagining things. The fire wasn't that big. And now the boys were safely crouched inside their blanket fort in the attic, panting hard as they stared at their prize. Light from the bare bulb overhead filtered through the blanket above them. "You can look," Con warned. "But you can't touch."

Davey nodded. He knew the rules. The Collar belonged to the Washington Pack. Davey was a warder, so he wasn't allowed to touch the Collar, not ever. He wasn't even supposed to know it existed.

He leaned close enough to see some sort of weird writing on the necklace's iron links. Con touched the closest one. "That's from the Boston Pack," he said, all proud, like he knew every pack in the world.

"Sure," Davey said, shoving Con's shoulder. "Like you can tell one group of werewolves from another."

Con glared. "I'm not a werewolf!"

"Full moon, shining bright," Davey taunted. "Shift a man for just one night."

"Take it back!" Con shouted. "I'm a real shifter, and you know it!"

"I don't know," Davey said, because it drove his friend crazy. "I think you're just a regular boy who got bit by a real shifter. Now you're stuck as a stupid werewolf, and you can only change when the moon is full." He chanted the taunt he'd heard shifters use with each other: "Poor little Connor, feels the moon's pull, can't shift at other times, powers are null."

"I can shift any time I want to!" Con stretched his right hand toward Davey, turning his fingers into razor-sharp claws.

Davey dove away. "Sheesh," he said, when he knew he was safely out of range. "I was only joking."

"It was a stupid joke," Con said, but he shifted his hand back. "No one wants to be a werewolf. Not when they can be a shifter like me." With his restored index finger, he touched the Collar again, a different link this time. "That one's from the Carolina Pack. And the twisted one is from the Southern Front."

Davey couldn't help himself. He had to touch the Collar. He had to see if he could feel the difference between the packs of shifters.

His finger froze against the metal.

But it wasn't freezing. It was burning. It was burning like he'd shoved his hand into the fire they'd set in the back yard. Like he was stirring a pot of boiling oil with his fingers. Like a volcano was erupting and he was catching the lava in his palm, except he couldn't drop it, couldn't spill it, couldn't get away.

He screamed as loud as he could, as long as he could. He

stood up, dropping the blanket as he tried to throw the Collar across the attic. He called on Hecate the way his father had told him he should, whenever he was in danger. "Blessed Hecate!" he cried, and his voice shook because he was crying, because it hurt so much.

He called on Hecate, but she didn't come to save him.

His father did.

George Montrose popped into the middle of the attic. One second, there was empty space at the top of the stairs, no boxes, no old furniture, just room for someone to straighten up and look around. The next, there was a full-grown man, a warder who shimmered into place through the ether.

Dad wore a black suit and a white shirt and the silver tie that said he'd been working at the court that morning. That's why Davey had come to Con's house in the first place, because Jimmy was taking his nap, and Mom said her ankles were swollen and her back hurt and couldn't she just have one single minute of quiet. Davey had gone to Con's house so he wouldn't get into trouble.

But he was in trouble now. The Collar was still fused to his hand, to fingers that didn't hurt anymore, that couldn't even tell if they were frozen or on fire. And Dad was clutching his sword, Deathrose, in both of *his* hands. The weapon flickered in the attic light, cold steel rippling like it was alive.

Dad was going to kill him. Right then, right there, even if Con saw everything.

"I didn't mean—" Davey started to say, but before he could get the words out, feet pounded on the attic stairs.

Not feet.

Paws.

Davey barely knew he was flying through the air before he crashed against Con's old crib. The wood splintered into a thousand pieces, but Davey didn't care, because he was lying flat on his back, the ruined railing digging into his shoulder blades as a wolf stood on his chest.

"Dad!" Con shouted, but Davey barely heard him. Instead, he was holding his breath, trying not to choke on the smell of raw meat. Mr. Hold—because the snarling wolf had to be Con's father —shifted his paws on Davey's chest, gouging holes with claws that felt like steak knives. Davey opened his mouth to say something, anything, but he started to gag when hot spit dripped off the wolf's teeth and splashed against the back of his throat.

He snapped his lips closed. He scrunched his eyes shut. He wished he could block his nose and ears, that he could shift the heavy weight crushing his heart beneath his ribs.

"Dad," Con begged again, but his voice was softer now. It came from a lot farther away.

Then there was a whoosh of air, and a smell like the bleach Mom used when she washed clothes. Davey opened his eyes, because he had to see what was happening. He had to know what new magic Mr. Hold was using.

But it wasn't Mr. Hold. Dad stood above him, feet planted by Davey's head. His arms were held out straight, angling Deathrose between Mr. Hold and Davey's face. The sword's sharp edges gave off the smell of bleach, wave after wave, rising and falling like the sword was breathing in the dusty attic.

"Yield!" Dad said, the single word a command that echoed in Davey's bones.

Mr. Hold snarled and flexed his paws.

"Yield!" Dad said again. "In the name of the Eastern Empire I charge you, Kenneth Hold. Yield your ground and let this boy rise." He flexed his wrists, raising Deathrose a single inch.

Mr. Hold raised his head and howled to the rafters. The sound echoed in the attic, rippling through Davey's bones and the wooden railing of the crib that felt like it was breaking his back.

Dad didn't say anything then. He only tightened his fingers on
Deathrose. As his knuckles stood out, the sword caught fire—flickering with purple flames that rolled off the metal without melting it.

Snarling, the wolf stepped back. He lifted first one paw, then
the other. He turned his head to the left. He thrashed his tail back
and forth. But in the end, he gave Davey room to stand.

Dad forced himself between Davey and the wolf. Mr. Hold
backed up more, one step and another and another, until his
hind paws almost touched the stairs. Dad nodded then, twisting
just enough to touch Deathrose's point to the bottom of the
Collar that still gripped Davey's hand.

The iron necklace slipped toward the ground.

Before it could hit, Mr. Hold leaped forward, snatching the
links between his teeth. At the same time, Dad closed his hands
on Davey's shoulders. Somehow, Deathrose had disappeared;
Dad must have pushed the sword into the ether. And then, before
Davey could look for Con or say anything to Mr. Hold, Dad was
pulling *him* through the ether.

There were ways to make the trip easy. Dad could have
protected Davey's mind, cushioning him like a crystal wrapped in
a sock. He could have held Davey's body inside a magic cape, safe
and secure against the ether's cold.

But Dad didn't care about making the trip easy.

They emerged in Dad's study. Davey shivered like he'd just
come in from the North Pole. His head felt like someone was
pounding the inside with marbles, shot after shot, in time with
his heart. His chest ached, like it did when he and Con chal-
lenged each other to see who could hold his breath the longest.

Dad's office door was closed. The desk was empty, not a piece
of paper or a pen in sight. Afternoon sun streamed through the
windows, which seemed strange, because Davey thought hours
must have passed since he and Con had run inside from the fire.
Hours or days or weeks.

He stared at his hand. It should be black, burned to ash by the

Collar. Or maybe white, frozen solid. He flexed his fingers, and they moved normally, like he hadn't been ruined by magic. "How —" he started to ask, but Dad cut him off, shouting.

"What the hell were you thinking?"

"We just—"

"You could have started a war back there!"

"We thought it would be fun—"

"Maybe it was *fun* for Connor to take the Collar. He's a shifter. It's a prank for him. But it's a blatant act of war for any other imperial—any supernatural creature in the entire Eastern Empire—to steal the shifters' sigil!"

Davey couldn't think of anything to say. Dad paced to the door and back.

"Ken Hold can demand you be brought before the Night Court." Dad turned on his heel. Crossed back to the door. Back to his desk. "Is that what you want?" Another lap. "A vampire judge deciding whether you stay with your mother and me, or if you get locked up in prison?"

Davey shook his head. Of course he didn't want that. It was all a mistake. An accident.

Except for one thing.

Davey had known the Collar was special. That's why he and Con had built their fort in the first place, to have a secret place to bring the stolen necklace. That's why he'd sneaked the matches instead of telling Dad he wanted to practice building a fire. That's why he'd stood watch outside Mr. Hold's office, because he'd *known* the Collar was magic, that it belonged to the shifters, and only the shifters.

Dad stopped his pacing, standing in front of his desk. Davey swallowed hard but forced himself to meet his father's eyes. "I was wrong," he said. "I shouldn't have taken the Collar."

Dad didn't react.

Davey bit his lip. He didn't want to say anything else. But if he was going to grow up to be a warder, he had to do hard things. He had to ask questions he didn't want to ask. He swallowed and forced himself to say, "Are you going to hit me now?"

"Hit you?" Dad's howl was louder than Mr. Hold's.

Davey nodded toward his father's waist, toward the leather belt that held up his pants. He'd heard stories from other boys in his warder classes. In his mundane ones, too. "Mr. Hutchinson makes Zach say how many times he should get hit when he's bad. When he forgets to feed the dog, or when he leaves the garage door open."

"Sweet Hecate," Dad said, whirling around the desk and throwing himself into his chair. "I'm not going to hit you," he said, after he'd taken three deep breaths. "But I'm going to tell you this: You're my oldest son, David. You're the one I should be able to trust with magic. I'm disappointed in you. You let me down today, and I don't know how long it will take for me to trust you again."

Davey's belly froze into a block of ice. He wondered if he could change places with Zach Hutchinson and live the life of a mundane boy, even if that meant getting hit with his father's belt.

Because one thing was absolutely clear. If Dad couldn't trust him, Davey would never, ever get to be a warder.

6

P *resent Day*

David had been inside Seymour House dozens of times before. He had plenty of specific memories of the wolf shifters' home. He could have anchored an astral thread and *reached* into the brick townhouse's kitchen directly.

But Connor had sounded desperate. And no warder on earth was foolish enough to transport directly into an unknown conflict, against unidentified enemies who might outnumber him with unbeatable odds. So David concentrated on the street corner half a block from the wolf shifters' communal home in DC's Petworth neighborhood. Better to walk a few hundred yards than be taken down before he was ready to fight.

A whiff of jasmine distracted him as he studied the brick townhouse. With a conscious effort, he pushed away his awareness of Jane Madison. He'd done all he could with the witch for tonight. He'd believed her when she said she wasn't going to work any more spells—at least right then. He'd be better served by concentrating on Connor, on whatever had scared the shifter—whatever was threatening the Collar—enough to summon him on the night of the full moon.

Wet leaves plastered the house's front steps. Cast iron chairs rested on the porch, rust stains circling their feet. No lights were visible inside, on either of the two floors.

The place looked like every other home on the street, sleeping quietly on a mid-September night. But Connor wouldn't have called him for nothing. David made his cautious way toward the front door, remembering to step over the creaking second step on his way to the porch.

Listening outside the house, he took a moment to strip his tie loose and tuck the length of silk into his breast pocket. Connor would never attack him, even in wolf form. Thirty years of friendship guaranteed that. But there was no reason to give anyone—any*thing*—else a noose to cinch tight.

Warder powers didn't extend to the canid sense of smell Connor took for granted. David lacked lupine hearing as well. But he had one clear advantage his shifter friend could not command.

Reaching into the ether, he envisioned his fingers closing around Rosefire, the sword his father had given him the day he began warder training. As a cadet, David had barely been able to lift the thing. As a man, he took comfort in the blade's solid weight and the leather-wrapped grip that had molded to his fingers long ago.

He pulled the sword into the physical plane and raised his left hand to knock. Before his knuckles made contact, the door jerked open. Connor stood inside, still in human form. He beckoned with one pale hand, moonlight glinting off his black-framed eyeglasses.

David's attention was stolen by a massive white wolf who paced in front of the brick fireplace. Her tongue lolled as she panted, and her golden eyes followed Connor's every move.

"All right," Connor growled at the beast as he closed the door behind David. The she-wolf only whined. "He's here. Get back upstairs so the neighbors don't see you." The white beast lowered her muzzle to her paws. This time her whine was softer.

"Go, Tala," Connor said wearily, pointing toward the townhouse stairs.

David had never seen Connor's mate in her wolf form. As a human, she was tall and blonde, a Norwegian Amazon inclined to wear plaid shirts over short skirts, with leggings that would have made him look twice if he'd been willing to wrestle Connor for the privilege. She was as smart as her librarian glasses made her look, and he'd never seen her back down from a debate.

But she was in wolf form now, and her alpha had issued a direct command. She slunk up the stairs, belly low, tail flat.

As she left, David's nostrils flared at the acrid tang of human sweat in the room's close air, strong enough to sense even without a shifter's gifts.

Connor wiped his palms on his stovepipe jeans and started pacing in front of the fireplace. His bearded face was pale above his faded T-shirt with its jagged legend: *I am Tyler Durden.* His bare feet looked like alabaster in the silvery moonlight.

That was the second pair of bare feet David had seen that night. Once again, he dragged his thoughts from Jane Madison because he was in a cold, dark townhouse now, with an unknown threat lurking somewhere nearby.

David glanced around the room. "Where's the rest of the pack?"

"Down at...the Den." That was the farmland Connor owned, a hundred acres on Virginia's Rappahannock River. The pack ordinarily retreated there during the full moon so they could run in the pine forest without risk of discovery.

David shifted his fingers on Rosefire's grip as he made a survey of the townhouse living room. "What happened?"

Even with the full beard framing Connor's lips, David could see how hard his friend worked to find words. Four, nearly five, hours had passed since the full moon had risen. Instinct must be pulling on every muscle in his body, ripping at his human flesh with white-hot pincers. He must be losing control over his inner conversion, organs shifting beneath his skin. This long after moonrise, complete transformation could only be reined in by sheer force of will.

"Salamanders," the alpha finally said. A spasm tightened his face, and his eyes clenched shut as he denied his agony. "Apolline Fournier," he managed to whisper.

Of *course* it was salamanders. It was *always* salamanders, where the wolves were concerned.

Wolf shifters were tied to the power of the moon, to the silver-lit night. Salamanders found their strength in the sun's unadulterated fire. The races sparred wherever they shared common ground.

With a snort of disgust, David banished Rosefire to the ether. No need for the blade now—any salamander who'd worked mischief in the wolves' home was long gone. "Dammit, Con," he said, suddenly exhausted. "I told you last time. I'm not fighting salamanders anymore."

Connor's face twisted. "Their...fault... They—"

"It can't be worse than your breaking that water main last December, flooding the salamanders' winter quarters."

Connor struggled to shake his head. "Ap—" He choked on the salamander queen's name. It took him three tries before he gave up and just said, "Different."

"Right," David agreed in disgust. "And it was *different* when you exposed her lair near the Capitol, back in March. When you sent the fire department to that stash of fireworks in May. It was *different* when you reported their midsummer bonfire to DC police! They were on a deserted island, Con! In the middle of the Anacostia River! The salamanders weren't hurting anyone!"

That last one resulted in Connor being dragged before the Eastern Empire's night court, with David called as a witness. He'd used personal leave to attend the trial, but Pitt had docked his salary anyway, making up some regulation about embarrassing Hecate's Court in front of other imperials.

But Pitt's petty vengeance was nothing compared to the salamander queen's retribution against the shifters. She'd torched their suburban mansion, leaving behind nothing but a stinking pile of ash.

Faulty wiring, local firefighters said. Bottom-feeding, scum-sucking fire-lizards, Connor insisted to any imperial who would listen.

David had nightmares about his own beloved farmhouse burning to the ground.

Despite his refusal to get involved, David glanced around the room now, searching for evidence of salamander fun and games.

Everything seemed to be in order. The usual assortment of fedoras hung unharmed on the coatrack beside the door. A ball of yarn rested on the coffee table, skewered by a pair of bamboo knitting needles. A coffee mug nestled on the floor near the couch, emblazoned with the words *Ceci n'est pas du cafe*. Half a dozen books were stacked haphazardly beside the vintage armchair: *Urban Beekeeping for Beginners*, *Taxidermy Tales*, *Bookbinding for Modern Libraries*. A tin of mustache wax crowned the pile.

There wasn't a scorch mark anywhere in the room. Not a whiff of ash. David shook his head. "What did they do this time?"

Connor's first reply was lost in a groan as he clutched his belly. Polished fingernails morphed into dark claws, only to be forced back to human form after a long, hissed breath. "Knocked," he forced between gritted teeth. Another struggle, and this time it took him longer to subdue his emerging paws. "Knocked over hives," he finally managed.

David shrugged. The insects would find their way home. "So they got the bees."

"No!" Connor insisted. "Bees—" His shoulders hunched toward his ears, and his head twisted hard to the right. "Just—" He clamped emerging fangs onto his lower lip in a bootless effort to stop the change. "Di... Diver.... Collar!"

"Sweet Hecate," David breathed. The bees had been a diversion, allowing the salamanders to strike at the wolves' core. He didn't wait for Connor to choke out more. Instead, he pushed past the alpha and ran down the hallway, into the small study on the ground floor. A drafting desk hulked against one wall, anchored by an architect lamp and several rolls of paper. A framed photograph of Fallingwater leaned against the opposite wall. The corner of its frame had shattered against the floor.

The blast marks on the wall said the salamanders who breached the safe behind the photo had valued speed over precision. They hadn't bothered cracking the safe. They'd just melted its metal door—melted it and clawed inside with imperial hands inured to fire.

David had seen the contents of the lockbox before, when Connor paid off the bear shifter lawyer who'd represented him before the Night Court. The wolf alpha had counted out crisp hundred-dollar bills, peeling them from the pack's accumulated wealth.

Now, similar stacks of money stood untouched in the safe. There was a diamond brooch that had belonged to Connor's mother. A strand of pearls. A handgun.

But the most valuable thing Connor had ever possessed was gone. The Washington Pack's Collar had been stolen.

Connor whined like a hamstrung dog. "Help..." he groaned.

And he ceased being a man.

Fabric ripped across his writhing shoulders. His tortured jeans split along their already-damaged seams. Connor tossed his head, sending his eyeglasses flying onto the desk. David's own belly twisted as the shift took over his friend's face, pulling out a muzzle, pushing back his jaw.

David's Torch cut into his fingers as he clutched it for comfort. He'd read imperial books. He knew a shifter's transition was a merger of pain and pleasure, that the final release into native form flooded the animal brain with endorphins.

Nevertheless, he looked away as Connor's body flashed between man and wolf, between bare flesh and furred flanks. He closed his eyes to the contortions, but he had no way to shut his ears to the grinding sound, the slurping. He only looked again when he felt a cold, wet nose against his palm.

He'd seen Connor's wolf form countless times. He recognized the brindle pelt and amber eyes. He understood the shake of the lupine head, the tilting of pointed ears toward the drafting table. A Blackwing pencil lay there, stark against a creamy sheet of paper. An address was blocked out in Connor's architectural script. *Apolline*, the note said. And an address in Kalorama, an exclusive neighborhood in the northwest quadrant of the city.

Connor whined, nosing at the pencil. He must have written the message after calling David, suspecting he couldn't hold off transition long enough.

"Okay," David said, automatically setting a steadying hand on the wolf's strong neck.

Sure, he'd vowed never to get between the wolves and the salamanders again. But the Collar changed things. And Connor was helpless as a wolf; he couldn't act for himself for nearly twenty-four hours, until the next moon rose.

As a warder, David was bound to uphold order in the Eastern Empire. He was obligated to protect those who could not defend themselves.

He picked up the address and said, "I'll go."

The wolf pulled his lips back from razor-sharp canines to sniff at David's right hand, the one that had held Rosefire. A firm nudge made his intention clear. "No," David said. "It would be a declaration of war to show up armed."

Connor whirled to face the savaged safe. When he growled, long and low and fierce, the hair rose on the back of David's neck, but he repeated, "No. That's your battle. I'll tell her to return the Collar, but I won't give her grounds to charge me with assault. Pitt would see me banned as a warder forever."

Connor growled again, and David couldn't be sure if the aggression was directed at Apolline or at him. Maybe even at Pitt. In the end, none of it mattered. He'd deliver the wolf pack's message. And then he'd return to his own crazed life, to a father who thought he was a failure, to a boss who wanted to destroy him, to a novice witch who somehow managed to own the greatest hoard of magic materials in the history of Washington DC.

He let Connor lead him out of the office, back to the townhouse's door. He worked the knob himself, raising his chin before striking out for the sidewalk. Connor growled once more and nosed the door closed.

David didn't take out his phone until he reached the streetlamp at the corner. There was no way to use his warder powers to transport to Apolline. He'd never met the salamander in person or been inside her lair.

Uber would have to do instead. At least that way, someone would have a record of his last known whereabouts if the salamanders attacked.

7

D avid stood in front of a wrought-iron gate in the luxurious Kalorama neighborhood. His fingers itched to pull Rose-fire from the ether. He was certain that would be a mistake—gripping a double-edged sword as he walked down the pre-dawn sidewalk in front of homes occupied by Supreme Court justices, former presidents, and billionaires. As it was, the scattering of black SUVs in front of prominent addresses made the nape of his neck itch. How many contained Secret Service agents and how many hid private security guards?

Guards, like the one who manned the small green hut beside the gate he stared at. "May I help you sir?" the salamander asked, stepping out of his shelter. His voice sounded like it had been dragged over a rocky riverbed. His right hand rested comfortably on the butt of a handgun.

So much for the element of surprise. "I'm here to see Apolline Fournier."

"Ms. Fournier isn't seeing visitors at this time of day."

"Tell her David Montrose is calling, on behalf of Connor Hold."

"Ms. Fournier isn't seeing visitors at this time of day." The guard repeated his words without a ripple of variation, his eyes unblinking.

"If you'll just call her—"

"I'll call the DC police," the guard offered instead.

"There's no need for that," David said. It took an effort to sound dismissive, rather than nervous. The last thing he needed was to attract the interest of mundane law enforcement. Too much human attention, and David could find himself in front of the Eastern Empire Night Court—as a defendant this time, instead of as a character witness.

The guard said pointedly: "Not if you're heading down the street."

David hesitated. There were tools he could apply, warder's magic. All it took was a quick touch, flesh to flesh, and he could make the guard forget David had ever stood at the gate. But a bout of amnesia wouldn't do any good if the various security forces on the street saw him act. And he had to suspect that a salamander guard had *some* sort of arcane protection against warder magic.

Not to mention the fact that any work he did could potentially be monitored by Pitt. In theory, the greasy rat would still be locked in his own bolthole, enjoying the sleep of the damned. But with a three-year run of bad luck behind him, he wasn't about to take chances.

"Look," he said to the salamander in his most conciliatory voice. "I don't want to make waves here." From the guard's skeptical glance, his best hadn't been conciliatory enough. "Can I leave a message for Apolline? Write a note?"

"Does this look like the Post Office?" the guard asked irritably.

"Of course, I'd make it worth your while," David said smoothly, as if he'd planned on bribing the fire-lizard all along. He fished his wallet from his pocket and slipped out a few bills. Folding them into a discreet rectangle, he moved to shake his adversary's hand.

The guard pocketed the bills with the speed of a striking cobra.

David retrieved a leather-bound notepad from his breast pocket, along with a Montblanc pen. He didn't bother shielding his note from the guard's curious eyes. He had no delusions that his message would be kept confidential.

I am authorized to discuss your recent acquisition. All reasonable offers will be considered.

He printed his name and added his cell number. As he handed the slip to the guard, he mentally adjusted the definition of "reasonable." Apolline would compensate him for his cash outlay—one way or another.

He walked a full block before he took out his phone and shot a message to Connor. *A in lair. Message left. Call me after shift.*

Shift. The word worked equally well to refer to Connor's lupine status or his own work at the court—work he needed to report to in less than four hours.

But he had other responsibilities too—more mundane obligations than salamanders or wolf shifters. Spot was waiting at home. The black Lab could come and go through his doggy door, that wasn't a problem. But he couldn't handle a can opener on his own.

Besides, there was still time to snag a couple hours of sleep. Then a hot shower and a cup of decent coffee, not the sludge they served at the court.

Wandering down a side street, David vaguely remembered a public park within a couple of blocks. He reached it in minutes—a couple of tall pine trees towering over matching marble benches. He took the nearest seat, slumping in the darkness beneath the massive trees.

He looked left, then right, then left again, making sure no one had seen him take refuge. Finally satisfied the coast was clear, he closed his eyes and took a deep breath. He closed his awareness around the sturdy steel rope that led across the astral plane to the farmhouse he called home, deep in the Maryland countryside.

He pictured the cornfields, sere brown from the summer heat. He smelled the fresh grass that surrounded his clapboard house. He felt the breeze blowing on his face. Clutching the familiar guidewire, he *reached* toward home.

8

David's eyes were bleary as he sank into his office chair. Three hours of sleep hadn't been enough to clear his head. He reached for a cup of coffee that was strong enough to strip paint before he thumbed on his computer. A message flashed in the corner of his screen: *My office. Immediately.*

He didn't need to check the sender to know he was being summoned by Norville Pitt.

Sure enough, the man crouched behind his government-issue desk like a frog on a putrescent lily pad. The overhead fluorescent lights made him look seasick. His plastic pocket protector tilted forward at a dangerous angle, threatening to spill his pens onto the chaos of papers before him.

He barked out a question before David could say a word. "Where are you on re-entering yesterday's forms?"

It seemed as if Pitt had deleted the records a lifetime ago. Of course he had to know exactly how much progress David had made; he could track every keystroke through his supervisory computer account.

David kept his voice carefully neutral. "I've completed all but one."

"One left. And yet you had time to spend your night roaming around the city like some self-appointed vigilante."

All vigilantes are self-appointed. But David concentrated on the silver ring on his left hand, reminding himself of the self-control he'd mastered at the Academy. He didn't say the words out loud.

Pitt licked his lips, glaring at David through his fingerprint-mottled eyeglasses. Apparently Pitt thought David was more naive than a high-school freshman. No self-respecting warder would voluntarily admit anything he'd done the night before— not his trip to the cottage in Georgetown, his side visit to Seymour House, or his stop in Kalorama. Keeping his mouth shut was the only way to find out exactly how much Pitt knew.

In the end, David had more patience.

Pointing a finger directly at David's chest, Pitt leaned back in his chair and said, "You're a warder of Hecate's Court."

Congratulations, Master of the Obvious. David could think the words. Emphatically.

His silence clearly irritated his boss. Pitt slammed a hand down on his desk as he once again lost their battle of wills. "You have no business getting involved with shifters. It's not your place to play message boy to the salamanders. Have some dignity, son."

Pitt was only ten years older than David.

Ten years older, but he'd obviously invested some of that time developing a spy network. David wondered who'd ratted him out. He could only hope they'd needed to pay Apolline's security guard a hell of a lot more than he had.

Or maybe Apolline had brought his message to the court herself. She could have complained about David getting involved in salamander business. He'd left his name there, after all, in simple block letters. He couldn't have made her task any easier.

Pitt shook his head in sneering disgust. "Cat got your tongue, Montrose? Let me keep this simple: I'm. Watching. You. I know everything about you. And I'm telling you, in no uncertain terms:

Do *not* get between the shifters and the salamanders. Have I made myself absolutely, one hundred percent, perfectly clear?"

David wanted to shout that Pitt *always* made himself perfectly clear—the man was as subtle as a black cat in a snowstorm. Even more, David wanted to argue that he *had* been acting like a warder. He'd been trying to resolve conflict in the Eastern Empire, guaranteeing that the world was a safer space for all the witches and warders who worked there.

He wanted to say that Pitt had no right to police him, no right to interfere.

But he swallowed every one of his protests. They went down like lye, but he pressed his lips closed until he was certain he could say, "I understand."

Those two words, and nothing else. Because that was the only way to get Pitt to dismiss him. The only way to head back to his office.

And the entire way there, every step down the drab corridor with his fingers rubbing the familiar swirls of his Torch, David heard the words Pitt *hadn't* said. He didn't know anything about the *Compendium.* Anything about the Osgood collection or Neko. Norville Pitt didn't know Jane Madison existed.

And David would do anything to see that Pitt never discovered the truth.

9

D avid sat in a sturdy Adirondack chair on the front porch of his farmhouse, watching the sun set over the nearby woods. Spot lay at his feet. The enormous black Lab occasionally flicked his tail against the floorboards to prove all was right in his world. David took a long pull from the bottle of beer balanced on the arm of his chair. He deserved it, just for making it through another shift in Norville Pitt's nightmare of a clerk's office.

He'd spent the day on another useless project, transcribing a collection of eighteenth-century wills into an outmoded database. Pitt had vetoed four different proposals to make the documents more useful.

Still, David hadn't argued too strenuously. He knew his work would be deleted on some pretext in the near future, and he'd have to re-create the wheel. Again.

As always, he'd repeated to himself, "Hecate's will be done." He just hoped the goddess end this particular torment in short order.

At least the mindless work gave him a chance to reflect on Jane Madison and the Osgood collection. When he'd left the witch, she'd seemed determined to forget all those books in her basement, never to work a spell again. Not likely. Magic called to magic across the miles, across the centuries. The Osgood collection had summoned Jane Madison to that garden cottage, and it wasn't going to let her walk away after liberating one free-spirited familiar.

David needed to consult with Linda. But he hadn't dared contact her from his bugged office. And now she was occupied all evening, celebrating his father's birthday.

David drank deeply again, determined not to think about George's sixtieth or Linda's earnest invitation. He wasn't going to dwell on his middle brother James—who was probably even now rattling off NASDAQ numbers like a living computer—or his youngest brother Tommy, who would have everyone laughing with his imitation of jurors at yet another high-toned indie film festival.

He wouldn't think about his father, lips grim, eyes hard, and judging, always judging. Finding David wanting in everything.

No. He wouldn't reach out to Linda tonight. The problem of Jane Madison could wait another day.

An hour after moonrise, a Mini Cooper turned down the long driveway. As the car made its way toward the house, Spot climbed to his feet. Staring into the silver-lit night, the dog whined deep in his throat. David set a comforting hand on his head.

Connor Hold took his time unfolding his lanky frame from the small car. His cuffed jeans looked black in the moonlight, emphasizing the length of his thin legs. He wore a sweater vest over a plaid shirt. His eyeglasses glinted in the darkness.

A nightingale's song crested in David's mind, the familiar marker his powers had long ago bestowed on the Washington alpha. Connor approached the three porch steps and locked eyes with Spot. Feet still firmly planted on the ground, he extended one hand to the dog, keeping his fingers curled in a loose, non-threatening fist. Spot sniffed with interest, whuffing deep in his throat. After a moment, his tail wagged, slowly at first, then faster. He crouched into a play bow, tongue lolling.

"Not tonight, pal," Connor said, reaching up to tug at Spot's ears. The man's voice was rough, as if he'd cheered himself hoarse at a concert.

The dog tried a few more bowing invitations, but Connor only sank into the Adirondack beside David. He accepted a beer, clinking the glass neck against David's bottle before he nodded approval of the artisanal microbrew.

"Sorry about last night," Connor rasped.

David grunted, not looking at his friend. They'd carried on countless conversations before, both staring out at the darkness —on this porch, at the Petworth townhouse, at the wolf shifters' old house on Seymour Street, the one the salamanders had burned down.

"Holding off the shift is...exhausting," Connor said.

"Sorry I couldn't get there sooner."

Connor shrugged. They drank peaceably for a while before he asked, "Any word from Apolline?"

David shook his head. "Not to me. I think she called Pitt, or maybe I was followed. He read me the riot act, anyway."

Connor's frown was almost lost in his beard. "Sorry about that."

Now it was David's turn to shrug. They were both sorry about a lot. "So she's not willing to negotiate. What will you do?"

"What *can* I do? I need to get the Collar back. The younger wolves are already getting squirrelly without it."

"Squirrelly how?" David pictured all sorts of havoc the shifters could work in their inner-city neighborhood.

Connor grimaced. "Ethan brought home a porterhouse for dinner."

David raised his eyebrows. He'd long ago accepted his friend's unconventional choice to live as a vegan—at least in human form. As a wolf, of course, all bets were off; Connor could demolish a doe in one long weekend.

But the Washington Pack followed its alpha in all things, even agreeing to eschew meat as humans. If Ethan—one of the younger brutes in the pack—had brought home a porterhouse, he was violating a basic rule.

David said, "That must have gone over well."

Connor sighed. "Extenuating circumstances. I made him grill it outside. And I looked the other way when Sondra and Noah helped him finish it off."

David's look was sharper at that. One young shifter straying wasn't a complete surprise, not with the pack in emotional free-fall over the theft of the Collar. Three, though, was a definite cause for concern. Connor's authority was on the line.

Commenting on the obvious wouldn't help. Instead, David said, "Here's what I don't get. The salamanders don't have a pack structure. What the hell do they want with the Collar?"

Connor looked uncomfortable. Finally, he said, "It's the were-wolves' fault."

"Werewolves?" David knew that full-blooded wolf shifters created lesser werewolves by biting unsuspecting humans on the night of a full moon. Every shifter alive viewed werewolves as second-class citizens—too weak to shift by force of will alone, destined only to gain wolf form on future full moons.

"Two new ones," Connor said, sounding frustrated. "Brutes, turned last year, when we moved into the new house." He took another long pull of beer before he faced David directly. "I thought they were comfortable with the pack. That they under-stood how things work."

David waited. Something had gone catastrophically wrong.

Connor set down his beer bottle with a distinct ring. He ran his hand down his face before he said, "They wanted to impress me, wanted the pack to think they were equals. So they broke into the salamanders' burrow and stole the karstag."

"Sweet Hecate," David swore, suddenly wishing he'd opted for something stronger than beer.

The karstag was the salamanders' most sacred artifact. The obsidian blade had been forged in the primeval volcano that gave rise to all salamanders throughout the world. It was a symbol of the creatures' history, their twin god and goddess of fire, all they held holy.

If the werewolves had taken the karstag, it was no wonder the salamanders had retaliated by stealing the Collar. In fact, it was a miracle the salamanders hadn't burned Seymour House to the ground. Seymour House, and the entire city block it sat in. And every other pack stronghold on the eastern seaboard.

"How'd they manage that?" David asked, amazed that two recently turned werewolves could defeat an entire nest of salamanders.

"I'm not sure yet. We're still getting all the facts. All I know right now is the wolves took it in their human form last night, a couple of hours before moonrise. They managed to get it down to the Den before they turned."

"So where's the damned thing now?"

"I don't know."

"You don't *know*?" David's shock made Spot whine. He barely remembered to stroke the dog's broad head, to calm him back to a dark shadow on the porch.

Connor let his hands dangle between his knees. "They buried it somewhere at the Den. There's a hundred acres down there. We could search for years and never find it."

"Make them show you where they put it!" David's voice crackled with outrage. Connor Hold was alpha of the Washington Pack. He had to know how to manage a couple of wayward brutes.

"It's not that simple. They're werewolves, not shifters. They don't keep any conscious memory of what they do in wolf form. They know where they stood when they turned last night. And they know where they woke this morning. But everything between is lost."

David suspected his frustration was nothing compared to the alpha's. Nevertheless, he started half a dozen sentences before he settled on, "So that's it? It's gone forever?"

Connor sighed. "Not forever. They can take us to it next month, when they've turned again. But I can't wait that long to get it back. Not with the rest of the pack grilling steaks in the back yard. Apolline will have to negotiate."

"You don't have a leg to stand on!"

"I have four," Connor said, his lips quirking ruefully inside his beard. He sobered and said, "I just need you to explain all this to the salamanders."

David's laugh was harsh. "Can't do it. Pitt is waiting for any excuse to terminate me."

Connor flexed his fingers, taking care to show David the flat of his left palm. Not just the flat of his palm—the long white scar that bisected his flesh.

Reflexively, David glanced at his own hand, at the matching scar glinting against his silver ring. "Forget it," he said.

"Blood brothers," Connor answered. And just like that, David was back in the basement of his father's house, bracing Rosefire against a workbench with his left hand, biting hard on his lip to find the courage to slash his palm against the blade.

"We're not ten years old anymore," he said, folding his fingers into a fist to hide the evidence of boyish folly.

"I need your help," Connor said. "Back me up at just one meeting. I can't lose face with the pack when they're already straying."

I can't. I'm afraid of the consequences.

But that's not what Connor would have said, no matter what enemy they faced, no matter how much personal danger loomed. "Con..." David said, fighting for the right words.

"You need to stand up to that bastard," Connor said.

For just a moment, David pictured doing just that. He could best Pitt in any physical fight; that wasn't a question. He was willing to stake his magical ability against his boss's any day. But David was a creature of rules and regulations. He'd learned on his first day in the Academy that any warder who openly declared war against another would automatically be deemed unfit to serve a witch.

And there was one witch he was pretty sure would need protecting, sooner rather than later. No matter what promises she'd made to him the night before. One witch whom Hecate had led him to...

"What?" Connor asked.

David was annoyed he'd given something away without saying a single word. "Nothing."

Connor sniffed, reminding David that the shifter had a whole range of senses beyond the human. "You weren't thinking about Pitt there." Another sniff, more of a snort this time. "Who is she?"

He wasn't surprised to hear the question—chagrined, but not surprised. And he knew damn well he couldn't get away with a lie. Connor was like a dog with a bone when he'd caught scent of a secret. "A new witch. I met her last night, just before you called."

"What's her name?"

"Jane. Jane Madison."

Another telling sniff. "You like her!"

"I barely know her."

Connor whistled, long and low. "Oh, how the mighty have fallen."

David shook his head. "She's a pain in the ass. Worked her first spell without a clue. She woke a familiar on the night of a full moon."

"Sounds like she needs a little expert...guidance." Decades of familiarity turned the last word into a dirty joke.

"Get your mind out of the gutter. *If* I work with her, I'll be her warder. Nothing more. But it's a moot point anyway. She promised not to work any more spells."

"Whatever you say, dude." Connor's shoulders shifted beneath his sweater vest. "But you warders are way too uptight. You need to give in to your wolfish side once in a while."

Right. Like your brutes did, stealing the karstag. But David recognized his friend's need to blow off a little steam. So he settled for flashing Connor an obscene gesture before he fumbled for another beer—anything to take a break from the current conversation.

Before he could snap the cap off, magic splashed across his consciousness. A wave of jasmine rolled on a torrent of golden light that flooded every synapse in his brain. For just a heartbeat, he thought he was trapped in the past, reliving the moment he'd first been summoned to the cottage in the garden. But no drumbeat rolled across his astral hearing this time. No steel string pulled him toward the Osgood collection.

Jane Madison was working another spell.

10

H e materialized on the threshold of Jane's cottage, having left behind Connor, Spot, and a perfectly good evening relaxing in the privacy of his own home. The power of the witch's spell was different this time—bigger, wider, and filled with more pure potential than he'd ever imagined a witch could have.

But she'd promised not to work more magic, so he closed his fist around the Hecate's Torch in his pocket—the symbol of his own vow to keep witches safe—and he turned his words to iron as she opened the door. "Miss Madison," he said.

Her cheeks were flushed. She was dressed in black stretch pants and an over-size T-shirt, as if she'd just strolled in from the gym. One hand rested on the doorknob, and the other curled around a highball glass that sported a cloudy half-circle of liquid in the bottom. Green flecks of mint clung to the side. "Would you like a mojito?" she asked.

He pushed into the living room. "I thought we'd reached an agreement."

"We did," she agreed readily enough. "I didn't work a spell."

He didn't even need to voice his skepticism. She read his

expression flawlessly. "Well, I didn't mean to," she amended. She looked at her arm, as if she expected it to fly away under its own power. "Um, I'm not even sure it worked."

Just that morning, he'd gotten Pitt to divulge everything the toad knew, just by keeping quiet. He applied the same technique again, tightening his jaw and waiting to see what Jane Madison would confess. She broke even faster than he expected.

"I don't even know what it was supposed to do!"

"And that is *precisely* why you should have some guidance. Some training." He sighed and gestured toward the basement door. "You might think that this is all *Bewitched*, but I can assure you it is not. There are consequences for your behavior."

"My behavior! What about Neko! He's the one who made this happen. He's the one who gave me the stick—"

"Neko." He raised his eyes to the kitchen doorway. Sure enough, the familiar stood there unabashed, holding his own mint-traced glass.

David craned his neck and caught a glimpse of a spell-book on the kitchen table: *A Girl's First Grimoire*, opened to the love spell. He recognized the formula because Haylee had once tried to work the same magic on him. She'd thought she had enough raw power to get past the spell's automatic block on a witch's own warder. She'd been wrong, but the attempt had proven mortifying for both of them.

And now Jane Madison had tried the same working.

In the presence of a mundane.

Because a third person stood in the kitchen, a woman. She was short, barely as tall as Neko, and she was dressed in the same gym gear as Jane Madison. Her shoulder-length blond hair was blunt cut, and her eyes were shrewd.

Apparently he passed whatever inspection she made, because she nodded and ducked back into the kitchen, only to reappear holding a pottery plate sporting some sort of chocolate-covered pastry. She ducked her head and peered up at him through glistening eyelashes. "Lust?" she asked.

Caught by surprise, he blushed.

Neko gasped.

David couldn't say whether the familiar reacted to the woman's blatant flirtation, or if he was shocked to catch a discomfited warder. In any case, his voice was gruff as he demanded of Jane, "Who is this?"

"My best friend. Melissa White. She's a baker. Almond Lust is her specialty."

Well, that explained the come-on. Hopefully.

"Look," Jane said. "I had a really crappy day, and she brought the bars over, and we decided to make some drinks, and she asked about the library downstairs, and Neko brought up one of the books." Apparently realizing she was rambling, she caught a deep breath.

And he nodded, because he knew all about really crappy days. But none of that explained why she'd worked a spell, especially after she'd explicitly promised to leave magic alone. Even if *she* were inclined to experiment with the books in her basement, her familiar should have known better. David turned to glare at Neko.

The creature was suddenly fascinated by his empty glass. "Whoops!" he said. "Time for a refill!" He dashed into the kitchen with a theatrical flair.

The familiar's antics gave Jane Madison the moment she needed to regroup. David watched her steady determination as she crossed the room and collected her friend's pottery plate. She settled the pastry on the coffee table in front of the two couches. Without any visible hesitation, she sat on one of the overstuffed cushions, adopting an unconscious air of authority.

In other words, she acted like a witch.

So he acted like a warder.

He sat beside her, scarcely waiting for Melissa White and
Neko to follow suit. "This has to stop," he said. "You don't understand. Witchcraft is powerful. The surges you released from the
house tonight could be felt for miles."

"Felt?" Jane Madison's voice was suddenly very small.

But he drove his point home, fully intending to put the fear of
Hecate in her. "By warders. And other witches. And by the creatures that seek them out."

She rubbed hard at her arms. Still, she set her jaw defiantly.
"Now you're just trying to frighten me."

"I hope that's what I'm doing." He leaned forward and
reached for her glass, settling it on a slate coaster. Her fingers
were cooler than he expected. "Listen. We can end all this right
now. The Covenants grant priority to any witch who actually
possesses the materials—books, runes, crystals. You don't have to
take advantage of that presumption, though. If you'd like, you can
give back everything in your basement."

"Give it back?"

The three words shot adrenaline into his heart. He didn't
want her to know her options, even if he was bound to tell her. He
forced himself to say, "The coven would gladly accept them. As it
is, they'll likely contest your ownership, but things move slowly
in Hecate's Court." Then, because she had to understand, he used
her first name. "Jane, this is serious."

Neko snorted.

David rounded on the familiar. "Laugh all you want. But
you'll be the first thing transferred if Hecate's Court takes over.
And no other witch will awaken you on the night of a full moon."

Neko squirmed for a moment before looking away. David
returned his attention to Jane, only to find that he couldn't look
away. Her eyes were hazel, dark gold flecked with green. A spray
of freckles splashed across her nose. When he'd seen her the
other night, he'd thought her hair was brown, but in this light, he
could see it was shot through with red.

For just a moment, he imagined kissing her.

Connor had planted the thought, damn his wolfish abandon. The baker friend hadn't helped, with her coy offer of Lust.

He could smell mint on Jane's fingers, along with lime. He'd taste mojitos on her lips, sweet rum beneath her own hidden flavor.

She felt something too. He saw that—in the flush of her cheeks, in the sudden softness around her eyes. She leaned toward him, just a fraction.

And her motion broke the spell.

Spell.

She was a witch.

He was a warder.

And Hecate wasn't likely to be impressed with his kissing a newfound witch, a woman vulnerable with power she'd scarcely begun to understand. He should be spending more of his energy thinking about how to please the goddess than how to seduce Jane Madison. A hell of a lot more of his energy.

"So," he said, pulling himself back to the edge of the couch. He ordered himself to think about ice storms. Blizzards. Glaciers calving in the Arctic Sea.

She blinked hard, clearly coming to her own senses. "So, what now?" she asked.

She phrased it as a question, but he could hear the decision in her tone. She'd already accepted his basic proposition. She'd stand against the court. She'd fight for the Osgood collection.

Neko understood that too. He started bouncing up and down on the couch, like a kid who'd been handed the keys to a candy shop. Or a City Center fashion boutique, as the case might be. "Yes!" the familiar exclaimed. "This is going to be *perfect!*"

The mundane best friend lagged behind. "What?" Melissa asked. "What's going on?"

David looked back at Jane. "Will you tell her, or shall I?"

She swallowed hard before she pieced the words together.

"I'm going to learn about this. I'm going to learn how to be a witch."

"First things first," he said, glancing toward Jane's empty glass. "No more alcohol."

"For tonight?"

"For good."

Melissa laughed like he'd told some sort of joke. "Well *that's* not going to happen," she said.

As Jane glared, he addressed his reply to the mundane. "It will, if she wants to learn more."

His words set Jane off. Her spine straightened, and her eyes narrowed, as if she were looking at something in her past. She broadcast the air of a strong woman who wasn't about to let any man tell her what she was going to do or when she was going to do it.

Meeting his eyes, she said steadily, "I won't drink when I'm working with you. I won't drink when I'm being a witch."

Neko laughed. "You're not the one who gets to set the rules!"

Jane scowled at her familiar before she turned back to David, her gaze as hard as jade. "I'm serious," she said. "It's not like Melissa and I get drunk every night. But I can't let this witchcraft thing take over my entire life."

"This witchcraft thing..." He shook his head. "You don't understand—"

"And I'm not going to, if you set rules that change who I am. I won't let you lock me up in a convent."

Convent? Where the hell did *that* come from? He definitely wasn't thinking of Jane as a nun.

But her furious blush made him realize he had to give her something. Hecate would want one of her witches to think she'd won. And he needed to impress Hecate, if he didn't want to work for Pitt another year.

"Very well," he said.

"Very well?" Neko squeaked.

David chose his words carefully, crafting a compromise syllable by syllable. "Very well. You may have a drink, or two. But not when you're working magic. And not when we work together."

It wasn't perfect. His father never would have agreed to a pact like that. Pitt would throw an absolute fit if he found out.

When he found out. Because this arrangement was going to end up front and center at the court, at the Washington Coven, everywhere. There was no way a witch of Jane's power could be kept secret.

But David extended his hand, waiting to see if she'd accept his offer.

Her lips curled into a wide smile. She took his hand firmly and shook three times, as if she'd just negotiated the land-grab of the century.

He didn't allow himself to consider the meaning behind the wave of relief that threatened to swamp him. Instead, he said, "We'll start tomorrow." But it was already nearly midnight. He clarified. "Rather, Wednesday. With dinner."

"With dinner."

David nodded decisively. He'd gotten what he wanted. He could see a clear path to the future. To Samhain, even. And beyond. Before anyone could say anything to set things back, he headed toward the front door.

But then he remembered that pottery plate with its glistening chocolate pastry. He hadn't eaten dinner; he'd planned on feeding Connor roots and leaves and whatever else he could summon from his refrigerator to satisfy the vegan shifter.

He rounded back on the table and scooped up one of the bars before anyone could say a word. The first bite was heaven—shortbread and almonds and that coating of rich dark chocolate. "Mmmm," he said, chewing carefully before he swallowed. "Lust, indeed."

Melissa's jaw dropped, and Jane's face flamed crimson again. Which didn't exactly make him unhappy.

He met his witch's eyes. "Until Wednesday," he said.

"Until Wednesday," she echoed as he stepped into the night.

11

"Very slick, Montrose."

Pitt spoke from the shadows before David made it halfway across the garden. David swore silently.

He hadn't lied when he told Jane her spell had been felt far and wide. Sure, he'd gotten a stronger blast, because he'd already been *reached* by the collection. But every witch and warder in DC knew something powerful had happened on the grounds of the Peabridge Library that night.

At least David had gotten to the cottage first. And now Jane was stepping up as the rightful owner of the Osgood collection.

For now, a stinger of doubt weaseled into his brain.

Swallowing hard to chase away the last vestige of pastry, David planted his feet on the gravel path. For just a moment, he imagined telling Pitt he was quitting his job at the court. He was going to work for Jane full time.

But she wasn't ready for that. She might crumple the first time he told her about the true extent of modern witchcraft. Their dinner might be a disaster. And then he'd be back at square one, without proof of his dedication to Hecate, and Samhain looming even closer. So he closed his fingers over his Torch and managed to keep his voice mild as he answered Pitt's sneer. "Nothing slick about it. I'm sworn to protect witches, wherever they're in need."

"That one's a stumbling child. A babe in the woods."

David pretended to be shocked. "Are you suggesting a new witch isn't worth protecting?"

"I'm suggesting," Pitt hissed, "that she won't last past Samhain. This is all glitter and fairytales for her now. But wait until the first time she feels Hecate's power in her veins. She'll run screaming for her mother."

David thought about how Jane had pulled herself together to reject his initial terms. "She's stronger than you think."

"She'd better be," Pitt said. "Because when news gets out that the Osgood collection's been found, every witch on the eastern seaboard is going to stake a claim."

"There's not a witch on the eastern seaboard—or anywhere else—who has a right to those materials. Hannah Osgood died without an arcane heir. The collection was fairly found by a witch who was able to wake the familiar."

"On the night of a full moon."

Pitt had only just learned about Jane. He shouldn't already know about Neko's untimely awakening. Unless, of course, Pitt had a witch he could consult, a woman with her own familiar who was tied into the network Neko had accessed. And toad or not, Pitt was important enough in the hierarchy of Hecate's Court to have any number of witches on his side.

David dug in. "She was fully within her right to awaken her familiar, whenever she saw fit."

"She didn't have the first idea what she was doing."

"For all you know, she trained in every magicarium from London to Shanghai."

"Tell yourself lies, Montrose, if that helps you sleep at night."

"I sleep just fine."

"Your witch is wild. She'll lose the collection as quickly as she found it. And she'll take you down with her."

"I'm not going anywhere, Norville. I'll be at my desk tomorrow morning."

"The court gave you a second chance after you struck out with Haylee James. But there are no third chances in the world of witchcraft. Fail now, and you'll never ward a witch again."

The words cut David to the bone—his greatest fear, laid bare.

He could accept disappointing Linda. He could deal with explaining a new reality to Connor, telling the shifter he was no longer a citizen in good standing of the Eastern Empire. And Hecate knew he'd long ago grown used to his father's disapproval.

But to never feel warder's magic again? To never know the thrill of transporting from one place to another, *reaching* through the astral plane? To forget the healing, the soothing, the comfort he could summon with a twist of magical thought?

He could save himself now. He could tell Pitt he'd been mistaken. He could ask forgiveness and slink back to his clerk's post with his tail between his legs, all in hopes of eventually working his way free from his clerk's job some day. Some year. Maybe a decade or more in the future.

But the cottage behind him held the *Osgood* collection. And the witch inside was *Jane.*

He was willing to take the risk. Whatever it cost.

He surged past Pitt without a word.

12

S tanding on the sidewalk in one of Washington's most expensive neighborhoods, David folded his fingers over the scar that matched the one on Connor's palm.

"There's another one," he muttered under his breath, trusting to the shifter's superior hearing. He didn't dare incline his head toward the salamander leaning against the lamp post on the street corner. A thin stream of cigarette smoke curled from the imperial's lips as he watched David and Connor approach Apolline Fournier's mansion.

There hadn't been any fire-lizard spies when David tried to gain access to the salamander queen the morning before. But the skeletal guy with the glare burning holes between David's shoulder blades was the fourth they'd seen in the brief walk from the subway. Their leather jackets marked them as if they were members of a 1950s biker gang.

"Come on," David said, approaching Apolline's formidable gate. "Let's get this over with."

David couldn't tell if the guard was the same man he'd seen the day before. He had the same black hair, short and sleek against his smooth skull. He had the same black eyes too, narrowed with evaluation. He even had the same lean fingers, resting on the butt of his gun.

"Mr. Montrose," he said, and he had the same gravelly voice. "Mr. Hold."

Glaring at both of them, he turned a heavy key in a solid iron door, allowing David and Connor to pass through the gate. As the door closed behind them, five men glided from the shadows behind the green hut. At a glance, they looked like clones of the spies on the street—identical leather jackets, whip-thin bodies, and sculpted faces.

"This way," the apparent leader said. He hesitated a moment before he added, "Gentlemen."

David gestured for Connor to go first. The four silent salamanders immediately fell in behind them. David prayed to Hecate that he'd have time to summon Rosefire if all the fire-lizards pounced at once.

The leader opened an unlocked front door, ushering them into a black-painted foyer, complete with an onyx floor. Daylight leaked in from a trio of small windows above the door, only to be swallowed by the dank space.

The salamander leader ignored the twisting staircase that led to the second floor. He didn't glance to the left—a formal dining room—or to the right—an equally formal parlor. Instead, he opened a pair of double doors and bowed slightly from the waist, inviting his guests to pass through to some sort of living room.

Living room. Devil's lair. Whatever.

Blackout shades blocked a full wall of windows. Dark leather couches crouched on a textured white rug, kneeling before a chrome-and-glass table like acolytes before an altar.

A fireplace filled the wall to David's right—obsidian slabs surrounding a maw large enough for a man to enter upright. Gold-red flames flickered from a bed of blackened stones, and the blaze was reflected off a smoked glass mirror on the wall to his left.

A man glided forward from his station beside the fireplace. His mane of grey hair was immaculately combed, and his close-trimmed beard set off stark cheekbones. His black suit melted into the gloom behind him. He nodded a curt command to the five salamanders.

The leader backed out of the double doors, closing them behind him. The four foot soldiers took up positions to either side of that escape, snapping into parade rest poses.

The man barely acknowledged David's presence as he turned to Connor. "Mr. Hold, I presume."

He didn't offer a hand to shake. In fact, his right hand remained buried in the pocket of his impeccably tailored trousers.

The social slight might have been a good thing, given the expression on Connor's face. The shifter's jaw was set and his eyes were wary, unable to keep from glancing at the wall of fire. He failed to offer his own hand. In fact, David wasn't at all certain his friend was capable of moving.

Well, in for a cauldron, in for a safehold. David had already put his job on the line, using this extended lunch break for Connor's shifter business. He might as well speak up, if the Washington alpha couldn't.

Pushing past Connor, David planted his feet on the black marble floor. He met his host's eyes directly and said, "You have us at a disadvantage. You know Connor Hold. I'm David Montrose. And?" He kept his voice perfectly neutral, barely allowing his question to curl into the air.

"I'm John Brule," the man said, betraying the slightest wisp of a French accent as he softened the J, as he lengthened the U in his last name.

"We're here to speak with Apolline," David said.

"Ms. Fournier is not available." Brule loaded an emphasis on the salamander queen's surname, a reminder that this summit required courtesy.

"She has something that belongs to Mr. Hold."

"And Mr. Hold returns the favor." With one cocked eyebrow toward Connor, Brule looked like an international jewel thief. His statement was emphasized by a leap in the fire pit flames. Connor shied back as if Brule had swiped a torch across his face.

Brule had choreographed this confrontation like a master, knowing full well that a shifter would be set off-balance by the open blaze. Wolves and fire had been bitter enemies since the dawn of human time. But David had seen the tell-tale flicker in Brule's arm, the barely-there tightening of muscles above his hidden hand. The salamander had some sort of remote control device in his pocket. He'd simply increased the gas feed to the fire pit.

"You stole the shifters' Collar," David said evenly. "Return it, and we won't need to disturb Apolline."

Brule's eyes narrowed at the continued use of the salamander queen's given name. His voice was oiled as he directed his reply to Connor, matching David's tone exactly. "You stole the salamanders' karstag. Return it, and we won't need to disturb the Eastern Empire Night Court."

That was the challenge, wasn't it? If this dispute went to court, Connor was lost. He'd have no choice but to offer up his errant werewolves. He'd likely be locked up himself, for failure to keep his pack under control.

The alpha remained silent, leaving David little room to maneuver beyond saying, "Mr. Hold can't bring you the karstag."

The salamanders' reaction was immediate—all four guards hissed their displeasure. At the same time, Brule snapped out a command: "Seize them!"

As David fought to grab Rosefire, the room filled with fire-lizards—the four guards by the door and reinforcements that rose up from the shadows. One kicked at the back of David's knee, sending him stumbling toward the edge of the fireplace. Another dropped the hard edge of a hand on the back of his neck, spraying white-hot stars across his vision. Another blow, lower on his neck, and his arms went numb. He had no hope of bringing in Rosefire.

A third salamander picked up a poker, red-hot from the edge of the fire. He sliced it through the air like a saber, putting the full force of his lithe body behind the attack.

David dodged one slash, and he ducked under another. But he was brought up short by the whisper of an obsidian blade against his carotid.

"Move, warder," a salamander urged, his lips close by David's ear. "Just give me one excuse to cut."

From this angle, on his knees, neck stretched back, perilously close to the fireplace, he could see that Connor had fared no better. The shifter's lip had split, and the blood trickling into his beard looked black in the firelight. A salamander had one arm locked across his throat in a chokehold. Another held an obsidian blade over his kidneys, the needle tip reminding him not to attempt to twist free.

This wasn't right. It wasn't fair—eight against two.

Even now, David could reach his warder's magic. He could call upon the Guardians of Water at least, asking their aid in this battle against fire. If he could stretch even a fingertip to reach Connor, he could spirit them both away, transporting them through the ether to someplace safe.

But any show of magic, and Pitt would know David had disobeyed a direct order, leaving his post in the middle of the day. He'd chosen shifter business over his work at the court.

He'd never be able to do anything else to help Connor. He'd never be allowed to ward Jane.

Brule strode into David's line of sight. This time, Apolline's lieutenant barely spared him a glance. Instead, he glared at Connor. "Perhaps you'll bring the karstag to us now," he said.

Connor's lips curled back over red-stained teeth. "Never," he mouthed, before the salamander behind him cut off his air supply. The knife above his kidneys pinked his dark plaid shirt.

"Enough," Brule said, flexing his arm and making the fire leap nearly to the ceiling. "Brand them both, and take them to the pit. Perhaps a little salamander hospitality will make them more inclined to speak. And if not... Well no one will hear them scream, if they need a little...encouragement."

David watched the closest salamander pick up another poker, this one still glowing red from its time in the fire. The writhing lizard carved into the tip looked like it was alive as the iron swung closer to his eye.

13

"Wait!" David shouted.

Brule flashed a harsh hand signal to his men.

Connor tried to toss his head, but the salamanders' restraints were too brutal. Clearly, though, the alpha was telling David to stay silent.

But he had to speak. He'd come to this parley as Connor's second. His job—ludicrous as it seemed now—was to protect the shifter. The odds against them were laughable, but David had to say: "He *can't* bring the karstag to you."

"Perhaps he merely needs the right incentive," Brule said. Looking past David, he nodded to the man who held the brand. "Continue!"

Even as David shut his eyes against the heat, against the light, against the poker's rippling lizard, he shouted, "It's locked in a moon-bound case."

Brule must have issued another silent command. The poker didn't pull away, but at least it grew no closer. "Moon-bound case?" Brule asked at last.

David had never heard of a moon-bound case in his life. But

he was willing to make one up, right there, right now, whatever it took to keep the salamander with the poker at bay. "The shifters put it there for safekeeping." And then, because it was always easier to sell a lie with a bit of the truth, he added, "It was locked on the night of the full moon. The shifters can't retrieve it until the next full moon."

That actually sounded reasonable. If the Washington Pack *didn't* have a formal storage system tied to the moon's cycle, they should. That's what the werewolves had effectively done, in any case.

But Brule was unimpressed. His only reply was to crank the device in his pocket. Flames soared in the fireplace.

David would have flinched if his captors had left him enough room to move. As it was, he watched Connor shrink away, choosing the biting knife over the blaze.

Brule reached past the edge of the fireplace. He took his time selecting a crimson coal, discarding two small ones before settling on a burning knot the size of his fist.

David's stomach turned as the salamander pulled his fingers out of the flames. Logic said his hand should be ruined. His flesh should be black, his bones cracked under the withering heat.

But Brule merely rubbed the coal between his thumb and forefinger, polishing it to a metallic sheen. "One month," he said. "My orders were to get back the karstag now or send you both to the pit."

Of course David knew salamanders were immune to fire. He'd seen proof only two nights before—the melted door of the shifters' safe. Nevertheless, he could not take his eyes from the coal that Brule raised to Connor's face. He couldn't look away, even when the crimson glow illuminated the shifter's lips, his nostrils, the shriveling edges of his beard.

The Washington alpha whined just a little, a sound almost too faint to hear above the roar of the fireplace. But David did hear. And he glanced down to see Connor's open palm, the white line of the oath they'd sworn to each other a lifetime ago. Connor had nothing to offer. Nothing the salamanders would value.

But David did.

"Leave him alone," he said, the words heavy on a sigh.

Brule merely arched an eyebrow.

David managed a ghost of a shrug despite his captors' grip. "In my pocket," he said. "Front right."

After a moment to weigh the risk, Brule nodded. One of his minions plunged a hand into David's pants. He wasted no time fishing out a keyring. The tangle of metal immediately caught light from the fire—nickel and brass keys playing next to the Lexus's sturdy electronic fob.

"You surely don't think I can be bribed with an automobile." Brule's voice was so dry it was a miracle he didn't go up in flames himself.

David merely gestured with his chin. The salamander followed his silent command, turning over the pile of metal. And there it was—etched in silver, sculpted into a lean, swirling shape. The fire made the emblem look as if it were dipped in blood. David felt like it had been ripped from his heart.

"Hecate's Torch," Brule said, not able to mask his surprise. Even a salamander knew the Torch was a warder's symbol of his bond to uphold Hecate's law, to protect the defenseless, to preserve order throughout the Eastern Empire.

"David," Connor said, finally breaking through his horror of the fire.

But David cut him off. "Until the Hunter's Moon," he said to Brule. "Keep it as a sign of our good intentions."

Brule twisted the Torch free from the keys. He held it up to the flickering firelight, turning it so it seemed to kindle. Then he slid it into his pocket, making it disappear beside whatever device he used to control the fire. "The Hunter's Moon," he agreed.

He nodded then, signaling his henchmen to step back. He watched through slitted eyes as David and Connor climbed to their feet. He let them twitch their clothes into place, allowing them to draw a dozen deep breaths each.

"I'll convey your respects to Ms. Fournier," he said.

Fury rose in David's chest at the thought of the salamander queen pawing at his Torch. But that desecration was better than being carried off to the pit. He'd have his Torch back in less than four weeks. A trip to the pit could—almost definitely *would*—last a lifetime.

Brule flicked a hand toward one of the guards, and the double doors opened to the foyer. Other salamanders worked the mansion's front door, then the iron gate, and soon enough David and Connor were limping down a sidewalk, three full blocks from the salamanders' lair.

"You shouldn't have," Connor finally said.

"What choice did I have?"

"But your Torch—"

"You'll get your wolves under control, won't you?" David tried to keep his words light. He didn't want to admit, even to himself, how unbalanced he felt without the Torch in his pocket. It proved he was a man. Proved he was a warder. It was the magical ballast he needed to serve Hecate.

Connor nodded. "But it's not fair—"

"It's not fair that I spent my lunch break locked inside the second circle of Hell," David said, even managing a laugh to accompany the words. After digging in his jacket pocket, he passed a handkerchief to Connor, indicating he should staunch his lip. "Everything will be fine," David said.

The words were automatic, a warder's insistence on order. But he didn't feel fine, not at all. He felt like a man who'd spent a lifetime on an ocean-tossed boat, suddenly trying to find his way on land. His body seemed disconnected from his mind; nothing was where he expected it to be—the sidewalk, the streetlamp, the stop sign at the end of the next block.

Without his Torch, he was literally and figuratively off-kilter.

But none of that mattered. He had to stand. He had to move forward. He had to get back to the office before even more time had passed. Because Torch or not, he had to keep Pitt from discovering anything was amiss.

14

By nightfall, he'd almost grown accustomed to the strangeness of losing his Torch. He'd stopped swallowing hard, trying to get his ears to clear. He'd given up blinking to bring the world into focus. He'd almost trained his fingers not to close on doorways and railings in an attempt to ground himself as he walked through a world that seemed just a bit...off.

He reminded himself that he was still a warder. He'd completed his Academy training, swearing his life to Hecate. The metal charm he'd forfeited was merely a symbol. Its loss didn't change who he was.

Besides, he'd promised to take a witch to dinner. He'd even sent her a text during the day, suggesting when and where to meet—La Chaumiere, in the heart of Georgetown.

As a warder, he automatically sat with his back to the wall in the cozy French restaurant. He continually scanned the other diners, the waiters, and the hostess at the front of the room, examining everyone for any hint of trouble. They were all mundanes, though, not affiliated with the salamanders.

His survey was interrupted by Jane hurrying to the table. "I'm sorry I'm late!" she gasped.

He stood automatically, placing his hands on the back of her chair and edging it forward as she sat. He tried not to think of the wood beneath his palms catching fire, of the flames that had reflected off his Hecate's Torch in Apolline's lair.

Fighting the urge to shake his head, he told himself to focus on Jane. She wore a sleek black dress, something that looked like it was designed for cocktails at the White House. A green necklace caught the light in her eyes. She seemed nervous.

No matter how off-kilter he felt, it was his job to put her at ease. He shot his cuff and glanced at his watch, letting the routine gesture calm his own galloping heart. Forcing a smile, he said, "Actually, you're right on time."

Still, she fiddled with the stem of her water glass, startling like a rabbit as the waiter swept down on the table. "Would Madame like a cocktail?"

She looked to David for permission, her lips trembling with uncertainty.

They certainly weren't working magic tonight. Not with him so distracted by the loss of his Torch. Not with Jane so nervous. He cleared his throat to get the waiter's attention and said, "I'll have a martini."

"Vodka gimlet," Jane countered immediately. She waited until the waiter was out of earshot before she said, "So, we're not actually working tonight."

"Not in the sense that you mean. We're getting to know each other better. You're learning to trust me. To trust yourself and what you can be."

Her cheeks flushed pink. He thought about saying more but decided to wait until she was fortified with liquid courage. After the waiter brought their drinks, he raised his martini and said, "To new beginnings."

She touched her glass to his and repeated the toast. He couldn't help but watch as she swallowed. Her neck was long and graceful. He caught himself staring as the tip of her tongue touched her lips.

Mentally kicking himself, he took a second slug of his drink. This wasn't a date. He wasn't here to seduce Jane Madison. Or to be seduced.

But she *could* turn his life around. He could prove he was able to serve her, to support her to Hecate's satisfaction come Samhain. Jane could be his ticket back to life as a true warder, to freedom from Pitt's tyranny.

So he schooled himself to rigid diplomacy when the waiter came back to take their order. Then he kept his voice perfectly dispassionate as he passed Jane the bread basket, asking, "So? How was work yesterday?"

He hoped she'd realize he was asking about the grimoire she'd used, about whatever poor sap she'd targeted with her love spell.

And she did understand, because she leaned forward with a conspiratorial whisper that tightened his chest. "It worked. The spell worked."

He nodded silent encouragement, and that was all the permission she needed. She started telling him about the man who'd succumbed to the working—Harold Weems, a janitor at the library.

As much as he wanted to disapprove of the spell she'd managed, he had to admit her enthusiasm was contagious. She rattled on about other men she believed had been caught in the backdraft of her working—someone who'd ordered coffee from her, a professor, three other guys who'd hung around that afternoon.

Of course, David knew the true limits of her spell. His own attraction wasn't based on *magic*. He was just off-balance without his Torch, intoxicated by the mere thought of serving as a warder again. And she couldn't actually be strong enough to have ensorcelled all those men. No witch was.

But her face was flushed with success, and her eyes glinted happily in the restaurant's dim light. There'd be time enough to explain her limitations later. For now he let the conversation meander as they ate their appetizers and moved on to their entrées.

She surprised him when she asked, "But what do you do when you're not watching me? I mean, what did you do before I worked that first spell?"

He didn't want to tell her about the court, about Pitt. And there no way in hell he'd mention following a wolf-shifter into the salamanders' lair. He settled for the least of all available evils and said, "I warded another witch until three years ago."

"What happened three years ago?"

Of course she asked that. Any idiot would. And Jane Madison definitely wasn't an idiot. He flattened his voice, hoping she'd realize he wanted to change the subject. "I was fired."

That got her attention. She practically shouted, "What?"

"I was fired," he repeated. And then he bit the proverbial bullet. "My witch decided I was too conservative for her taste. Too restrictive."

"Imagine that," she drawled.

Then he had no choice but to tell her about working for the court. He didn't waste time wondering why he tried to make it sound like something he'd done a long time ago, before Jane had ever dreamed of entering the basement of her garden cottage.

Soon enough she was back to disturbing territory. "So, the witch who fired you. You were her teacher?"

She was so naive. "No. Most of you are educated in a magicarium."

"Magicarium?"

"A school for witches. It's a boarding school. Girls start when they first come into their powers, usually around eight years old. They practice the Rota, a series of basic spells, repeating each one dozens, maybe hundreds of times until they have them mastered."

"Is that what we're going to do?"

"Absolutely not."

He wasn't teaching her anything. He was her warder. At least he would be if Hecate deemed him worthy by Samhain.

But maybe the best way to protect her *was* teaching the basics of witchcraft. Pitt's threat had been perfectly clear—the Washington Coven was coming after the Osgood hoard. Jane had to know a lot more than a love spell if she wanted to survive.

It wasn't actually *forbidden* for a warder to teach a witch. It was just that no warder had ever thought to do it before.

He reached for his Torch automatically, seeking the reassurance of the familiar metal beneath his fingertips. A fresh wave of loss made him choose his words with care. "Most young witches don't have the power to awaken a familiar. Or to broadcast their spells across all of DC. You don't need to start at the beginning. And I don't have the patience to repeat lessons forever."

Mercifully, she headed off on a tangent. "So, who are these witches? Is it hereditary? Like your being a warder?"

"Usually, it is. Hereditary in the mother's line. But it doesn't always pass, not even from a strong witch to a first daughter." He looked her directly in the eye. "Is your mother a witch?"

She hesitated. He hadn't meant to ask a trick question; he just wanted a few more details about her life. But her discomfort was clear before she finally said, "I don't know. I haven't seen her since I was a year old. My grandmother raised me."

He nodded. "And is *she* a witch?"

"Gran!" She laughed out loud. "Absolutely not. She's a little old lady. She drinks Earl Grey tea. She sits on the board for the Concert Opera Guild. She's my *grandmother*, for God's sake."

"Precisely."

But the mere thought of a magic lineage clearly agitated her.

Having launched the uncomfortable line of inquiry, he had to help her now, had to make it better.

Drawing on his years of Academy training, he settled his fingers against her wrist. Her power was sparking wildly, sending bursts of static through his fingers, up his arm, across his entire body.

At least he knew how to manage that. He'd mastered the technique as a third-year student, working with a nervous lab partner in Elemental Summoning 101. Without hesitation, he spun a net with his own steel-grey powers and cast it around her wrist. As the strands settled over the golden thrum of energy fluctuating there, he thought the command: *Relax*, forcing the order through every fiber of his web.

His steel absorbed the errant sparks from her powers. He let her energy jangle into his own bloodstream, kicking his heart into overdrive and squeezing air from his lungs. Then, with a warrior's concentration, he calmed his own responses, permanently banishing her anxiety.

"She's your grandmother," he said reasonably, repeating his command: *Relax*. Again, he absorbed her unease before he elaborated, "And you came by your power from somewhere."

She pulled her arm away.

He'd gone too far. He should have waited long enough to build a natural bond, for her to trust him without magical enhancements. When she finally spoke again, her voice was impossibly small. "Is there any other way?"

She clearly needed separation between the women in her family and the life she'd built for herself—not to mention the new life she was just coming to accept. He understood that. He'd insisted often enough that he was his own man, not just his father's son.

"There is," he said. "Sometimes, power skips generations. Every once in a while—in a very, very rare while—it appears spontaneously. But there hasn't been a wild witch in the Eastern Empire since Salem, since 1692."

A wild witch. Pitt had warned of that in the Peabridge gardens after Jane worked her love spell. A wild witch stood outside the boundaries of Hecate's Court, separate and apart from all her sisters. Jane might wish to be declared wild so she could justify her powers, but the label of "wild witch" would set her on a lonely road. One where she wouldn't need a warder. Wouldn't need him.

"So it's not likely," she said.

"Not likely." He returned to his neglected pork loin and tagliatelle. As he placed the last bite of pasta in his mouth, a drop of sauce fell on his lapel. His lips twisted into a wry smile as he mopped up the spill with his napkin.

The mistake seemed to put her at ease. If he'd known that was all it took, he would have spilled food earlier.

"So, the books," she said, leaning forward. "How did they get to be in the Peabridge's cottage? I mean, isn't that a strange coincidence, that I just happen to be a witch and my employer just happens to have a secret stash of spellbooks?"

That was his opening to tell her about Hannah Osgood and the collection. He'd done his research that afternoon, just in case she asked. So he drew out the tale of the powerful Washington Coven Mother whose life was destroyed during the 1918 flu outbreak. She lost her husband first, then six of her daughters. Only the seventh survived, the youngest, who sadly lacked the awesome power of her mother.

"Magic reaches out to magic," he concluded. "Like magnets, jumping across space to be joined together. Or quantum physics, with particles influenced by actions an entire universe away. The books sensed your powers and influenced the world around you. Your dormant powers sensed the books."

He could see she wasn't convinced. But she thought about

what he was saying—at least until the chocolate soufflé arrived. The waiter put on quite a show, breaking through the dessert's crust and pouring a steady stream of vanilla sauce into the resulting hollow. He served up generous bowls and disappeared into the kitchen.

Jane took her time savoring a spoonful. He couldn't help but grin at the ecstatic expression on her face. "Good?" he asked.

"Heaven."

And that marked the end of Jane Madison's first lesson about witchcraft.

Together, they let the conversation drift to other things—the traditional Halloween parade that would take place through Georgetown at the end of October, the questionable quality of the first autumn apples at the Safeway up the street, whether the temperature would actually dip to freezing over the weekend.

As they talked, he found himself more and more attracted to the woman across the table. She was funny. She was self-deprecating. She observed the world around her closely, making note of the little things that mattered. And she had one hell of a sexy laugh.

By the time he eased her coat over her shoulders, he realized he'd made a decision. Screw tradition. He'd be Jane's teacher. So he said, "We're agreed, then? You'll continue meeting with me to learn more about your powers?"

"Of course." She sounded surprised, as if she'd assumed they would work together. It wasn't until they were walking back to the Peabridge that she asked, "But what sorts of things are you going to teach me?" she asked. "I mean, what can you tell me that Neko can't?"

She really was new to all this. "Neko is your familiar. He can magnify your powers. To some extent, he can even focus them. But he can't raise them in the first place. There are many skills you can learn besides reading spells."

"Such as?"

"Reading runes to predict the future. You'll find some in the basement; Hannah owned antique sets of jade, wood, and clay. There's herb magic too—using plants to enhance good traits or minimize bad ones. You're the owner of a large collection of crystals now. Different stones enhance different powers, and you can learn all about those."

She shivered, clearly overwhelmed by the possibilities. He wanted to tell her she'd be all right, that she wasn't in this alone. He'd be there for her, no matter what happened.

But he didn't trust himself to find the right words. Maybe if he'd had the ballast of his Torch. Maybe if the sidewalk didn't feel as if it was slipping sideways with every step they took.

They reached the garden gate sooner than he'd anticipated. Jane turned to face him. "Thank you," she said. "For everything. I had a lovely time tonight."

His ears heard proper, polite words. But his warder's senses were suddenly awash in night jasmine. He felt the *power* of this witch, amplified a thousand-fold by proximity to the collection that had awakened her. He was tipping, falling, even though his feet were planted on the flagstones. He wanted something, needed something; he longed for the swirling confusion to stop.

And so he kissed her.

He tangled his fingers in her hair. He tasted chocolate on her lips, and surprise and arcane force. He pulled her close, matching her body to his, and she sighed a little, opening her lips. He didn't hesitate to press his advantage.

For the first time in hours, he felt sane again. The world stopped spinning. He had Jane. He didn't need his Torch.

No.

That was wrong.

He was a warder. He was *Jane's* warder, Hecate willing. Until the goddess said otherwise, he was Jane's warder, and she was his witch, and he had absolutely no business kissing her.

He forced himself to pull away, his arms falling like dead

weights to his sides. The temperature seemed to drop a hundred degrees.

He didn't want to meet her eyes, to see her inevitable surprise. But he was a warder, so he forced himself to meet his witch's gaze. "That was wrong," he whispered. Her hazel eyes widened, and he cleared his throat, saying the last word again. "Wrong."

"No! I mean— I wanted—" She fell silent, succumbing to yet another blush. And this time the color in her cheeks shamed him.

"I shouldn't have done that," he said. "I'm your warder."

"So what does that mean?"

He could feel her trembling beside him, but he didn't trust himself to offer a steadying hand. "I shouldn't have blurred the boundaries. You're my witch. I'm your warder. We're going to work at being friends. It is too complicated for us to do anything more. Not while you're still coming into your powers. Not while you're still learning."

Rebellion sparked across her face. But doubt was there, too. Uncertainty, which made her look toward the cottage, toward the Osgood collection.

Following her gaze, he caught a glimpse of Neko in the window. Wonderful. The last thing he needed was a smart-mouthed familiar ready to drag up this momentary indiscretion whenever the manipulative creature wanted the upper hand.

But there was nothing to be done. No way to make it right. Except...

He extended his hand. "Friends?" he asked.

"Friends," she managed, with a single nod.

"Get some rest, then. We'll continue with your training. And be kind to poor Harold Weems."

She smiled wanly before walking to her front door. He waited until she was inside, and he heard the deadbolt shoot home. Then he stepped into a shadow and *reached* toward his own house, before he could change his mind and do something irrevocably stupid.

15

David's phone rang, interrupting his sorting forty years of receipts from a long-defunct emporium of magical herbs. Edging his index finger between the stacks for oregano and orris root, David reached for the telephone handset. "Montrose," he barked, just as the slippery receipts broke free and cascaded to the floor. He barely smothered a curse.

"The pack is out of control." Connor's voice crackled with tension, drowning out the nightingale that whispered at the back of David's mind.

"I can't talk now," David said, mindful of Pitt's ever-present spies.

"They aren't listening to me," Connor said, as if David hadn't responded at all.

"*You* aren't listening to *me.*"

"It's like they're pups, all over again. I can't keep them in line until—"

"Penn Quarter," David snapped. "Farmers Market." He slammed down the phone.

The Farmers Market was the first place he could think of where there'd be a crowd. People would be moving in and out of the booths. No one would linger to remark on an odd overheard conversation.

He was halfway to the stairs when Pitt stepped out of an office. "Going somewhere, Montrose?"

"Taking a lunch break." David never took a lunch break. Except for the day before, when he'd spent the time being roasted in the salamanders' lair.

Pitt's bulging eyes indicated he recognized a lie when he heard one. "At three in the afternoon?"

David barely resisted the urge to barge past the troglodyte. He couldn't linger to debate his imaginary lunch plans. Connor had sounded like he might snap—quite literally—if any mundane crossed his path.

"Fine," David said, sighing as he crafted another lie. "I'm working on the accounts from Green Life. They sold an unusual amount of dill and fennel. I want to bring in some fresh samples. Maybe one of our people can use the herbs to trigger some connection I'm missing."

It was a desperate gamble. Dill and fennel were both used as defenses against witches. If Green Life actually *had* sold a surfeit of the plants, then they might have been double-dealing, working agains the interests of the women who'd kept them in business for three generations.

The story was sheer fabrication, of course. Once he procured his fresh herbs, he'd get Linda to do the reading, one that would show absolutely no connection to malice. Then, he could admit he'd misread the sales numbers, that Green Life had never engaged in any suspicious behavior at all.

For now, he was dangling an impossibly attractive temptation in front of Pitt. David had admitted missing a link. He'd confessed to failure, no matter how minor, hoping his boss would pounce like a tabby on catnip.

"Well, don't waste your time standing around here," Pitt said irritably. "Pick up whatever you need and get back to your desk."

David headed for the stairs at double-time. He didn't want to give Pitt a chance to change his mind.

It was faster to walk to the market than to call an Uber. As David filled his lungs with brisk September air, he tried to tamp down his worry. Connor wasn't a newborn pup. He'd fought hard to gain his alpha position last February. If he lost it now, because he couldn't regain the Collar promptly enough to satisfy the pack...

That type of instability was bad for every imperial in DC. The old saying that nature abhors a vacuum was doubly true when the nature in question was a pack of hormone-addled wolves, rebelling against their leader and fighting for territory in the city streets.

The Farmers Market was in full swing when David arrived. Half the booths sold fruits and vegetables. The other vendors covered a broad range of artisanal products—fresh-baked bread and handmade empanadas, hypoallergenic soap and cold-pack pickles.

David started to seek out the largest purveyor of organic fruits and vegetables, figuring that was where he could get his herbs. Along the way, he found a small stand selling kombucha, the fermented drink glistening like amber in sealed mason jars. David stepped to the side and waited.

In just a few minutes, Connor made his way through the crowd. It was a sign of his distraction that he didn't purchase any tea for himself. He didn't even pause to join in the discussion about the best way to obtain a SCOBY to start a home-brew operation—despite one particularly naive customer proposing to order one from Amazon.

Instead, the shifter sniffed the air sharply and turned toward David with unnerving accuracy. His eyes were hard as both men drifted over to a booth selling mushrooms.

"We can't wait for the new moon," he said, without preamble.

David pretended to be interested in a clutch of thread-like enokis. "You can," he said. "And you will."

"We have to raid the lair tonight."

The aproned woman behind the counter turned from loading a huge chicken-of-the-woods fungus into a customer's bag. From the alert look in her eyes, she'd caught Connor's tone, if not his precise words. It was time to move on.

David led them in the opposite direction from the Mennonite farmers selling organic beef, pork, and chicken, figuring the scent of meat might be enough to push Connor over the edge. Instead, they took refuge in front of bushels of apples and pears. David started searching for the perfect honeycrisp.

"If you do it tonight," he said, purposely keeping his tone conversational, "you'll be branded by dawn. You saw Apolline's guards yesterday. They're on high alert."

"I lost a pup last night!"

A woman with a nose ring and a hummingbird tattoo on her forearm looked up from the Jonagolds. "Did you call the Animal Rescue League?"

Connor started to snarl a reply, but David cut him off, saying, "Great idea."

The woman started to elaborate on shelters or puppies or the glorious autumn weather. Desperate to avoid small talk, David hauled Connor down to the end of the long counter where four baskets of late peaches baked in the strong sunshine.

"You've got to get a grip," he said. "Empire rules."

They'd grown up with the Eastern Empire held over their heads, the ultimate sign of power and influence in the supernatural world. David's life might be controlled by Hecate's Court, and Connor was beholden to the shifters' Council. But as children, they'd been routinely threatened with the Empire Bureau of Investigation, the most powerful police force east of the Mississippi, charged with keeping the existence of supernatural imperials secret from all humans.

Old habits died hard. The reminder about the EBI made Connor glare, but he kept his voice low as he repeated, "I lost a pup."

"What does that even mean?"

"Liam came in with a rack of spare ribs. He sat down at the dining room table like he owned the place. When I told him to take them out back, he refused to move."

David could see that merely retelling the story cost the wolf alpha. He expected absolute obedience from his pack. The thought that a pup—a shifter too young to have sworn allegiance to the pack—would challenge his authority was virtually unthinkable. "What did you do?"

Connor glanced around, confirming no one was paying attention. "I shifted. A nip or two on a flank is better than throwing punches."

David wasn't certain of that. But before he could protest, he discovered that the peaches had attracted the attention of a mother with an infant strapped across her chest. With a pointed look at Connor, David stepped over to the next stand, which boasted an extensive display of baked goods.

Feigning interest in piles of sweet-glazed croissants, scones loaded with currants, and glistening rounds of coffee cake, David asked, "Then what happened?"

"He left." At David's sharp glance, Connor clarified, "He got up on his own two legs and walked out of the house. He left the ribs behind for me to dispose of, and he made it perfectly clear he's not coming back. Not to Seymour House. And not to the Washington Pack. He'd rather be a lone brute than serve under me."

Well, at least the shifter hadn't exposed the pack by roaming DC in his animal form. David edged away from the sweets, taking refuge between loaves of spelt bread and amaranth sourdough. "So you've lost one," he said, trying to sound reasonable. "And you might lose one or two more before the next full moon. But once we get the...heirloom back, they'll all come home."

Connor stared at him. "You don't know."

"Know what?"

"I just assumed, with your Tor—, with your own *contribution* yesterday, you would have sensed..."

"Sensed what, Con?" David barely remembered to keep his own voice low.

"They broke it last night." Connor's hands clutched the edge of the table, threatening to topple the neat stacks of bread. Even without shifter blood, David could sense the effort it took for the alpha to refrain from rippling into his wolf shape.

"The Collar?" he asked, because even here, even in public, it was absolutely vital that he understand what Connor was telling him.

The wolf spared him one tight nod. "One of the links, the one from the Vermont Stake. It's been melted through." David pictured the heavy iron links and imagined how much heat it would take to separate the iron. The salamanders were capable of that. Of more. Much more.

He'd thought offering his Torch would secure the Collar's safety until the next full moon.

He'd been wrong.

"Did they melt it down?"

Connor shook his head tightly. "Not yet. Just cut it loose."

"Then you can fix it next month."

"I'm not waiting a month!" That was loud enough to gain the attention of half a dozen people. Scowling, Connor stomped off, barreling through the line of people waiting to buy bread and cookies. Exasperated, David followed him to the edge of the market.

"I'm not waiting a month," Connor repeated defensively. "I'm taking it to the Eastern Empire court. Tonight."

"You can't. Not unless you can give them back their—" He was playing a dangerous game conducting this conversation in public. He couldn't say the word karstag aloud. He settled for the far less descriptive: "Knife."

Connor's jaw was set beneath his beard. "I'll be fighting every member of my pack before the month is up."

Damn shifters, with their alphas and hierarchies. Connor held his position by the mutual assent of the wolves he led. Any one of them could challenge him to a duel at any time.

"Let them call you out," David said. "You won't have to fight until the next full moon. Three and a half weeks. And you'll have the...knife...by then."

Connor whined, deep in his throat. "I should have gone after her Sunday night."

"You couldn't—"

"As a wolf," Connor interrupted.

David glared. So much for keeping their conversation bland enough for mundane ears. "That's what she wanted. That's why she acted when she did."

"Strike fast. Strike hard. If I'd done it then—"

"You'd be in a holding pen in the Empire courthouse."

"It's not murder, if an imperial acts to save a relic. The Collar counts."

"Not murder, no. They wouldn't get you for harming Apolline. They'd get you for disclosing the Empire to mundane eyes."

Connor's own eyes glowed with rage.

"Go home," David said. "Eat something. Talk to Tala. I promise this will all work out."

"You can't promise that."

Connor was right of course. But David merely firmed his voice. "Go home."

Connor glared. For just a moment, David thought he might actually lose his battle for control. He might let his fingers transform into claws here, in broad daylight.

But the shifter hadn't become alpha of the Washington Pack

by being weak. He jammed his hands into the pockets of his skinny jeans. He hunched his shoulders beneath his blue plaid shirt. He raised his chin in frank defiance and said, "They won't stop with one link, you know. They're declaring war. And there's nothing you or I can do to stop it."

He turned on his heel and stalked into the crowd. David didn't make any attempt to follow him. Instead, he waited until the shifter had disappeared before he turned back toward his office.

That's when he saw the salamander.

The leather jacket was unmistakeable. The close-cropped hair. The dead onyx eyes, staring at David without blinking.

Apolline was having him followed.

He resisted the urge to clutch the tangled keys in his pocket. Once again, he was adrift without his Torch, without its sense of steadiness, its voice of calm.

Lacking his familiar solace, he forced himself to walk toward his office at an even pace. He was halfway there before he remembered he needed to buy dill and fennel.

Doubling back, he found no salamanders in sight, but he was certain they were still there, watching from the shadows. He couldn't find organic herbs either, but by then he didn't really care. The inevitable challenge from Pitt seemed preferable to staying exposed in the marketplace. He'd face down a self-important martinet any day, rather than confront the fire-lizards.

At least he had the choice.

For now.

16

The headache started as David *reached* for home at the end of his Friday workday.

He'd been using his powers to move from place to place since he was five years old, when his father first showed him how to move from the kitchen to his own bedroom. In those early days, he had to concentrate to anchor his steel guide-wire to his destination, picturing the sight and sound and scent of his goal. He had to weave his awareness through the wire and fight his way across the astral plane.

During every single transfer, there was one delicate moment when he was neither *here* nor *there*, when his physical form had completely transferred to the ether. He was vulnerable then, open to both astral and mundane attacks. His training had taught him to minimize that time, reducing it to a matter of heartbeats.

But that Friday night, after a week filled with Jane Madison and Connor Hold and Apolline Fournier and more imperial crises than he'd grappled with in years, he had trouble making the simple connection home. He became too aware of his own heartbeat. He heard his breath inside his lungs. He felt every ridge on his fingertips, each whorl and arch imprinting on the steel-grey cable of magic.

He dragged himself home by sheer force of will

The transport cost him. A vise closed around his temples, and his heart pounded into triple time. He had to blink hard several times to clear the jewel-toned lights that danced before his eyes.

And the worst part was, he couldn't close his Torch inside his fist. He couldn't use the familiar silver lines to relax, to slow down, to return his body and his mind to stasis.

Three fingers of the Macallan didn't begin to take the edge off.

He forced himself to eat—scrambled eggs and toast, the type of food his mother had fed him when he was sick as a child. The meal was one hell of a letdown, especially after French onion soup and pork with tagliatelle the night before.

At least he wasn't in danger of humiliating himself, here in the safety of his own kitchen. He couldn't kiss a witch, letting himself get carried away by her heady cocktail of raw power and touching naiveté. He wouldn't have to pull back like some over-eager high school kid, schooling his thoughts to cold showers and arctic ice floes and sparkling banks of virgin snow.

What in the name of Hecate's sweet breath was he doing with Jane Madison?

Linda had told him to offer himself to the goddess by Samhain, and part of him had scoffed at the deadline. He had a better chance of becoming Norville Pitt's blood brother than of proving himself to Hecate in less than six weeks.

But another part of him had risen to the challenge. He *could* teach Jane—about crystals and herb craft and runes. He'd learned enough watching Haylee fling her powers around. He understood how a witch grounded her powers in the natural world, in Air and Fire, Water and Earth. He could teach that, at least enough to get Jane started on her magical path. To make any bond between them valid in Hecate's eyes.

But did he truly dare?

Something about the woman called to him, something beyond his warder bond to her *Compendium*. Sure, she was fresh and strong, untainted by the endless political currents of the Washington Coven, but that wasn't all.

No. The thing that drew him, the reason he'd kissed her, had nothing to do with witchcraft. It was an older bond, the even more ancient attraction between man and woman. She'd made him laugh. She'd let him relax. He'd had fun.

He'd told her the truth as he backed away. He shouldn't have blurred the boundaries. But *damn*, he wanted to. Right now, sitting alone at the end of the day, when his best friend mourned the possible end of the Washington Pack and his boss plotted yet another way to fire him...

He wanted Jane.

But he couldn't have her. Not that way. So he started to pour another whisky.

He barely stopped himself, knowing alcohol was only a stop-gap. Instead, he whistled to Spot, and headed out for an evening walk.

The black lab wagged his tail, clearly unable to believe his good fortune. The moon—five days past full—was bright enough for David to easily see the path to the woods on the far side of the garage. He'd walked the trail thousands of times. His feet knew every dip along the way. His legs automatically braced against the slope to the lake.

Spot took thunderous side trips into the trees, scaring up half a dozen squirrels. He snuffled at one large trunk, digging hard at the roots until David called him to heel, sparing some woodland creature's home. The dog loped down the path, clearly eager to reach the boat shed and its cache of gnawed-bare tennis balls. It was still warm enough for David to toss a ball far out into the lake, letting Spot retrieve it with single-minded joy.

The dog's whine was the first clue that something was wrong.

The sudden stillness in the woods around them—not a single

bird trilling on a branch, not a solitary bustling squirrel—was the second clue.

The black shadow lying in the ditch beside the path was the third.

In the patchy moonlight, David thought he saw a child. The girl's face was white against her jacket, snowy against the loden green of her collar. Pushing back Spot's concerned muzzle, David was vaguely aware of a tailored shirt that matched the jacket, of trousers in the same dark shade.

He expected the girl's brow to be icy, but he was surprised to find she burned with fever. Peering close in the moonlight, David could tell her lips were chapped. Her hair was damp with sweat.

And he could see that she wasn't a child.

She was a sprite.

David had seen a few of the woodland creatures before. As a race, they were shy and elusive. They avoided contact with humans; even the most gregarious among them limited exposure to other imperials.

Sprites were water creatures. They were bonded to flowing water—creeks, streams, rivers, and the like. Now that he knew what to search for, David could see that this one had buried her hands in the damp ditch searching for a healing flow. She'd smeared mud on her sleeves, on her knees, on the ruined toes of her shoes.

Spot whined in the darkness, dancing back a few steps as if begging David to move away. But David couldn't abandon a feverish sprite in the woods he was bound to protect.

Feeling as if he should apologize for the familiarity, he worked one arm under her shoulders and the other under her knees. He braced himself for the dead lift, but he needn't have worried. The sprite felt as light as dandelion fluff—raging, fevered dandelion fluff.

He could carry her up to the house and get her into the light to see if she suffered any visible injuries. He could wash her and force some food down her throat, some drink.

But the sprite hadn't been dragging herself toward the house. She'd been working her way toward the spring-fed lake, the clear, fresh water that had been David's own destination.

He made his way down the rest of the path, the sprite cradled close to his chest. Spot stuck close, not sparing an ounce of attention for squirrels, for sparrows, even for a sibilant slither that might have been a snake winding through fallen leaves.

It was harder to kneel with the sprite than it had been to stand. Her head lolled at an improbable angle, and one arm dropped into the water at the edge of the sandy beach. Her legs splayed.

David dug out his handkerchief. The square of white cotton gleamed in the moonlight as he soaked the cloth. He bathed her burning forehead first, letting water trickle into her colorless hair. Again, he soaked the handkerchief and let cool, clear water trickle onto pale flesh, washing over her muddy hands.

As David worked, Spot circled around to splash in the lake. The dog's whined concern made David look up, made him see another possibility, another chance. He shifted the sprite's closest arm, making sure her hands rested in the lake. The loden jacket turned black as it soaked up water. The weight of the fabric pulled the sprite onto her side.

Spot pranced closer, sending up a cool spray. David started to call the dog off but before he could speak a command, the sprite stirred. Her eyelets fluttered as droplets of fresh lake water fell on her lips.

David splashed her face again. One more time. And then the sprite was pulling herself into the water, submerging her head in the cold lake for longer than any human could have survived.

Her legs twitched. Both hands scrabbled at the sandy bottom. She pulled herself even deeper, ignoring the man, ignoring the dog.

David made a single curt hand gesture, summoning Spot to shore. The dog obeyed reluctantly, keeping his attention on the creature who lay face-down in the water. David let his fingers stroke the dog's velvet neck; he needed his own assurance that he wasn't watching a sprite drown.

Just as David resolved to rescue the creature, water-spirit or not, she finally rolled onto her back. It took a moment for her eyes to focus and even longer for her to plant her elbows in the sand and push herself up on one side. Finally, she sat, one hand braced in the lake, the other wiping water from her face.

"Thank you," she said, her voice breaking on the second word.

David nodded. "Is there something I should get you? Someone I should call?"

"No, Montroseson."

David shuddered at the name. This sprite knew him. She hadn't arrived at the farm by accident.

He watched her fingers trail through the lake water, growing straighter, stronger, as if she sucked sustenance through her fingernails. "I'm Bourne Morrissey," she said at last. "And I owe you my life, Montroseson."

He answered the sprite's declaration with a touch of formality. "You have me at a disadvantage. You know my name, and I know yours. But what brings you to my land? How far is your stream?"

Bourne's face tightened. "I have no stream."

David waited, recognizing a story in her hesitation.

She didn't disappoint. "The humans diverted my stream. It was in their Howard County, near their city of Baltimore. They built houses there and destroyed my home, so I took to mundane roads."

"But that's thirty miles away"

Bourne nodded. "Flowing water is scarce between here and there. I found two streams, but they were home to other sprites. I could not steal my siblings' beds."

"What brought you here?"

"I knew the Montroseson before you." Bourne knew David's father. "He called upon my aid once, decades ago as you warders count time. In return, he offered me sanctuary at his croft."

Croft. That was the old term for a warder's territory. Now most warders didn't bother with land at all. They guarded their witches and lived in cities.

But this farm had been George's croft before David's mother insisted on moving to DC. David couldn't remember the last time James or Tommy had come back to the property. George either, for that matter. But to David it had always been home—the house and the barn and all the land around them.

The lake too.

"I've never seen a sprite around here," he said.

Bourne looked across the water. "There was one, long ago, tending the stream that feeds the lake from the north. He faded away seven, no, eight of your decades ago."

David shivered. A breeze had picked up, cutting through his wet pants. He glanced at the soaked sprite. "You must be freezing. Come up to the house and get something to eat."

Bourne tore her gaze from the far shore. "I need no food. Not tonight."

David's first instinct was to argue. He was in charge here. He was supposed to protect the weak, to nurse the ill.

But Bourne didn't look weak any longer. Her limbs were clean and straight. Her lips were smooth in the silver light of the moon, as if they'd never been rough and chapped. "You've given me life, and yet I ask another favor. May I hold your stream?"

Hold.

The sprite was asking to take up permanent residence. She wanted to claim the ancient waterway, to nurture it, to tend its needs.

David was charged with protecting the croft. The sprite's presence could only make the stream stronger—the stream, and the lake, and the land that surrounded it.

"I'd be honored," he said, inclining his head.

Bourne laughed, and the sound was like a river rolling over stones. She held out her hand, water dripping back into the lake. "The honor is all mine, David Montrose."

As the sprite spoke, Spot tossed his head toward an ancient oak that nestled on the lake's edge. Following the dog's gaze, David looked up until he saw a flash of white surrounded by night blackness. An osprey, he realized—one of the great fisher-hawks that nested on the edge of the water.

The birds approved of the sprite's arrival. And that was good enough for him. He clasped hands with Bourne and shook on their new bond.

17

B ack in the farmhouse, David found himself too restless to settle down. He should take a seat on the grey couch in the living room. Pour himself a drink. Read a book. Watch a movie.

But too many distractions spun through his head.

He wondered how Bourne was doing at the stream, if she'd settled in, what it *meant* for a sprite to settle in. He wondered how Connor was faring back at Seymour House, whether any of the wolves had come home with steak or ribs or some other verboten food. He wondered whether Apolline Fournier was destroying another link of the Collar, if she was going to keep poking and prodding the shifters until open warfare was the only option.

He wondered about Jane.

She'd denied any witches in her family tree. Sure, it was possible she was the first wild witch in three centuries. But it was a hell of a lot more likely she just hadn't mapped the tree properly.

His interest was more than personal. Wild witches stood beyond Hecate's Court. He could never watch over Jane if she were a wild witch. And more and more, he wanted to watch her powers develop.

He needed to impress the goddess, and he might just do that by determining Jane's lineage. Surely Hecate would reward a man who brought a long-lost line of witches back into the fold.

His first step would be talking to Jane's mother. Well, maybe not her mother. Jane had made it perfectly clear her mother wasn't part of her life. With her grandmother, then.

The court maintained access to thousands of databases, magic and mundane. He used his official login to track down Jane's grandmother in a few keystrokes—Sarah Smythe at a staid DC address in a pre-war apartment building near Rock Creek Park with a 202 phone number.

In fact, it took him longer to debate whether he wanted Pitt to know what he was doing. But Pitt would find out anyway. He always did.

He glanced at the clock on his phone. 9:37. Too late to call a stranger, especially an elderly one, even on a Friday night.

His palms itched. He couldn't wait till morning.

One ring.

Two.

He couldn't trust his message to an answering machine.

Three rings.

He prepared to end the call.

"Smythe residence. Sarah speaking."

At least it didn't sound as if he'd woken her. "Mrs. Smythe," he said, trying to swallow his gratitude. "My name is David Montrose. I'm a security specialist for the District Court, and I'm calling about a security clearance requested for one..." He paused, as if he were shuffling papers on a desk. "Jane Madison. I understand she's your granddaughter?"

"Yes?" The answer came out sounding more like a question.

He pushed his advantage before she could think to ask for more details. "In order to complete our clearance process, we need to speak with at least one direct relative of the applicant.

Due to the sensitive nature of our inquiry, we prefer to conduct our meetings in the privacy of our interviewees' homes."

"Oh dear, I don't think—"

"Of course, you're more than welcome to have someone else present. Perhaps another relative?" He loaded the words with just a little warder's magic. If she were a mundane or a registered witch partnered with her own warder, his tone would have no effect at all. But if she carried magic in her blood and was unpaired, his glamour might reach her. She might feel safer, more relaxed.

"My daughter will be coming over tomorrow morning. You could stop by then."

He tried to smother the excitement ignited by her words. Focusing on spinning out a little more of his warder's magic, he said, "Excellent, Mrs. Smythe. What time should I be there?"

"Why don't we say nine o'clock? You can join us for a bite of breakfast. Let me give you the address. Do you have a pen and paper?"

"I've got the address, right here," he said. "On Jane's application form."

He hoped his answer dispelled any lingering doubt in the old woman's mind. Hanging up, he glanced into his kitchen. Now, he could pour himself that drink—and spend the rest of the night planning his fact-finding mission to the satisfaction of the goddess he longed to impress.

18

"Please, Mrs. Smythe," David said. "You shouldn't have gone to all this trouble. And on a Saturday morning, too."

"What trouble?" she asked. "Breakfast is the most important meal of the day."

David could see where Jane got her irrepressible attitude. Sarah Smythe reminded him of some sort of bird, full of energy and excitement. She perched on the edge of her chair, head tilted to a curious angle, bright hazel eyes taking in his slightest movement. Her snow-white hair was held off her face by a pair of combs that looked like genuine tortoiseshell. Her hands fluttered toward the array of plates and bowls displayed on the coffee table. She seemed unaware that her knuckles were swollen, with her fingers twisted into delicate claws.

"Please, Mr. Montrose," she insisted. "Help yourself."

He leaned forward and put a small clump of grapes on his plate.

She sniffed in disapproval. "I *said*, Mr. Montrose, *help* yourself."

Hoping to build further rapport, he added three cookies to his plate. When Mrs. Smythe still looked disapproving, he picked up a slice of pecan-laden banana bread. She finally nodded, appeased.

Then she filled her own plate. A fistful of grapes. Three walnut-stuffed dates in tiny gold cups. A hefty slice of cheddar. Cookies, banana bread, and a chunk of sugar-laced coffee cake that filled the room with the smell of cinnamon.

As she settled back on her throne, her daughter came in from the kitchen. *Clara*, David reminded himself. *Clara Smythe*. Jane's mother.

The woman balanced three teacups with matching saucers on a tray. David sprang to his feet to help, but she laughed at the attention, tossing back a mane of hair tinted a red that could never have been found in nature. "Here you go, Mother," she said, passing a cup of mud to Mrs. Smythe. "Decaf for you. Full test for our visitor." She nodded toward David's cup before picking up her own. "And tea for me."

He got a whiff of smoky oolong—a preference she shared with her daughter—but the brew in her cup was nearly the color of rainwater. As David eased back into his chair, Clara helped herself to a single grape, popping it into her mouth as she settled into a lotus pose in the middle of the couch. She had her mother's hazel eyes, the same as Jane's.

"So," Clara said. "Mother says you're here about a security clearance for Jeanette."

"Jeanette?" he asked.

Clara's laugh sounded like she'd found it at the bottom of a bottle of cheap whiskey. "I keep forgetting. *Jane*. She doesn't go by the name I gave her."

He wanted to learn that story, but he had more important tasks that morning.

He took a sip of coffee. Instant. He fought to keep from grimacing as he returned the cup to its saucer and searched for the right words. "I might have been a bit misleading over the phone," he said. At the alarmed look on Mrs. Smythe's face, he hastened to add, "But I only have Jane's best interests in mind."

"I knew it!" Clara exclaimed. "I knew you were lying the minute you walked through that door!"

"Clara, dear," Mrs. Smythe murmured.

"Just look at his aura, Mother! Can't you see how muddled it is?"

Hecate grant him patience. Clara was a New Age believer. The type of aura she claimed to see didn't exist. And the type of aura *he* was trained to detect—the after-image of a magical working— would never be visible to a non-warder.

"Mr. Montrose," Mrs. Smythe said, obviously discomfited. "My daughter is quite interested in esoteric studies."

"I'm glad to hear that," he said, trying for a sincere note. "Because what I've come to tell you might be difficult to believe. The more familiar you are with...auras and esoteric studies, the easier this will be."

Clara leaned forward on the couch, drinking in his every word. At the same time, Mrs. Smythe started to worry the edge of her napkin.

Time to lay his grimoire on the table. "Mrs. Smythe," he said. "Clara. I have reason to believe that Jane is a witch."

He was ready for almost anything. Furious denunciations and demands that he leave the premises at once. Hysterics and palpitations and collapsing to the floor. Stunned denial and the need to repeat his declaration multiple times until the impossible words were processed.

But he wasn't prepared for laughter.

Mrs. Smythe threw back her head. Her silver hair shook. Her eyes watered. She fought for breath.

David leaped to his feet, barely rescuing her over-full plate before those dates rolled to the floor. "Mrs. Smythe?" he asked, when she finally came up for air. "Did you hear me? I said your granddaughter is a *witch*."

"Of course she is!" Mrs. Smythe said, wiping tears from her cheeks.

David passed her plate back to her. "You already knew?"

"All the women in the Smythe family are witches."

"Mother!" Clara said. "You never told me that!"

Mrs. Smythe reached across to pat her daughter's arm. "Believe me, dear. You didn't need any more excuses to be odd."

If Clara were insulted, she recovered quickly. "What magic can we do? Are all Smythes attuned to the Vortex the way I am? Can we all read ley lines? What about auras, and horoscopes and—"

David interrupted the catalog of claptrap. "Do you know your lineage, Mrs. Smythe?"

"Not precisely," she admitted. "But we're descended from Abigail Somerset of the Massachusetts Somersets. She had the good sense to leave Salem thirteen years before all that nonsense started. Changed her name to Windmere and said she was a widow to avoid hassles on the road. She married Theophilus Carroll, bought a farm in Connecticut, and never looked back."

David wondered if he looked as stunned as he felt. Hecate's Court tracked every descendant from Salem. The court had gone back ten years before the witch-hunting madness exploded, tracing the bloodlines of anyone who'd fled Salem as accusations bubbled to the surface.

But *thirteen* years? And a double name change, along with a move to a different state? Abigail Somerset was completely invisible to Hecate's Court.

David fought a frisson of excitement as he said, "I work for Hecate's Court. It's a secret organization dedicated to protecting witches. Jane recently came to our attention because of...skills she demonstrated."

"Our Jeanette!" exclaimed Clara, pressing a hand to her heart. "I knew it! Didn't I tell you, Mother? My horoscope said it was time to come back to DC. 'A loved one has need of your aid.'"

Mrs. Smythe's frown expressed everything she believed about horoscopes. "Mr. Montrose," she said. "What exactly do you want from us?"

"I want what's best for Jane," he said quickly. "Often, we find that witches mirror their mothers' power. With three generations of Smythe women working together, harnessing the raw power we've already seen from Jane…"

Mrs. Smythe shook her head. "I don't think that will be happening right now," she said.

"Excuse me?"

"This is not the time to push my granddaughter."

"With all due respect, Mrs. Smythe, this is *exactly* the time to encourage Jane to explore her strength. She's already awakened her familiar, and she's worked her first spells. If she collaborates with the two of you to grow and expand her reservoir of power—"

"No."

"Maybe I haven't made myself clear—"

"You've made yourself perfectly clear, Mr. Montrose. But you're speaking about the potential of a woman you've barely met. I'm speaking about the emotional well-being of a granddaughter I know and very much love. This is not the time to turn her world upside down." Mrs. Smythe took a prim sip of her decaf, settling her cup back on its saucer with a delicate clink of china on china. The sound seemed to help her reach a conclusion. "All right, Mr. Montrose. I wasn't going to say this. It's nobody's business but Jane's. But I honestly believe you want to help her."

Nevertheless, Mrs. Smythe hesitated, looking at her daughter while her lips thinned with some unexplained tension. But by the time she turned back to him, the old woman was a mountain of resolve.

"Jane ended a long-term relationship nine months ago," Mrs. Smythe said. "Her employer is financially insolvent, which places her job in jeopardy. And just this week, she learned that her mother—Clara—is alive and well and interested in being part of her life after more than twenty years. In fact, she's going to meet her mother this morning."

Now David understood Mrs. Smythe's furious devotion to Jane. But he couldn't give up. Not with Samhain only five weeks away and his career hanging in the balance. "I can't walk away from Jane's potential, Mrs. Smythe."

The old woman's lips twisted in a resigned grin. "I'm not asking you to. I suspect Jane won't let you, either. But Clara and I can't get involved. We can't be part of her training in any way." She sipped at the sludge in her coffee cup and eyed the platter of sweets as if the secrets to the universe were written in pastry. "Why don't we try this? The three of us will keep this little talk a secret. David, dear, you go on and teach Jane whatever you think she's ready to learn. But Clara and I? We'll just pretend this little meeting never happened."

It felt wrong. She was asking him to lie to his witch.

No. She was asking him to lie *for* his witch. She'd known her granddaughter since Jane was an infant. She knew what was best.

"All right," he said at last.

"Excellent!" Mrs. Smythe crowed. And she settled back in her chair and finished every last bite on her plate.

19

David edged past the stack of bankers boxes in the hallway, then brushed at the dust on his sleeve. He'd come straight from Sarah Smythe's apartment, intent on using his Saturday to investigate the story she'd told him.

He wasn't surprised that a quick computer search on the mundane Internet had yielded no information about Abigail Carroll, née Somerset. He'd hoped for a little more from the court's internal filing system—if not a reference to the witch in conjunction with Salem, then some mention of her name with regard to artifacts she'd once owned, properly recorded on Request for Protection forms if nothing else.

His senses had jangled as he ran a dozen quick searches. Relics that he'd logged personally set off a symphony of sounds, an explosion of tastes at the back of his throat. He saw a few flashes of light, and one long-orphaned rowan wand ignited the sting of nettles across the backs of his hands.

But none of those items connected with Salem, Massachusetts was actually tagged with Abigail's name—not the relics he'd cataloged, nor ones that had been docketed by any other warder.

Knowing his task was hopeless, he'd checked birth records for the Boston Coven. They'd exercised control over Salem for decades before the seventeenth-century disaster. He called up membership records for fifty years after the mad events brought on by a handful of mundane girls and the intolerance of a church threatened by the strength of perfectly ordinary women.

Nothing. Not a hint of Abigail Somerset Windmere Carroll's life. And so he found himself walking down a dusty basement hallway, shoving aside boxes of old records and feeling the grit of countless years under the soles of his shoes.

Warders weren't big on libraries.

Classrooms, where they were drilled on magical workings, on obligations to witches, on their ancient obligation to the elemental Guardians and Hecate—check. The Academy occupied the top eight floors of the building.

Gyms, where they mastered swordplay and martial arts and a dozen other disciplines to best protect their witches—check.The warders' gym filled the entire third floor.

Offices, where the least-accomplished among them wasted hours inputting computer data to satisfy power-mad bosses—check. The first and second floors were filled with offices.

Individual witches might accumulate collections of books, like the Osgood trove Jane now possessed. And covens might pool their resources, sharing rare texts among themselves, as the Washington Coven did. But warders didn't rely on book knowledge. They simply had no need to study spells and runes, herblore and crystals.

Therefore, this was the first time in his entire career that David had strayed into the library of Hecate's Court. He'd double-checked the basement room number, just to make sure he knew where to go.

The door at the end of the hall was painted a dull green that some industrial psychologist had probably recommended fifty years earlier, claiming it would calm whoever worked there.

There wasn't a lock or any other indication that precious materials might lurk inside.

David turned the doorknob and shoved the door open, half expecting it to creak on its hinges like the cheapest of special effects in a horror movie. There wasn't the groan he anticipated, but it took him a moment to find the light switch, farther down the wall than any contemporary designer would have recommended.

Blinking in the dim yellow light, he made out a dozen dilapidated boxes, mostly crushed on at least one side. A few wooden bookcases slouched against the walls, sway-backed shelves indicating they'd once held something heavy. A handful of books—no more than a couple dozen, all told—was scattered on the shelves. *Who Wards the Warder?* asked one, its title picked out in lurid red letters on a yellow background. *The Care and Feeding of Warders* announced another in scrolling black letters across a field of dusky blue.

A dozen metal bookcases filled the rest of the room, empty except for banged-up shelves canting at unlikely angles. A single glance confirmed that no wealth of historical records lurked in the abandoned room.

Why had David thought he could find information about a lost line of witches here, where no warder had passed for ages? It had been yet another stupid idea, one more off-base decision, probably the result of his astral senses being warped without his Torch.

He started to turn back to the hallway when an army charged in from nowhere.

No. That wasn't an army stampeding across the room. It was one man snorting—loud enough and long enough that David glanced at the ceiling, fearing the fluorescent lights would shake loose from their fixtures.

As David froze, the gargling throat-clearing settled into a series of ratcheting snores, each one louder than the last. He only edged toward the noise when he was certain the asbestos tiles wouldn't crumble above him.

A bare mattress lay in the far corner of the room, wedged between the last bookshelf and the wall. A man sprawled on his back, limbs splayed across the blue and white ticking. He wore stained grey sweatpants and an undershirt that might once have been white. His feet were shoved into torn Chuck Taylors, with no socks in sight.

It looked as if he'd have an easier time shaving his head than working a comb through his tangled hair. His beard, more salt than pepper, wasn't in better shape. The one hand David could see looked calloused, with torn hangnails around the thumb.

A tattered box of Pop-Tarts rested above the man's head. Three different bottles of wine bled their dregs into the mattress.

David's first thought was to call Court Security. They could get the homeless guy out of the building with a minimum of fuss.

Before he could back away, another snore sawed through the air. Amazed by the vagrant's lung capacity, David glanced at the guy's chest.

That's when he saw the Torch—fashioned out of silver and strung on a fine-linked chain that was almost lost against the filth of the T-shirt. The man was a warder.

And he was awake.

That last snore must have been more than even the drunk sleeper could ignore. Laser-sharp blue eyes peered out from a network of fine wrinkles. Before David could speak, the man rumbled, "You're George Montrose's boy, aren't you?"

David was a man, his own man, had been for a decade and a half at least. But he owed respect to the older warder. Those were the strictures of Hecate's Court, keeping the world safe for witches and mundanes alike.

"David Montrose," he said, offering to shake after only a second's hesitation.

The other man ignored his hand, using his elbows to haul

himself into a sitting position. "Aidan," he barked, by way of introduction. "Aidan O'Rourke."

Of course David knew the name. Every young warder did. Aidan O'Rourke had warded Maggie Hanes, a witch in the Boston Coven. He'd watched over her for twenty-two years. But she'd killed herself in the most public way possible, raising a fiery circle near the swan boats in the Public Garden. Mundane police had investigated for months. Local television shows had interviewed traumatized kids who'd seen the whole thing. Entire websites were devoted to dissecting the supposed cover-up of some vast terrorist conspiracy.

Aidan O'Rourke had done nothing—not to save Maggie as she slipped into despair, not to hide her actions on the night she took her life, and definitely not to deflect unwelcome mundane attention during the scrutiny that followed. As a result, the warder had been burned. The Boston Coven Mother had told him his services were no longer needed. The Academy had rejected him as a potential teacher of impressionable youth. The court had refused to consider him for any job, even one as lowly as clerk. He'd been cast out from the society of warders.

O'Rourke's name became synonymous with failure. "At least I didn't pull an O'Rourke"—David had heard it for years. Linda had said it to him when he'd debated working for Pitt: "Take the job as a clerk, David. At least you can build on that. It's not like you pulled an O'Rourke."

The ruined man haunted every living warder. If asked, David would have said O'Rourke was dead by now. If not in a grave, he must be imprisoned in some mundane jail. Maybe, just possibly, he'd fled the Eastern Empire altogether.

But, surprise of surprises, Aidan O'Rourke was very much alive. And if he hadn't hit bottom yet, his feet were scraping the jagged edge.

The grizzled warder looked suspicious as he asked the question David was thinking. "What the hell are you doing down here?"

David was surprised enough to answer honestly. "Looking for genealogy records."

"Down here?"

He shrugged. "It seemed like a good idea at the time."

Those eyes pinned him again, more alert than they had any right to be. "What family?" he demanded, as if that was a perfectly normal response.

It couldn't hurt to tell him. It might even help. O'Rourke had been tied to the Boston Coven for decades. "Carroll," David said. "Or Somerset. Witch's name, Abigail. She came from Salem originally."

Silence, while whatever rusty wheels that passed for memory turned inside O'Rourke's skull. Finally, a short shake of his head. "Never heard of her. There's a Carroll family in Connecticut, though. Near Old Salem, if that's not confusing enough."

That would be the farm Clara Smythe had mentioned. But David wasn't going to learn more about that place here. Not amid nearly-empty shelves with a wreck of a warder peering at him through dangerously bright eyes. He offered a shrug and kept his voice even. "I guess I'll have to look somewhere else."

"I guess so."

Feeling awkward, David crossed to the door, but he turned back before he left. "Do you need anything? Food? Something to drink?"

O'Rourke jutted his chin toward the Pop-Tarts. "Got food."

And David didn't want to bring O'Rourke another bottle of wine. He hesitated a moment longer, though, his hand hovering near the light switch. "Lights on?" he asked.

O'Rourke snorted. "How's a man supposed to sleep around with the lights on?"

David argued before he thought better of it. "You're going back to sleep? It's the middle of the afternoon."

For reply, O'Rourke muttered under his breath and turned over on his mattress. His T-shirt rode above the waistband of his pants, and David stared at the knobs of his bare spine. There wasn't anything else to say. Not "Good night," because the sun was still high above the horizon. Not "See you later," because David never wanted to see the other warder—the symbol of abject failure—again. Not "Good luck," because there was no luck involved in O'Rourke's fate at all—he'd been a warder charged with protecting a witch, and he'd failed.

Shrugging, David turned off the light and headed upstairs, no better off for his trip to the warders' lousy excuse for a library.

20

By the time he'd climbed back to the first floor, David was planning his visit to Jane. The steely thread to her cottage was anchored in his memory, its cool strength calling him like the placid surface of the lake back at the farm. By now, she'd met her mother. She'd had coffee or tea or one of those amazing pastries her friend baked. She'd confronted her past, the dark memories, the hard questions that had shuttered her expression over dinner at La Chaumiere.

He couldn't just travel to Jane, though. Sure, he had his warder's magic. It would barely take an effort to *reach* for Georgetown.

But he wasn't supposed to know about Clara. He wasn't supposed to know anything at all about Jane's family—her mother, her grandmother, any of it. And he couldn't trust that his desire to see Jane was based on helping her. He suspected at least part of his interest sprang from his memory of that kiss, the one he never should have allowed to happen.

Of course, meeting Clara might drive Jane to explore the Osgood collection in her basement, and then she'd need a warder. She might retreat from her complicated family life to research arcane lore in her newfound books. She might even study the crystals or runes or herbs she now owned.

He could help Jane with that. It was his *obligation* to help her.

He flexed his powers and reached into his memory like a tired man testing a bad tooth. He remembered the sound of the kettle-drums perfectly. But the *Compendium* wasn't summoning him now.

There wasn't any flash of emerald light, either. Neko wasn't flexing his power as a familiar.

No scent of jasmine anywhere. No hint of Jane.

He stopped dead in the middle of the atrium. He was as bad as a lovelorn schoolboy. Jane was an unwelcome *complication* in his life—the witch and her familiar and all the items in the Osgood collection. He should be grateful he wasn't needed.

Had O'Rourke felt grateful after his witch was gone?

What the hell kind of question was that?

Once the words had come together in his mind, however, he couldn't let them go. What sort of life did the old warder have? Pop-Tarts and wine and clothes worse than rags...

Dammit. He couldn't go to Jane. And now he couldn't go back to his own home. He needed to help the man in the basement. At least he could get the guy a decent meal.

Alas, David realized as he stepped onto the sidewalk outside the anonymous building that housed the Academy and the court, buying a meal was easier said than done. It was Saturday after-noon in the middle of a downtown block more accustomed to housing lawyers and lobbyists than a single well-intentioned warder. The sandwich place on the corner was locked as tight as the drums he still remembered at the back of his thoughts. The three banks and the cell-phone store in the middle of the block were shut down as well.

But there was a Starbucks across the street, and it was open, because no Starbucks anywhere ever seemed to close. He darted across F Street, easily avoiding the lonely red-and-grey taxicab cruising hopelessly for a fare.

The display of travel mugs solved one problem—he could buy coffee and keep it warm until O'Rourke managed to claw himself back to wakefulness. A cooler held an array of sandwiches; David picked up three without paying attention to the labels. He grabbed some overpriced organic free-range gluten-free chips as well, the type of thing that would send Connor over the moon. If, that was, Connor ever deigned to set foot inside a Starbucks. The shifter was partial to independent coffee shops with small-batch artisanal pour-overs. Of course.

O'Rourke wouldn't be as picky. David added some packaged almonds, a few pieces of fresh fruit, a box of cookies... In the end, he spent close to a hundred bucks.

Something about the purchase felt like a ritual of atonement. But that was ridiculous. David hadn't done anything wrong. Not exactly. Not like O'Rourke. Haylee's practicing dark magic was nothing like Maggie Hanes's committing suicide. David had never officially been burned.

He barely resisted the urge to reach for the Torch he knew wasn't there.

He was exiting the store, juggling two bags of food and a sealed coffee mug, when an incoming customer bodychecked him. Barely managing to keep the mug from crashing to the sidewalk, he scowled in annoyance. The kid who'd almost bowled him over was glued to his phone and barely looked up.

Barely. But the guy *did* glance up from his screen for long enough to stammer, "M— Mr. Montrose!"

David tried to place the red hair, the freckled face, the wide green eyes that looked like they might belong to Jimmy Olsen of *Superman* fame. No luck, even though the kid had jammed his phone into his pocket and was frantically, desperately trying to shuffle left, right, left again, intending to give David the right of way but matching him step for step in some sort of crazed ballet.

"Stop!" David finally barked, and the kid froze. David maneuvered out the door, only to have Jimmy follow him onto the sidewalk.

"I'm sorry, Mr. Montrose. I should have been looking where I was going. My mother always tells me—"

"No problem."

"But Mr. Montrose—"

"Don't worry about it."

"Can I help you carry your...lunch back to the office?"

Office. That meant the kid worked for the court. Not that David cared. "I'm fine," he said, but he wondered if the boy really thought he could eat all that food in one sitting.

"It's no problem, really. I don't even need a cup of coffee. I just came over here because I'm waiting for the D1000 update patch to load onto the 703A system."

A connection finally clicked inside David's mind—a tiny spark of peppermint oil across the back of his throat as he recalled emails he'd received from the Help Desk. There'd been instructions about new systems, reminders about security measures, apologies for outages. "Kyle," he said. "Kyle Hopp."

A blush started at the tips of the kid's ears, quickly flooding down his face to the V of his shirt. "Yes, sir. Mr. Montrose, sir."

David interrupted the enthusiastic reply. "David," he said.

"D— David."

After that, Kyle seemed out of inane things to babble. David finally nodded toward the office. "I'll just be getting back—"

"You don't want to do that s—, David."

"Why not?"

"Mr. Pitt came down to the Help Desk about fifteen minutes ago. He asked me to track you down through your cell phone's signal, and he didn't seem to be in a very good mood."

As if Pitt was *ever* in a good mood. Well, so much for going back into the building. The last thing David wanted was to lose what remained of his Saturday doing Pitt's make-busy work. But that meant he had no way to get his over-priced coffeehouse fare to O'Rourke.

"And what did you tell Pitt?" David asked. The kid had warned him off going back into the building. Maybe he could actually be trusted as an ally.

"I told him we weren't allowed to use Help Desk resources to track down a warder. Not without a completed Real-Time Resource Monitoring form, submitted in triplicate with counter-signatures from at least two court judges."

"I'm sure he loved that."

Kyle looked uneasy. "He threatened to report me to my boss. And he demanded to talk to someone else on duty. But there wasn't anyone else. Not on Saturday."

Aren't you a little young to be left in charge?

Something in his expression must have given away his thoughts, because Kyle said, "I'm allowed to staff the Help Desk!"

David lied. "I didn't think—"

"I got permission from the headmaster to work at the Help Desk on weekends."

So, the kid was still in the Academy. Most boys his age spent their weekends working on fighting forms and swordplay, maybe even memorizing a few rituals. They played pranks on each other and whichever teachers they thought they could harass without incurring overly egregious penalties.

But Kyle Hopp preferred to spend his weekend staffing the Help Desk. He must be finding Academy life...challenging.

The kid's phone buzzed. David glanced down in time to catch the flash of a crimson notification on the screen. He recognized the form immediately, although he'd received his by email back when he'd been in school.

Clearly embarrassed, Kyle jammed his phone into his pocket. He looked like he might cry.

"Demerit?" David asked sympathetically, because he'd served enough hours when he'd been a student.

Kyle nodded.

David cocked his head. He couldn't imagine what Kyle had done to earn the punishment. He certainly didn't seem the trouble-making type. Except...

"What class are you failing?" David asked.

"Swordplay," Kyle answered, whispering like it was a filthy secret.

And David suddenly saw a solution to his own dilemma. "Here," he said, shoving the bags and the coffee mug into Kyle's surprised hands. "Take these back to the office for me. Then we can meet tomorrow afternoon, in the Academy gym. I'll give you a lesson in swordplay."

The boy's eyes were larger than the sandwiches he now held. "You'd do that? For me?"

David shrugged. "You warned me about Pitt." He reached into his pocket for his wallet. Peeling off a bill for the kid, he said, "Buy yourself a cup of coffee. Then drop those things off at the door of the library."

"The library?" From Kyle's tone, David might have been speaking Egyptian.

"In the basement. End of the hall. Can't miss it."

Clearly awed, the boy shifted the bags and the mug, managing to clutch the money. "And you'll really do that? Help me at the gym?"

David remembered what it was like to get a demerit. His had been in penmanship, before George had finally convinced him that warders needed to write like gentlemen, as well as fight like them.

"Yeah," he said. "I'll help you out."

Once Kyle was headed into the Starbucks, David decided to make his own timely escape. The last thing he needed was to run into Pitt by accident on the empty DC sidewalk.

Hurrying, he made his way to a break between buildings, a narrow alley sheltered by high brick walls. He ducked behind a

Dumpster, taking care to look left, look right, then study the windows overhead. When he was certain no one was watching, he closed his eyes and *reached* toward home.

He materialized on his driveway. He never *reached* directly inside the house. That was a holdover from one of his earliest lessons as a warder—never place yourself directly in the path of a prepared enemy without a clear path to escape. By long-standing habit, he appeared in the shadow of his garage. The shelter gave him a chance to look over his property and make sure nothing was out of place.

Nothing, like the low-slung sports car that hulked in the center of his driveway.

Nothing, like the leather-clad salamander standing on his porch.

21

To the salamander's credit, he hadn't burned the house down.

He hadn't even singed the swing on the front porch.

But David could hear Spot barking behind the front door, his voice hoarse enough that David suspected the salamander had been in place for quite some time. Apparently that was the advantage of wearing a leather jacket—even a cold-blooded, dead-eyed killer dispatched by Apolline Fournier didn't get chilled.

Rosefire was such a comfort in David's hand that he didn't remember reaching for the sword. Ward-fire flickered along its edge, coruscating in the twilight.

The salamander immediately held up his palms in the universal signal for innocence. "No need for the sword, Mr. Montrose."

David planted his feet, regretting that the salamander had the literal high ground of the porch. "What are you doing here?"

"I was sent to bring you to an important meeting."

David let the sword's rippling flame burn higher. "I don't have any meeting scheduled."

"You won't want to miss this one." The salamander took a step toward the edge of the porch, but he stopped when Rosefire's tip angled to meet his heart. "You won't be alone," he said, his voice slick with amusement. "Your shifter friend is already there."

Not taking his eyes from his enemy, David reached inside his pocket for his phone. With his left thumb, he placed a call to Connor. "What color is the moon?" he asked, the instant the shifter answered.

"Silver," came the immediate reply.

The question was thirty years old; he and Connor had used it as boys. A silver moon meant the coast was clear. All was well. A blue moon would have warned David that the situation was unclear—a parent might be angry, but no immediate punishment was forthcoming. A crimson moon meant danger—ongoing parental inquisition, imminent grounding. Or, now, death at the hands of the salamander queen.

David thumbed off the phone and gestured with Rosefire, ordering the salamander off the porch steps. The imperial slithered to the ground, letting the motion carry him over to the sports car that crouched in the driveway. From this vantage point, David could see it was a Dodge Viper.

"Come on, Warder," the salamander said. "Don't make me tell my boss you're afraid to take a ride."

He wasn't afraid. He was rightfully cautious. But Connor had just told him he'd be safe enough—at least for now. And in a pinch, he could *reach* his way out of a moving car, back to the safety of home, or anywhere else. It wouldn't be easy, but he could do it. He slung himself into the car.

The salamander drove fast. He'd clearly studied the local roads, and he made it to the interstate without attracting any small-town law enforcement intent on meeting month-end quotas for speeding tickets. He opened up the throttle on the highway, edging close to ninety miles per hour.

David bit back a hundred questions as they hit the Beltway

and were slowed by traffic. Chances were, they were heading back to DC. But they didn't strike out for downtown. Instead, they crossed into Virginia. Cut through the suburb of Arlington. Ended up at the cemetery of the same name.

The salamander pulled into a low parking garage, gliding the Viper into a slot in the shadows, farthest away from the entrance to the burial ground itself. David followed the imperial up the stairs, past the Visitor's Center and onto one of the wide paths that cut through the bright green grass. Row after row of white tombstones marched across the hillside in hypnotic order.

He couldn't summon Rosefire in the middle of a public place, especially not in broad daylight. He had to trust to the crowds to keep him safe. Even if the salamander wanted to cause him grievous bodily harm, it wouldn't be worth the unrestrained wrath of the Empire Bureau of Investigation for revealing magic in a mundane setting.

Those reassurances gave David a semblance of calm as they climbed the steep footpath, passing the occasional funerary monument and equine statue. He only came to a stop on a grey stone platform, beneath the watchful eye of Robert E. Lee's Greek Revival home, where Union soldiers once buried their dead in the rose garden.

Here, in the heart of Arlington, broad flagstones were surrounded by grass. Individual markers lay flat on the ground, etched with names, birth dates, and death dates. John F. Kennedy. Robert F. Kennedy. Patrick Bouvier Kennedy. Arabella Kennedy. Jacqueline Bouvier Kennedy Onassis.

Above them all, a flame burned in the center of a circular stone, flickering pale in the afternoon sunlight. As David approached with the salamander, the color gradually intensified, darkening from salmon to tangerine to a vibrant, blaring orange.

The handful of tourists gathered around the memorial didn't seem to notice. They were too busy panting for breath after the steep climb, or taking selfies against the backdrop of Arlington

House, or turning around to capture the Washington Monument and the Capitol in the distance.

But David understood the power being exerted over the living fire. He saw the striking figure in front of the burning bowl—not Apolline, as he'd expected. Rather, John Brule wore a full-length trench coat, as black as the soot around the eternal flame. His silver hair caught on a breeze, flaring around his face like a halo.

"Well met," Brule said. "I thank you for indulging my... passion." He inclined his head toward the fire. At the same time, the flames brightened another notch, transforming from orange to liquid gold.

"What do you want?" David asked, fighting a visceral reaction against such a public display of magic. "Why did you bring me here?"

Brule spared him a smile, his onyx eyes glinting in the afternoon sunlight. "I thought you'd be more inclined to meet me in a public place. But let us join your friend. We can talk away from the crowds."

The "crowds" were a family wearing University of Montana gear, burgundy and silver emblazoned with grizzly bears. But another cluster of tourists was approaching from below, and a uniformed soldier stood almost within earshot.

Brule gestured toward the left. David followed the salamander's open hand and saw Connor. The shifter's feet were planted on the white stone walkway, his shoulders set as if he were barely restraining himself from taking his lupine form.

"All right," David said, when he and Brule had joined Connor. He could spot at least four salamander guards stationed on pathways in each of the cardinal directions. "You've got us here. What do you want?"

"Such haste!" Brule exclaimed, his sharp laugh sounding like the collapse of logs in a bonfire. The lilt of his French accent became more pronounced as he crooned, "Relax, *messieurs*. I owe you both an apology. Things at the lair became far more...heated than I'd planned. My men were understandably distressed when they learned you could not produce the karstag in a timely fashion. I'd only intended for them to...detain you momentarily. Not to harm you in any way."

Connor made a spitting sound, a blatant expression of disbelief. David had to agree with the sentiment—he could still feel the heat of the salamanders' fire pit against his cheek, and he'd had nightmares about that lizard-chased poker. But he'd been trained to keep calm when all was collapsing around him. He understood how to project steady confidence when an allied witch—or a shifter, for that matter—was on the edge of losing composure. So he kept his voice perfectly level as he said, "The karstag is safely in one piece. Which is more than I can say for the Collar."

At the mention of the wolves' relic, Connor growled but Brule was the first to reply with words. "Ah yes," he said. "One of my colleagues became a little...overzealous with regard to your Collar. I explained to her the folly of breaking that link."

Connor growled, "You can tell your *colleague*—"

Brule wasn't saying Apolline had done the breaking. But how many female salamanders could there be in DC? Everyone knew the females were as likely to poison each other as they were to say hello.

Brule was throwing Apolline under the bus.

David flicked his hand in a horizontal gesture, just enough to capture Connor's attention. The shifter cut off his spluttering protest in time for David to say, "What do you want, Brule? What's so important that you called us here on an autumn afternoon, in front of the entire mundane world?"

The salamander shook his head, issuing a trio of soft hisses like a dog owner calling off a puppy from a particularly appealing toy. "Such haste..." He offered another Gallic shrug. "We must work together, soldiers like us, on the front lines of war."

Connor balled his hands into fists. "We wolves work with allies. Not with yellow-bellied—"

Brule directed his next words at David alone. "The salamander who broke the Collar wasn't working alone. She had certain...encouragements to complete her work. Certain people who told her our nest would benefit from keeping you busy. You, specifically, David Montrose. You seem not to have many... allies...in that court where you work."

Hints and suggestions, that's all Brule offered. But David understood the story behind the salamander's words, the conclusions he was supposed to draw. A warder had spoken to Apolline. David was willing to bet his next year's salary that Norville Pitt had engineered the breaking of the Collar.

"Why would Apolline trust Pitt?" he demanded, using the words to tamp down his reflexive rage against his boss. It was one thing for Pitt to manipulate David's professional career. It was another for him to move against the shifters.

"Ms. Fournier," Brule corrected. "Yet we understand each other, you and I."

Connor bristled. "You two may have a perfect understanding, but I'm the one trying to keep the Washington Pack from breaking ranks. I need some show of good faith, Brule. I need to let my pack know there'll be a Collar left to trade for, come the next full moon."

Brule studied the shifter for a full minute before reaching some decision. Taking a single step back, he raised his chin, letting his coat fall in uninterrupted lines from his shoulders to his knees. He looked first at Connor, but he addressed his words to David. "The breaking of one link was just the beginning. You should know that Apolline Fournier is convening a Grand Congress."

That was the last thing DC needed, a gathering of all the salamander groups on the eastern seaboard. Before David could make some diplomatic response, Connor growled, "It's a free empire."

Brule raised one eyebrow. "You should exhibit greater concern, Wolf. At least about *this* Grand Congress."

"Stop playing games," David said, as much to irritate Brule as to remind Connor not to be sucked into the charade. "What is Apolline planning?"

For the first time, Brule didn't take exception to David using the salamander queen's given name. Instead, he used it himself, to emphasize his reply. "*Apolline* plans to do more than break your Collar. She will distribute the links among all the nests."

Connor moved faster than David could stop him. His fingers were dark against the salamander's throat, and his snarl raised the hairs on the back of David's neck. It took David leaning his full weight into the shifter before he could force the other imperials apart.

"Curb your dog, Warder," Brule spat.

David interposed his body between the two grown men. Trying to give the shifter time to regain control of his senses, he said, "If you show a wolf his dinner, don't be surprised when he bites."

Brule managed to look unimpressed, but he took a full step back as he shot his cuffs. "I'll match you, adage for adage: When the foundation catches fire, the whole house is lost. I called you here as a courtesy, because I thought it was better for the Empire if you knew what was being planned. My people—most of them, at least—aren't looking for a war. I thought you two were smart enough to avoid one as well."

"You tell us that your *people*," Connor sneered over the word, "intend to destroy what belongs to my pack. You're the one setting the match to the foundation."

"Don't play with fire, pup. You'll be burned every time."

But David wasn't distracted by personal fear for the Collar's welfare. He wasn't hogtied by his own pack having stolen the karstag. He was an outsider—and so he was fully capable of stepping back, literally and physically.

And from his new vantage point, he could see the true importance of Brule summoning them to the cemetery. He was speaking with Apolline nowhere in sight, with her closest spies out of earshot. Brule was offering a confidence, even if it came with posturing and threats.

"When?" David asked, his voice sharp enough to interrupt Connor's growled retort. Once he had the attention of both men, he repeated: "When is Apolline meeting with the nests?"

Brule turned toward David, as if to indicate that the Washington alpha wasn't worth his attention. "A week from tomorrow. Midnight."

"Where?" David pushed.

Brule nodded slowly, seeming to appreciate David's getting to the heart of the matter. "Underground. On the Mall. In the old garage beneath the Air and Space Museum."

David could picture the gaping entrance, a steep ramp blocked by bollards. The garage had been shut down decades ago, shuttered for security concerns years before the Twin Towers fell a few hundred miles to the north. After forty years of neglect, the garage should be dark and damp—perfect for salamanders plotting an ambush.

"Next Sunday," David confirmed, fighting against a shudder. "Midnight."

"She'll have the Collar," Brule said. "At least until it's reduced to a pile of links."

Before Connor could react—to the promise or the threat—Brule turned on his heel. He raised a hand, snapping once, and the sound echoed like a stick breaking on a forest footpath. The four salamanders David had seen glided to his side, along with another two who'd been hidden in shadows beneath nearby clumps of trees. All seven disappeared down the hill, well-trained soldiers swallowed up by acres of cemetery.

"What the hell?" Connor said, shaking his entire body as if he were just coming out of a trance.

"What the hell, indeed," David said. He glanced up at the eternal flame on the Kennedy gravesite. The fire was back to its usual pale self.

"Do you trust him?" Connor asked.

"Not one iota."

"Do you think Apolline sent him?"

David mused. "That isn't her style—announcing her plans ahead of time. I think Mr. Brule is going rogue."

"Why would he do that?"

David shook his head. "I don't know. But we have one week to figure it out. And to decide exactly how to take advantage."

22

That night, walking the perimeter of the farm with Spot, David was still contemplating Brule's actions.

It had taken resources to figure out where David lived and to send a minion to drag him out to Arlington. As a warder, David had made sure the farm's address couldn't be found easily. He wasn't in online phone books, and casual searching would send a computer user in circles. But there were expensive resources David couldn't control, and legal databases he couldn't corrupt. There were people who knew the location, people who might be charmed by Brule, or coerced.

So, Brule's sending his salamander chauffeur had been a show of strength. At the same time, the action was a gift, reminding David that his home was vulnerable. All the more reason to complete his evening survey of the boundaries—especially with a new imperial, the sprite Bourne Morrissey, living nearby.

Snapping his fingers to get Spot's attention, David led the way down to the lake. At first glance, everything was normal, exactly the way he'd last seen it. Sumac turned crimson on the edges of the forest. Late afternoon sun glinted on the weathered grey of the dock. An upended canoe leaned against the boathouse, near the two kayaks sitting on their rack. Looking across the water, he could make out the gigantic osprey nest in the old oak tree. The chicks had flown weeks ago. The parents would be migrating soon.

David sat on the edge of the dock, hanging his feet over the side. Spot settled beside him with a heartfelt sigh, strategically placing his head at the perfect angle to be scratched behind his ears. A pair of jays squawked somewhere close by, and a fish jumped in the lake.

No. Not a fish.

The concentric rings were too large, moving too fast for any fish in the lake. Pulse quickening, David peered across the water, automatically tightening his fingers around Spot's collar.

A face swam into view beneath his feet.

Pale blue hair swirled in the green-brown water. Wide eyes, all pupil, blinked below the surface. Lavender lips opened and sucked in water, then pursed and exhaled to create a fresh set of ripples.

Beneath the lake's surface, David could make out limbs— arms and legs that ended in clusters of flexible digits, something between fingers and tentacles. As he watched, minnows swarmed from the shallows, diving and weaving among the underwater fronds.

The creature's body was lean and lithe, moving in the under- water currents like the tail of a kite high in the sky. The silver torso twisted and rolled, sinking beyond the range of David's vision before it floated back to the surface.

Spot whined, a high-pitched greeting punctuated by the beat of his tail against the dock. David barely voiced the word, "Stay," before the creature rippled into a vertical position. Its head broke the lake's surface, and water streamed over sapphire hair.

"Montroseson," came the liquid voice, and David barely recognized the timbre.

"Bourne," he said, astonished to see the sprite so transformed.
"Your lake," she said. "It's a good home. A welcoming one."

"I'm glad you find it so." David responded with a touch of the
stiffness that always came from interacting with a new imperial.
By and large, the races got along well—salamanders and a few
other bad actors excepted. They all had a common interest in
keeping their existence hidden from mundane eyes. Nevertheless, a little respect could go a long way toward keeping the peace
when tensions did arise.

The sprite acknowledged David's courtesy, flipping backward
and rolling through the sunlit water. When she came back to the
surface, she blinked hard. "I've taken some liberties, Warder. I've
sung to the stream at the eastern edge of the lake. I've balanced
the flow a little more to the liking of the sunfish."

"I'm grateful," David said, his tone matching his words.

"And I've murmured to the duckweed on the southern shore,
encouraging it to spread thinner on the surface. It had grown a
little...exuberant with the summer heat. Understandable, with
the shallows as silty as they are." As if illustrating her gardening,
Bourne rippled her arms through the water.

"Excellent," David said, although he had no idea about the
appropriate balance of duckweed, or silt for that matter. But
speaking about water made him think about his last conversation
with Connor, of their plans to follow Brule's lead to the abandoned parking lot under the mall.

"There's a stream that flows out of here, isn't there? On the
western edge?"

"West by south-west," Bourne agreed, after trailing one
fringed arm along the surface for a moment.

"And where does it lead?"

"Eventually? To the Wild Sea. It flows from Four Streams
Meet, by way of the Bitter Water. It leaves your lake to reach the
Falling Water."

The cascade sounded like a recitation of clans, a family

lineage that would be at home in any mundane family Bible. The sprite's words rolled like their own river, rising and falling over the liquid syllables, as if meaning was conveyed by her very tone. The confidence behind the flowing song told David his blossoming idea was a good one.

"Can you trace water in your human form?"

The sprite undulated beneath the surface, swaying as if she were tempted to swim away. "Yes?" she finally answered, but only after another ducking, another sheeting of water from her hair. Even then, the response sounded more like a question than an affirmative response.

But that was enough for David. He began with some background: "A wolf shifter and I are meeting some salamanders."

He wasn't prepared for her response. One moment Bourne was rolling beneath the dock, entwining her tendrils around the wooden uprights like a woman caressing a lover. The next, her legs slapped the water, the sound echoing like a shot across the lake's surface. Spot barked at the disturbance, one sharp complaint followed by a flurry of angry snarls that tightened David's gut. He slashed a hand command for silence, but the lab continued to growl deep in his throat.

David peered into the gloom, suddenly aware of how much time he'd spent watching the sprite twist and turn in the water. Twilight came earlier in autumn. The sun had dipped to the tops of the trees. He'd be returning home in the dark, and he hadn't left a light on in the house.

"Easy," he muttered to Spot, settling a heavy hand on the dog's velvet neck. As he repeated the word, he wasn't certain if he was trying to calm the animal or himself.

He also wasn't sure if he should wait on the dock for Bourne to return. Maybe the sprite had taken fright at the mention of the salamanders or at the notion that David might be allying himself with the ancient enemies of water. Maybe she'd even decided to leave the lake, to follow the Bitter Water or the Falling Water, to seek out a better, safer home.

So much for building a new alliance.

Sighing in disgust at his ham-handed efforts, David pushed himself to his feet. Just as he turned his back on the lake, a loud splash echoed off the line of trees. He whirled back to the end of the dock in time to see a woman settle on the wooden edge.

It was Bourne, in human form. She was naked, every line of her body lean and hard. Water flowed from her close-cropped hair, streaming over a torso that was scarred with tight, white flesh. Her feet were planted on the dock, toes curving as if she anchored herself on a sheer mountain face. Her hands closed around a giant chunk of driftwood, a length of oak that might once have been a tree trunk.

The sprite's forearms clenched, and she hefted her club to her right shoulder. "Take me to the fire demons now."

As venom dripped from Bourne's words, David studied the mottling on her chest. She'd been burned before, badly enough to leave those scars.

"Not now," he said, forcing his voice to stay calm across the two syllables.

"Soon."

"Next Sunday," David said. "Eight days from now."

"Soon," Bourne repeated, her fingers tightening on the tree trunk.

"We go to make peace with them," David insisted, bracing himself as the sprite hissed disapproval. The spluttering sounded like rainwater falling on a bonfire. "Peace," David repeated, "because they have things we need." No reason to explain about the Collar now, or why he'd given up his Torch.

It took a moment for the sprite to process the words, then whistle and hiss and settle back on the soles of her feet. David couldn't believe this fierce imperial was the same broken creature he'd rescued on the path in the woods. For the first time, he began to understand what his father had seen in the sprite, why George had invited Bourne to come to the farm.

"Need," Bourne finally said, repeating his last word. She didn't sound happy, but she relaxed her grip on her club by a fraction.

"It would be nice to have an ally. Someone we can trust."

"Trust..." The sprite lingered on the syllable, as if she were tasting it and discovering exactly what it meant. She shifted her weight, settling more firmly on the soles of her feet. She swung the tree trunk off her shoulder, planting it on the grey dock with a resonant thud. "You can trust me," she said, her voice creaking as if she had not used it for centuries.

"You can't fly off the handle," David warned.

"You can trust me, Montroseson," the sprite repeated. And this time, she extended her hand. Her fingers were long and supple, as if the bones glided loosely beneath her flesh.

But when David shook, he felt the strength there. He felt a warning, not to him, and not to Connor, but to the fire creatures who were clearly the sprite's mortal enemies. His gaze shifted to the massive chunk of driftwood that still dripped onto the dock.

David was supposed to be an ambassador in this entire venture. His job was to support his friend—support the shifters and get his own Torch back. But he had to admit that he felt a little more certain of his success with Bourne Morrissey at his side—especially as he watched the creature dive off the end of the dock, twisting in mid-air and transforming to her native shape the instant she hit the water.

23

I n theory, David should have enjoyed what was left of his weekend, basking in the opportunity to avoid Norville Pitt for another thirty-six hours. Instead, he continued to worry about the upcoming parley with the salamanders—now only one week away. Sitting in his study, working through the detritus of bank accounts and bills and all the details of life in the mundane world, he kept straying back to the mess Connor had gotten him into.

He still missed his Torch, although he'd recovered from the worst of his disorientation. Until the emblem was gone, he hadn't realized how often he reached for it, how frequently he let his thumb brush against it in his pocket.

Of course, his loss wasn't only physical. Even with essential equilibrium restored, there were times when he felt like he was pushing through fog or swimming in cloudy water, victim of the silt Bourne had mentioned the night before.

On Sunday afternoon, determined to tear himself free from his languor, David headed outside. The sky was marbled, grey clouds scudding across a slate blue that hinted of rain. Ignoring the gusts of wind presaging a cold front, David strode to the massive oak tree that spread behind the house.

Splitting wood, that's what he needed. The satisfying heft of the maul in his hand. The thunk of the blade as it cut through a round of wood. The tension up his arms and across his back as he wrested the iron blade free. The twist as he swept the split logs to the side.

He burned through two cords of wood every winter, more when the weather was extreme. Every forecaster he'd heard was predicting a colder winter than usual, wetter, with a chance of record lows.

All the more reason to finish breaking down the maple that had fallen in an April storm. Back in the spring, he'd used a chain saw to carve the trunk into massive rounds. They'd been drying beneath the oak tree, taking on a grey hue as they aged. It was high time to get the wood split and stacked beneath a protective awning for winter.

Fingers moving automatically, he pulled on a pair of protective goggles. His wedge-shaped maul felt comfortable in his hand.

He gave himself over to the comfortable rhythm, thudding the maul into the edge of a round, sweeping the sheered-off wood from the block, shifting the round, bracing himself for another vigorous stroke.

Splitting wood had always been one of his chores at the farm. George hated the task, and David had always been stronger than his brothers, better at physical exertion. Hours spent at the woodpile had made him a better warder too, had kept him competing against older students, in swordplay especially.

Swordplay.

A memory swooped in from nowhere. He'd promised to help Kyle Hopp at the Academy's gym. Swearing, David checked the time. It was too late to shower away wood chips and sweat. Why bother, anyway? He was just going to work up a lather in the practice ring.

As he *reached* for the familiar setting, he wondered what the hell he was going to teach the young cadet.

After arriving, he saw that the answer was *Everything.*

Kyle crouched in a corner of the gym. He held a sword that was too short and too light, a practice blade far more suited to a first-year student than any young man in the senior class. His fingers twisted awkwardly around the grip; it was all David could do to keep from reaching out to rotate the weapon ninety degrees.

The kid's loose T-shirt hung to his knees, almost obscuring baggy flannel pants emblazoned with the emblem of Washington's football team. He looked like he'd stolen his big brother's pajamas.

Sweat streamed down Kyle's face, and his chest heaved as he fought for breath. At a glance, David saw he'd been sparring against the Terminator, an animatronic opponent used by students to test their basic skills. A blinding computer display above the mechanical device shouted out the bad news: twenty-seven minutes of active swordwork, with zero fatal blows, zero hits on an extremity, zero parries, and thirteen kills.

The last statistic showed the machine's success. Not Kyle's.

David cleared his throat, and the kid whirled around, automatically crouching as if he expected to submit to the fourteenth kill of the day.

"So," David said. "It looks like you got an early start."

He didn't think it was possible for the cadet's face to flush any more crimson. He was wrong. "I— I was already in the building," Kyle said, his voice breaking on the first try.

"Which form were you practicing?"

The kid scowled. "Dragon."

"With a sword that light?"

"It's the only one I have," Kyle protested. "My mother says it's stupid to throw good money after bad."

David heard an entire encyclopedia of background in that

protest. Kyle's mother managed his training. That meant no father was in the picture—grandfather either, or even an uncle. Kyle had no male relative still alive. His mother wasn't helping matters, either. She clearly didn't think her son had any potential as a warder or she would have taken *some* step to get him a half-way decent weapon. Maybe she couldn't afford one. Maybe she didn't understand why it mattered.

Maybe she'd already battered her son's confidence into dust.

Setting his lips tight against the first retort that sprang to mind, David reached into the ether. He brushed past Rosefire, ignoring the subtle hum of the blade that was always ready to serve him. Instead, he closed his palm around the leather-wrapped hilt of the sword he'd first learned on.

The weapon was a practice blade. It didn't have a name or lineage. But it had taught him everything he knew about the twelve basic forms—taught his father too, and his grandfather before him.

Pulling the sword into the gym, he automatically shifted his weight, accommodating the iron's heft. It was ice-cold, like all blades from the ether. A shimmer of frost reflected along the edge as he offered the grip to Kyle. "Try this," he said.

"S— sir?"

"The forms are easier when you have a decent weapon." He offered the sword again, barely biting off his frustration when Kyle backed away. "Take it," he ordered.

Another flush, this one a slow burn that painted the kid's throat. Kyle shrank into himself, refusing to meet David's eyes. His fingers slipped on the grip of his own inferior blade, as if they'd only danced over the plastic letters on a computer keyboard and never touched leather. "With all due respect, sir, this is a really bad idea."

"Noted," David said. That was his father's favorite response, when George had absolutely no intention of listening to whatever David had to say. "Rotate the grip in your hand. No. Like this." He pulled in Rosefire and demonstrated the proper placement of his fingers. "Now, forget about Dragon. Let's start with Snake."

Any ordinary student would have protested. Snake was a form for first-years. It required little training; it was specifically designed for a child to master in minutes, to gain confidence, to learn success.

But Kyle Hopp was no ordinary student. He merely hunched his shoulders, half-heartedly lifting his borrowed blade and dragging the weapon through the sinuous loop as instructed.

David's first reaction was to snort in anger. Smothering that— barely—his second reaction was to scoff at the kid's poor form. Instead, he forced himself to nod, taking a single step back to make time to phrase a proper critique. "Very good," he finally said. "You know the maneuver."

The kid's eyes shot up, as if he were searching for mockery.

"Now all you need to do is focus on the angle. Like this." Using Rosefire, David demonstrated the first sequence in the basic form, shifting his weight from his left foot to his right as he raised his weapon to shoulder height. "Now, you try it. Focus on *rolling* your weight forward."

It took three tries, but Kyle finally presented something related to a smooth shift of posture.

David didn't allow himself time to question how an Academy student could reach his senior year without ever focusing on the basics. Instead, he concentrated on breaking down every motion into its most elementary parts. Roll forward from heel to toe. Turn the wrist from left to right. Rotate the blade from flat to edge.

He'd never thought about the fighting forms that way. He'd only needed to watch his father work a combination once, and his own body had known the action. His fingers and toes, arms and legs, had all moved without conscious command.

Now, guiding Kyle, he discovered that Snake was a type of meditation. Each pull of muscle drew him deeper into himself.

Each shift of weight activated another part of his mind. The elements of the exercise spread across his senses—a pulse of violet light that faded into a tremor of birdsong, the sound melting into a pool of vanilla at the back of his throat only to stop hard against the sharp scent of juniper.

"Again," he urged, as Kyle finally completed one perfect Snake.

"One more time!" he cried, after the repetition.

"Excellent!"

Kyle came to a rest, his feet joined in perfect symmetry, the blade hanging like a metal spine at the front of his body. His arms trembled from exertion, but his eyes widened in victory.

Before David could comment, the sound of slow clapping filled the gym. Both student and teacher whirled toward the locker room door. As he spun, David's fingers tightened on Rosefire, but he quickly identified the man who leaned against the doorway.

Aidan O'Rourke had clearly availed himself of the locker room showers. His salt and pepper hair was still long, but now it hung in damp curls around his face. His beard was every bit as scraggly, but no crumbs—from Pop-Tarts or any other meal—remained. The man had traded in his stained T-shirt and baggy sweatpants for the practice-wear provided by the gym. The tight black T-shirt revealed too many ribs, and the matching cotton pants hung loosely from jutting hip bones, but the man was clean and upright. Sober, too, from his sharp gaze.

"You think training a squire will help tame that new witch of yours?" O'Rourke asked.

Flicking a glance at Kyle, David said, "Hit the showers."

The kid planted his feet in defiance. "No, sir," he said, actually raising the practice blade as if he intended to defend David from enemy attack.

"Now," David said. He didn't raise his voice. Instead, he used a lesson George had taught him, lowering his tone until the single syllable shook like an earthquake.

Kyle hiccuped and started to hand him back his sword.

"Keep it," David said. "Practice on your own until we meet on Wednesday. Five o'clock."

The kid nodded, barely remembering to sheathe the weapon in the ether. On his way to the locker room, he turned sideways to edge past O'Rourke, but he held his head high.

"He's not my squire," David said to the old warder, as soon as the door slammed closed.

Those piercing blue eyes merely narrowed.

"And I don't have a new witch."

"Noted," O'Rourke said.

David bristled, but there wasn't any way to respond to the acknowledgment. That's why George had always used it.

O'Rourke jerked his chin toward the locker room. "You know that one's never going to win any pitched battle."

"He just has to get out of the Academy with passing grades," David said.

"Why help a stranger?" The question was tight, as sharp as the edge of Rosefire's blade, and David knew they weren't talking about Kyle any longer.

"Because I can," he finally said.

For a moment, he didn't think O'Rourke would accept that. He'd press for more information, for a better reason. And David didn't want to give him one. He didn't want to say that sandwiches and coffee were a hedge against his own disaster. He didn't want to admit that *he* could be the next warder living as an outcast. He was one confrontation with Pitt away from becoming an object lesson as bitter as O'Rourke's.

O'Rourke finally nodded. "You've got a decent Snake there," he said, jutting a shoulder toward Rosefire. "What about your other forms?"

For answer, David nodded toward the rack of practice

weapons. He wasn't certain the disgraced warder had a sword of his own waiting in the ether. "Grab one, and I'll show you."

The warder took his time choosing a blade, testing the weight and balance of half a dozen before selecting one. When he returned to the practice court, he swept the sword in a curving arc, as if he were sanctifying a space to all the Guardians. He bowed to David, inclining his head in a ritual gesture before he bent from his waist. That was a deeper acknowledgment than any practice round required.

David accepted the honor with his own bent neck. Going any deeper would eliminate the other warder's gift.

Together, they worked the full Fire Cycle, from Snake to Phoenix to Dragon to Sun. David knew the steps, of course. He'd mastered them years ago, and he worked them on a regular basis, together with the Water Cycle, with Earth and Air. Not a week went by that he didn't offer up his sword in service to all the Guardians. It was the least he could do to display his worthiness to Hecate.

But never before had the sequences flowed from one to the other so smoothly. Never before had his muscles been as aware of the tiny linkages, the connections he'd discovered when he'd broken down Snake for Kyle. Never before had his senses rioted over the motions, scent and sight, taste and touch and sound breaking against his consciousness, drawing him in, linking him tighter and faster than ever to the ancient art of swordplay.

He only stopped when his arms were shaking and his thighs trembled from the exertion. His breath came in short, sharp gasps. His heart pounded against his sternum. Sweat dripped from his hair onto the floor beneath him.

The other warder still looked as if he'd just emerged from the locker room. He stood easily, not betrayed by a single muscle twitch. His chest rose and fell as if he were meditating, and his face was as placid as a cow's.

"Excellent," he said. David heard the tone that matched his

own, matched the compliment he'd given to Kyle. He wondered how much more he could learn from an outcast, abandoned warder.

Squaring his shoulders, he forced himself to raise Rosefire in a fighting stance once more.

"Again," he gasped. Because he knew he needed help wherever he could find it.

24

On Monday, David stopped by the Academy gym after work. He told himself his visit was a casual decision—just a chance to use the free weights in the corner, to watch the oldest cadets sparring in their first organized matches of the school year. In reality, he hoped O'Rourke would show. He could use some serious drilling on the Air Cycle—from Dragonfly to Moth to Crow to Eagle.

But the grizzled old warder was nowhere in sight. David thought about heading down to the library and trying to roust him from his makeshift bed. But that seemed a hell of a lot more intrusive than bringing the guy some food and coffee. And if O'Rourke was no longer camping out in the library, David would feel obligated to track him down, to make sure the old warder was safe.

At least Kyle came in, even if he was half an hour late for his scheduled class. He earned a demerit for tardiness and was sent off to practice Bear form with the first-years. The kid seemed to have forgotten everything he'd managed the day before.

Dissatisfied, David *reached* home, only to realize he hadn't spoken to Connor since leaving Arlington Cemetery. It wasn't unusual for a week or two to go by without contact from his friend—but not when the shifters' Collar had been stolen. Not when Connor was already on edge, preparing to fight for supremacy within his pack. Not when Brule had said their enemy would be gathered on Sunday night.

David texted, but he got no reply. He could phone, of course. Or better yet, head over to Seymour House. But that wouldn't change one basic fact: The Collar—along with David's Torch—was still missing.

At least he could still make out the faint trill of a nightingale, somewhere in the distance, almost out of range. Connor was alive. Not answering his phone, but alive.

Ordering himself not to fret, he made a quick dinner, pouring a can of soup over rice and heating the whole thing in the microwave. After Spot licked the bowl clean, they went on their nightly walk of the farm's boundaries.

He was still approaching the lake when Bourne rose out of the water, somersaulting onto the end of the dock. As she landed, the sprite transitioned from her imperial form to her human demeanor. He watched her tentacles shorten to fingers. Her lustrous azure hair seeped into her skull, growing shorter and paling to a blond that was almost white. The feral look on her face was enhanced by lavender lips that darkened to a more human shade.

"Salamanders?" she asked without preamble.

"Not yet," David said. Spot approached the sprite warily, snuffling at the water that still streamed from her shining skin.

"We should take them by surprise, Montroseson," Bourne said.

"They won't be gathered until Sunday."

The sprite tilted her head.

"Six moonrises from now," David clarified.

He caught her flexing her fingers, as if she were harvesting reeds on the edge of the lake. "Six," she repeated. "And then we'll kill them all."

David shuddered at the blatant violence in her tone. He knew how to fight, but the sprite brought vengeance to a whole new level. Before he could say anything, she dove backward off the dock, jackknifing in mid-air as she slipped into her imperial form.

After returning to the farmhouse, David considered *reaching* to the cottage behind the Peabridge Library—just to check on Jane, to make sure she didn't have any questions about her magical abilities. He remembered, however, that he had to leave the proverbial ball in her court. She was the witch, after all. He was just a warder. Not even *her* warder, no matter what O'Rourke had said.

He had a lousy night, unable to fall asleep. There were only so many times he could punch his pillow into submission. Spot whined from the floor at the foot of the bed, chasing something in his sleep.

On Tuesday, David stopped by the gym again. No O'Rourke. Hanging around, hoping the warder might drift by, he witnessed another spectacular failure by Kyle in front of his entire sword-play class. This time the kid was tripped up by Eagle Form.

At home, waiting for pasta to boil, David texted Connor for the tenth time since the morning. When the shifter still failed to reply, David resorted to placing a call. Voicemail picked up on the fourth ring. "You know what to do," Connor growled in his recorded message. David let his own voice reflect his frustration. "Yeah, I know what to do. But do you? What the hell is going on? Call me."

After hanging up, he got nine digits into phoning Jane before he banished his phone to his pocket. He told himself he was keeping the line clear, waiting for Connor to call back.

Nevertheless, he couldn't resist reaching out to Jane's familiar.

"Neko!" He sent the message searing across the ether, targeting

the creature's astral signature, the bar of emerald light that glowed in his memory.

"I didn't do it!" The response was immediate.

"Do what?" David's pulse quickened as he imagined Jane hurt, caught in a magical backlash as Neko failed at some essential service.

"Finish the cream." Neko's reply came after a long pause. David forced himself to take a calming breath as the familiar justified himself. *"It was sour. I had to rinse the container, or the whole kitchen would have started to stink."*

David bit off a frustrated sigh. *"Is Jane there?"*

"She's with Melissa. Girls' night out. Do you need her?"

David didn't *need* her. He just wanted to speak with her. And that wasn't reason enough to drag Jane away from her friend. Hecate would frown on a warder putting his own interests before a witch's. And the last thing he needed was Hecate disapproving of anything he did. Not with Samhain fast approaching.

"It's not important," he finally said. *"But you better replace that cream before she gets home. Use your ability to roam for good and not for evil."* He severed the link before Neko could come up with some self-serving reply.

That night, walking down to the lake, he heard movement before he arrived on the shore. Crossing the beach, he saw Bourne in her human form. She was dressed, head to toe, in what looked like midnight blue, but the precise shade was hard to tell in the silvery moonlight.

The sprite sat on the sand under the boathouse eaves, holding a stone in one hand and a tree branch in the other. Slowly, methodically, she was fashioning the branch into a spear, smoothing away all its deformities and sharpening the end to a single, lethal point.

She sang as she worked, liquid notes rolling across her tongue. David couldn't make out individual words. He had no idea what language sprites used among themselves. But the notes were stirring, like the soundtrack to an epic adventure movie. He found himself pulled into the circle of moonlight around Bourne's feet. He realized she'd already completed half a dozen spears.

"Five more nights, Montroseson," the sprite said by way of greeting.

"If we go at all."

"We'll go!" The sprite glared at him, her smooth face reflecting the moon as easily as the lake behind him.

"I haven't been able to reach the shifters. This is their battle. Not mine."

"Salamanders are everyone's battle," Bourne said. "Your shifters are preparing. As I am. As you should be."

David didn't have a reply for that. And Bourne wasn't interested in saying anything more. She merely reached for a new branch, starting yet another spear. David whistled Spot to his side and returned to the house.

Calling Connor again, he got a message from the phone company that the shifter's voice mailbox was full. It was just as well. All the things David wanted to shout were better left unrecorded.

Restless, he turned on the TV and forced himself to stare at the screen. An hour later, he couldn't remember if he'd been watching a sitcom, a reality show, or the nightly news. He went downstairs and ran on the treadmill for another hour. At least his body was exhausted enough for sleep, even if his mind fed him strange, disjointed dreams.

Wednesday. No O'Rourke. Kyle skipped class, despite the fact that David had promised to train him that day. Silence from Connor, from Neko, from Jane. David sent a text to Connor before he fell asleep: *I'm out if I don't hear from you by morning.*

That was a lie, of course. David couldn't be out. Not while the salamanders still held his Torch. Not while the nightingale still sang, however softly, however distant.

Connor didn't reply.

Once again, David ended his nightly patrol of the property down at the water. Bourne wasn't at the boathouse. She wasn't at the end of the dock. Calling Spot to his side, David sat at the edge of the water, listening to ripples lap the sandy beach.

It took half an hour for the rhythm to change. Even then it was hard for him to discern the sprite in the shallows. In her imperial form, she ebbed and flowed, weaving across the sandy shelf that led to the lake's depths. As he squinted, he made out sapphire lips, stretching, changing, just enough to shape human sounds.

"Montroseson," Bourne murmured.

"Bourne."

"Forgive me if I do not come ashore. I am channeling the flow from Bitter Water, changing the entrance to your lake, so the minnows will have sufficient shelter from the egrets."

The words flowed out of her, rising and falling like a stream skipping over stones. He realized that was the longest sentence he'd heard her speak. "I'm honored," he said. "And the lake itself is grateful."

"The lake is balanced," the sprite corrected. "Or it will be, before I leave."

"Leave? You're welcome to stay here," he said. "For as long as you need."

"Once, I thought my journey ended here, and I would live in your lake forever," Bourne said. "That was the gift of Montrose, honored by Montroseson." Her voice trailed off, lost like the strands of her hair in the water. "But that was before I knew we would fight salamanders together. Four more nights, Montroseson."

The tolling chilled his blood. Or maybe that was just the late September breeze, sifting through the oak trees on the distant shore. "You'll come back, though," David said. "After the battle."

But Bourne's lips had lost their human form. They opened

and closed beneath the water, cornflower shadowed by indigo. She floated toward the center of the lake, beautiful and terrible and foreign in the moonlight.

David had no choice but to snap his fingers for Spot to stay at his side. He thrashed through the woods, refusing to stop at the ditch where he'd found the sprite. That night, he didn't sleep.

25

O n Thursday, David braced himself to start the whole cycle again, at least running through Fire forms by himself in the gym. As he powered down his computer at the end of the workday, Linda Hudson stepped into his office. "Good," his father's witch said. "I caught you before you left."

"I was just on my way—"

"If you know what's good for you, that sentence will end with, 'to take you to dinner.'"

In a world where everyone seemed wreathed in secrets, Linda was the most forthright witch he'd ever met. Forthright woman. Forthright person, no modification needed. Despite himself, David smiled. "Why don't you tell me what you really want?"

"I want to talk to you," Linda said.

"We're talking."

"It's been almost two weeks since your father's birthday party."

"Ten days, but who's counting?"

She scowled at his glib reply. "At least pay me the courtesy of admitting you're avoiding us."

"I'm not," he countered automatically. "I've been busy. Connor asked for my help with a problem he's having with some sala-manders." At least that much was true. He wasn't about to explain the rest of his time, obsessing over old fighting forms with an absentee warder whose very name was anathema and a kid who didn't want the first thing to do with swordplay. And there was absolutely no reason to bring up the murderous sprite he harbored at the lake.

"You're a warder," Linda insisted. "You ward witches. You're not some mercenary, hiring out your sword to any imperial who asks."

"Good thing, too," David retorted. "Because Connor hasn't paid a cent for my services."

Linda set her hands on her hips. The look she gave him must have been part of the curriculum in magicaria the world over because her arched eyebrows left no doubt about her skepticism. Tight lines beside her lips made it perfectly clear she could lecture him for hours. Could. But so far, had chosen not to.

He sighed and spoke as if he were reciting lines in a play: "Linda, I was just getting ready to leave. Is there any possibility you're free for dinner tonight?"

"Good boy," she said, looking for all the world like she intended to pat him on the head.

He managed to maintain a facade of polite conversation as they took the elevator down to the street. The days were getting shorter. First frost was probably a couple of weeks off. Linda was already tired of pumpkin spice latte. David preferred mint.

At least she couldn't grill him about warding, not on a busy DC sidewalk. He tried to think of the busiest restaurant nearby, one where their conversation would most likely be overheard. With any luck, he could keep the discussion confined to the best movie he'd seen recently (none), his favorite beach read from the summer (none), and any plans he had for a weekend getaway before the holiday season began in earnest (definitely none).

But Linda was far more experienced than that. Before he

knew what hit him, she'd taken his arm and guided him down one city block, scarcely hesitating before she ducked through the heavy doors of Oceanaire. The high-end seafood restaurant catered to DC's elite lawyers and lobbyists, professionals who understood the value of privacy. They were soon seated in a high-sided booth, ample panels of dark wood providing the illusion that no outsider could overhear a word either one of them said.

Linda dispensed with ordering after the briefest glance at the menu. "A glass of Viognier," she said to the waiter. "And then I'll have a cup of the lobster bisque and a wedge salad. Chopped. Dressing on the side."

David might have been impressed with her decisiveness if he hadn't felt pressured to place his own order as efficiently. He settled on the grilled swordfish along with a Dewar's on the rocks.

After the waiter brought their drinks, Linda leaned toward him. She took a precise swallow of wine before she said, "It took me four days to catch up with you." The statement wasn't angry. Rather, she was relaxed. Inviting. Allowing him to welcome her into his life.

He sipped his Scotch for strength and said, "I've been hitting the gym every day after work."

"You?" She was right to be skeptical. David had never invested a lot of time or energy in formal exercise. He got enough of it splitting wood, patrolling the farmhouse borders, and keeping the old house in shape.

He nodded. "I agreed to help one of the cadets. Kyle Hopp."

"From the Help Desk?"

Of course Linda knew the kid. Linda knew everyone. He shrugged. "He did me a favor. Said he got a demerit in swordplay, so I offered to coach him."

"That *is* a full-time job. Is he getting any better?"

"We worked on Snake form on Monday. Enough to get him a passing grade."

Linda took another sip of wine, matching the earlier print of her lipstick exactly. Only after she'd placed her goblet in the precise center of her cocktail napkin did she ask, "What aren't you telling me?"

"How the hell do you do that?"

"Don't dissemble."

He refused to drink his Scotch because then she'd know he felt vulnerable. Instead, he met her gaze directly. "I got some instruction too. From Aidan O'Rourke."

"Oh, David..." She trailed off. He couldn't remember ever seeing Linda Hudson at a loss for words.

"What?" he finally asked, when it became apparent she didn't plan to elaborate.

"You know it would break your father's heart—"

He started to say he didn't know the first thing about his father's heart, that he was pretty sure George didn't *have* one, had never had one, and even if he did, one lousy training session with an antisocial outcast wasn't going to affect dear old Dad one way or another. Before he could launch his tirade, however, the waiter descended on their table, a laden kitchen runner hovering at his side.

"Lobster bisque for the lady. And one wedge salad, chopped, with dressing on the side. And for the gentleman..." David didn't listen to the description of his dinner. He'd lost all appetite for whatever the chef had prepared.

The instant the staff headed back to the kitchen, David tried a different approach. "Why would my training with O'Rourke break my father's heart?"

Linda stared at him, her spoon halfway to her lips. "You don't know."

"Know what?"

"Your father and Aidan O'Rourke were best friends. Aidan introduced your father to your mother."

"I'm talking about Aidan O'Rourke, from the Boston Coven."

"That's the only one I know." Linda lowered her spoon to

the saucer beneath her soup. "He was born and raised in DC. He only moved to Boston because he met Maggie at Midsummer Conclave. Your father was dead-set against his going—said they didn't know anything about Maggie, didn't know the first thing about her people. And your father turned out to be right."

David thought back to that morning in the warders' library, to the moment O'Rourke had called him "George Montrose's boy." No wonder the stranger had recognized him. The stranger wasn't a stranger.

"I still don't get it," he said, his fish cooling on its plate. "Why would Dad care about my sparring?"

"You know what happened to Maggie!" For the first time in their conversation, Linda's voice was heated.

"*Everyone* knows what happened to Maggie!" David matched her intensity.

"A good warder protects his witch, David. You know that. Aidan should have seen what was happening to Maggie. He should have brought her to her Coven. His only job was keeping her safe, and he failed."

She was talking about O'Rourke. Talking about Maggie Hanes. But David shriveled beneath the implied accusation that he hadn't kept *his* own witch safe. He hadn't kept Haylee from dabbling in dark magic.

He'd always known his father thought he was a piss-poor warder, after Haylee went dark. But somehow—in ways he couldn't even articulate—it cut *more*, knowing that George's rejection was because of something from his own past. George wasn't disappointed in David. He was disappointed in his long-lost best friend, in the man who'd introduced him to his beloved wife, to David's mother.

George didn't even care enough to despise David for his own failure. David was just collateral damage.

He folded his napkin and slid out of the booth.

"Where are you going?" Linda asked, scrambling to her own feet.

"Thank you," David said, as if that weren't a non sequitur. "Everything makes a lot more sense now."

"What are you talking about? Sit down and eat your dinner. Let's *talk* about this."

"There isn't anything to say."

She wrung her hands. Linda Hudson, the very image of arcane self-possession, stood in front of him, twining her fingers together like she was trying to gather the nerve to speak. "Please, David. Come out to the house. Talk to your father. We can't keep going on like this."

"We can," he said. "And we will." He fumbled for his wallet and tossed too much money onto the table.

"David, he's your *father*. The only one you're ever going to have. If you don't talk to him now, you'll regret it until the day you die."

David started to walk away. Stopped. Came back to the table. He towered over Linda. He knew he stood too close, knew he made her crane her neck to look up at him. "What did he say when you told him that?"

"What?"

"What did my father say when you told him that *he'll* regret not talking to *me* until the day he dies?"

She opened her mouth, struggling for an answer. He could read the reply on her face, though, as clearly as if she'd formed the words. His father hadn't said anything. His father hadn't cared.

He turned on his heel and strode out of the restaurant.

26

For the first time in three years, David called in sick to work on Friday. He didn't want to face whatever new hell Pitt had created for him. He didn't want Linda to stop by, full of sympathy and forgiveness. He didn't want his computer to crash, forcing him to open a ticket with the Help Desk so Kyle could come to his office and stumble through an apology for screwing up at the gym. He didn't want to run into O'Rourke.

So, he was standing on his front porch, nursing a cup of coffee and scratching behind Spot's ears when the first cars pulled up. Connor's Mini Cooper was in the lead, followed by two Jeep Cherokees, and a battered VW microbus. As David gaped, shifters fell out of each vehicle. Some had dark hair. Some were blond. A pair of ginger twins unfolded from the back seat of the Jeep. Every man was different, but every one was the same—tall and lean, with long-fingered hands and a hungry expression on his bearded faces.

"You're here," Connor said, approaching the porch with an uncharacteristic wariness.

"I live here." David clicked his tongue, calling Spot to his side.

"We've been busy."

"So I gathered."

"We've been training. Figuring out the best approach for going after the salamanders."

David looked at the men who stood by the cars. "We?"

"The males," Connor acknowledged.

Of course he'd only brought the brutes. The females would be safe back at Seymour House. David had been friends with Connor his entire life, but he'd never understand the shifters' social structure. No witch would tolerate for a day what the she-wolves regularly accepted from their mates.

"That's more than the Washington Pack," David said.

"I sent out a request to the rest of the Eastern Empire," Connor said. "They know about the Collar. The other alphas are here to keep the salamanders from dividing up the links."

This was a bad idea. The salamanders might move their meeting place. They could change their minds and call off the congress altogether. Brule might have been lying all along.

Even if the salamander could be trusted, it was risky having so many alphas in one place. Connor was strong enough to keep his own pack in order. But how long would the other shifters follow his lead? How long before he'd have to fight for supremacy, especially with his Collar at risk?

"I hope you know what you're doing," David said.

"I do."

"And why you're doing it here."

"We need space to practice shifting. The northern alphas weren't willing to travel to the Den."

Weren't willing to submit to Connor's absolute control, more likely. But David wasn't going to say that out loud. He wasn't going to do anything that might risk Connor's tenuous hold over his troops. "Tell them to stay away from the lake," he said. "There's a sprite living down there. She wouldn't take kindly to two dozen wolves muddying the water."

Connor's eyebrows shot up. "A sprite?"

"It's a long story."

"We could use all the allies we can get."

David pictured Bourne in human form, threatening to drive a tree trunk through the nearest salamander. He didn't trust her berserker fury. He wasn't sure she could be controlled, that she wouldn't strike out for her own reasons, without regard to the safety of her fellow warriors. "Not all the allies," he replied reluctantly. "Just the ones we can trust."

"You must have some warders who can join us."

A few years back, David would have had two dozen men to call—classmates from the Academy, warders sworn to Washington Coven witches, George and a handful of the senior warder's friends.

But those ties were broken now. They'd been shattered the instant Haylee James dedicated her powers to dark magic.

Now, he had a cadet computer geek who'd barely made it through Snake form. And maybe, on a good day, he had a rogue warder who was even more outcast than he was.

He shrugged. "No one I can think of."

Connor didn't seem surprised. "But we can shift here?"

David glanced toward the road. The farmhouse was secluded. No one could see the clearing without coming down the long driveway. Nevertheless, mail would be delivered sometime in the afternoon, and there was no telling who might drop by on unexpected business.

He waved toward the far end of the clearing. "Use the barn."

Connor nodded. "You'll join us?"

David had no desire to see that many shifts. "Go ahead. I'll be down in a few minutes."

Connor called out to the wolves as he led the way across the grass. Spot whined, his entire body straining toward the shifters. David snapped his fingers, breaking the dog's concentration. "No," he said firmly. "It's not safe." The lab ignored him, taking a dancing step onto the top stair.

David couldn't lock Spot in the house; he'd just slip out the dog door in the kitchen. Instead, he called the dog over to the garage door. A howl of betrayal rose, high and thin, as he turned his key in the lock. He hardened his heart and turned away.

Against his better judgment, he went to join a pack of wolves intent on destroying the largest salamander nest in the Eastern Empire.

27

After two days of drilling with the wolves, David couldn't say who was crazier—Connor for thinking he could manage half a dozen alphas along with his own brutes, or himself for thinking he had anything to do with the entire mess. Over and over, he'd watched alphas administer their own rough justice—nips to the heels of disobedient wolves, loose-mouthed grips on necks. Half a dozen conflicts had escalated to angry snarls. Once, Connor had faced them all down, planting his paws on the chest of the Manhattan alpha.

David had shivered then, frozen with the brutes who watched from the sidelines. He'd expected bloodshed and enough residual bad feelings that the entire mission would founder.

But attacks that looked savage to a warder were commonplace to wolves. Ultimately, the alphas knew they had a common enemy. The salamanders melded all the shifters into a new pack, one that was stronger and infinitely more determined than the Washington Pack could ever be on its own.

Three times, David traveled down to the lake, seeking out Bourne so she could coordinate her attack with the wolves. The sprite, however, was nowhere to be found even though the lake

seemed to be flourishing. In addition to healthy grasses at the
edge, David saw two great blue herons and a flock of ducks
wintering overnight. But Bourne had vanished.

David had no choice but to return his attention on the wolves.
And so it was that two dozen men gathered in the shadows of the
National Mall on a cold October night. That many shifters could
never have traveled in wolf form—they'd be exposed long before
they got to the abandoned parking garage beneath the Air and
Space Museum.

Instead, the men hunched human shoulders against the cold.
They'd worn the fewest clothes possible—over-dyed stovepipe
jeans and tight-fitting black T-shirts, anything to make them
disappear in the shadows. As they waited, their breath fogged on
the air. Traffic slowed on nearby Independence Avenue. Washington was as close to sleep as the capital ever got.

But the wolves weren't the only shadowy creatures on
the Mall.

Connor saw the salamanders first. His eyes and ears were
sharper than David's. The alpha whined softly, immediately
commanding the undiluted attention of every wolf beneath the
elm trees.

David squinted into the darkness. He knew what he *should* see
—slender men clad head to toe in black, with leather jackets
skimming their narrow waists and pointed-toe shoes stream-
lining their feet. Just as the wolves dared not shift in full view of
the public, no salamander would travel in imperial form.

Concentrating on the shadows closest to the abandoned
garage entrance, David finally made out a leather-clad human.
Security bollards blocked the ramp that led underground. The
massive concrete blocks were designed to keep a truck from delivering an explosive payload beneath the most visited museum in
the United States. Nevertheless, a standard-size door was cut into
the articulated steel gate beyond the concrete barriers.

As David watched, the metal door opened. The darkness

inside was so intense that he almost missed the shadow of a salamander slipping past. Connor tensed beside him. The shifter still
held his human form, but his face was frozen in the lupine intensity of a hunter.

David returned his attention to the garage door as another
salamander slipped into the garage. No. Two entered, followed
rapidly by another three men. David couldn't say for sure how
many salamanders had now entered the underground facility; his
eyes weren't strong enough to pick out every shape in the
darkness.

Somewhere on Capitol Hill, a bell tolled. David counted off
the tones in his head. Ten...Eleven...Twelve.

The shifters behind him vibrated with scarce-restrained
energy. Feet shuffled on gravel. Denim whispered against
lean legs.

Another shadow glided to the door. Apolline Fournier.

The salamander queen moved like a box office diva on the red
carpet at the Oscars. She wore the same black leather as her
minions, but her jacket was double-breasted and cinched tight at
her waist, with tails hanging almost to the backs of her knees.
Despite her stiletto heels, her ankles were rock-steady in her
thigh-high boots.

She paused on the threshold, glancing over her shoulder as if
someone had called her name. Her heart-shaped face was pale in
the moonlight, framed with a sleek black bob so perfect it looked
like a wig. Her lips glistened, probably painted scarlet, but
looking dark as pitch in the moonlight.

Behind David, Connor whined, a sound of pure animal need.
Knowing they only had one chance to make this attack work,
David caught his friend's wrist in iron fingers. Connor shrugged
himself free, but he mastered his keening.

A shadow appeared beside Apolline, a cloud of black with a
shock of silver hair that could only be Brule, speaking to his
mistress. David held his breath, but he could not hear the sala-

mander lieutenant across the distance. Apolline inclined her head like a goddess granting absolution. She listened, and then she nodded once. With one last look at the Mall behind her, she glided through the door into the abandoned garage.

Something was different about the door after she passed. David squinted, trying to make sense of what he saw in the darkness. The concrete bollards remained unmoved. The steel gate stayed the same.

But the shape of the doorway was different.

Not the shape. The shadow. Someone—it had to be Brule— had left the door ajar.

Connor noticed it too. He held up one hand, index finger high, to get the attention of his men. When he bent his wrist to point to the door, David felt the undivided attention of two dozen deadly predators shift to the entrance.

Having alerted his pack to their prey, Connor lost no time preparing for the hunt. He stripped off his clothes with remarkable speed, folding the garments with tight, controlled gestures. The other wolves followed suit, stashing their clothes beneath benches, in the shadows of the elm tree roots, and under the edge of a massive steel-reinforced trashcan.

This was the moment they were most vulnerable, more than a score of naked men loitering in a public park. Connor tossed his head back and summoned his shift. David's belly turned as it always did when he watched the transition; he imagined the torque on his own muscles, his own bones, his own flesh.

The other wolves followed Connor, completing their changes with speed and precision. Crouching in the trees' shadows, they were nearly invisible, only their eyes glinting in the moonlight.

Connor pressed his snout under David's hand. Then, he issued one short bark and led his pack into battle. David ran with them, his two feet making more noise on the gravel path than all their paws combined.

The door gaped open a few inches. Connor used his snout to

pry it wider before shouldering the door back on its hinges. He took care to keep the steel doorknob from crashing against the wall behind it. The wolves surged through the passage two abreast.

Entering last, David paused on the threshold, looking out at the deserted Mall. Even now, he expected Bourne to appear, gliding toward the garage ramp in a coordinated outfit of black or navy or the nameless color of dusty urban tree trunks. But the sprite was nowhere in sight, and David could not afford to wait.

He pulled the door closed behind him, leaving only a hairsbreadth gap to speed the shifters' escape. The last thing they needed was some heroic night watchman spotting the open door on a routine tour of the property.

Catching his breath, David peered into the gloom. The wolves huddled on a grooved ramp that curved away into darkness. They stayed clear of a glass-walled booth, domain of a long-absent parking attendant. A jagged piece of wood indicated where a yellow- and silver-painted arm had once regulated traffic; the plank had broken off some time in the past.

At first, David thought the only light in the space was the narrow sliver of grey that marked the barely-open door. But as his eyes adjusted, he realized that an orange glow rose from the bottom of the ramp. The color fluctuated, shading to crimson and dropping back to gold.

Someone had lit a fire inside the garage.

Now that he'd identified the source of the light, he could smell something burning—wood, maybe, or paper. The smoke dominated other odors—the musky scent of the wolves, a more pronounced funk of mildew, and the overarching stench of decay. The reek of gasoline was sharp and sweet beneath all the old garage's other smells, like the ghost of tourist dreams held over for decades.

David's ears carried information as well. Voices hummed beyond the bend, rising and falling in the normal buzz of conversation. Water dripped nearby, the steady ping of drop after drop striking a metal surface. The wolves panted, their rapid breathing almost in unison.

Connor glanced over his shoulder, surveying his pack's readiness. Apparently satisfied with what he saw, the huge brindled alpha led the way down the ramp. He placed his paws precisely, taking care to preserve the element of surprise.

The other wolves followed. Not a growl echoed off the high ceiling. Not a whine escaped to be heard.

David brought up the rear.

Looking down, he realized he'd pulled Rosefire from the ether, automatically dampening the steely ward-fire that flickered along the sword's edges. The weight of the weapon was reassuring as he dropped back two full paces to give himself room to swing without harming any of his lupine allies.

Each wolf rounding the bend in the ramp sank to his belly, minimizing his silhouette for the enemy. David approached the same curve with caution, turning sideways to present a smaller target.

The garage stretched out like a cathedral. Concrete support columns carved out a nave. The ghosts of white lines marked parking spaces across the floor, like massive flagstones in a church without pews.

Water glistened on the floor, puddles that had accumulated from the spiderweb of cracks along the columns and across the ceiling. White minerals had built up beside some of the breaks, drawing a stony roadmap into the past.

A maw gaped against the right wall, a dark too deep for fire to penetrate. Common sense said the hole led to another level of parking, but David's skin crawled as he imagined a direct ramp to Hell.

The salamanders were gathered in front of that pit. There had to be three dozen of them, maybe more. They stood in a tight clump, bodies swaying, arms stretched overhead. Here, in the echo chamber of the garage, David could make out a new sound. The salamanders hissed, their sibilant breath rising and falling in rhythm as they pulsed toward their leader.

Apolline Fournier stood on a concrete riser, the base of the spiral ramp that led to the parking level below. As David watched, she raised her arms above her head, her slender body echoing the swirl of poured concrete behind her. She rotated her hips, then rolled her torso and her neck. When the ripple reached the top of her head, she stiffened her fingers and pointed to the ceiling that was lost in shadow.

"Let the Salamander Congress be joined," she proclaimed, a whisper of a French accent beneath the words. Her voice was throaty and low, like a dirty joke told in a dark room. The fire-lizards hissed their approval, surging to and fro in a paroxysm of ecstasy. David watched the wolves crouch even lower, tails extending like rudders.

"Well-met, my nestlings," Apolline crooned, frothing up an even stronger response among her followers. "May the flames grow ever higher."

"May the flames grow ever higher," chanted all the salamanders in response.

As the congress chanted, "higher," a great blaze rose behind Apolline. It surged toward the ceiling in shades of pomegranate and tangerine and lemon, individual flames woven into an incendiary curtain.

The wolves flinched. Two or three broke out of their crouches, scrambling back toward David and the safety of the garage entrance. But Connor quickly glided forward half a dozen steps, rallying his pack.

David followed the wolves, taking refuge behind one of the garage's support columns. He eased around the barrier just far enough to glimpse Apolline's writhing figure.

"I stand before you, loyal nestlings, *avec un cadeau*. A gift to mark your loyal service." She nodded once as she finished her

proclamation, directing her obsidian gaze toward a single salamander in the crowd.

John Brule pulled himself onto the riser beside his queen, a
striking figure in his expertly tailored suit of black wool. Raising
his hands high above his head, he let an iron necklace cascade
from his fingertips. Each individual link captured the firelight,
tossing back glints to the ecstatic salamanders. Brule cast his gaze
beyond his queen and the dancing fire-lizards, all the way to the
wolves.

For a heartbeat, everything was still—Apolline on her dais,
Brule by her side, the crowd of salamanders gathered for their
prize. Then, Brule tucked his chin, inclining his head just a hair.

Connor took that as a signal. The alpha wolf leaped into
action, crossing the mottled floor with the speed of an avalanche
bearing down on an unsuspecting elk. The rest of the pack was
one pace behind, each furred missile directed to one target—the
Collar.

The wolves were strangely silent as they ran, wasting no
breath to howl. Instead, they launched themselves into the air,
ready to rain down fury on the thieves who had stolen their most
valuable possession. David swept behind them, Rosefire at
the ready.

The wolves might have been silent, but the salamanders were
not. Apolline issued a hissing screech of wordless fury as she cast
her hands high into the air. Bolts of fire shot from her fingernails,
jagged arcs of pure vermilion.

The nest reacted as one, whirling to face the wolves. The
fastest among the fire-lizards raised their hands, summoning
their own flames before they were battered by teeth and claws
and the force of fur-covered muscles hurtling at all-out speed.

The salamander queen rallied her troops from the top of the
curved concrete wall. "To me, loyal nestlings!" she shouted.
"To me!"

Fire-lizards surged toward their queen. Wolves yelped as bolts of fire hit home. Salamanders hissed as razor-sharp teeth slashed through leather.

Connor broke free of the pack to focus on John Brule and the Collar. The tall salamander had fallen to his knees after triggering the wolves' attack. He crouched at Apolline's feet, shoulders curved over his iron treasure.

Connor threw back his head and howled, loud enough and long enough that David's blood ran cold. As the echoes of that primal challenge bounced off the walls, salamanders froze. Most covered their ears. A few collapsed to the floor. Only a handful closest to the queen continued their fire-maddened dance, lobbing grenades of pure flame into the tangle of wolves.

David swung Rosefire like a scythe, determined to reach Connor's side. One step. Another. But then his feet slipped—on water or blood or worse—and he came down hard on one knee. Before he let himself feel the pain, he lunged at Brule, flashing a command to Rosefire.

Ward-fire surged.

A royal bodyguard leaped in front of Apolline and Brule, but David swept his flaming sword toward the warrior. Ward-fire kindled the golden crown embroidered on the guard's leather jacket, spreading rapidly to his slick black hair. The salamander bellowed and whirled, toppling sideways into the abyss behind his queen.

Connor was snapping at Brule, jaws slavering. The fire-lizard's eyes flickered in the reflected light of salamander flames and the steely glow of ward-fire. David poured more energy into Rosefire, extending his burning reach as far as he dared with Connor so close.

Brule raised his hands, cradling the Collar like a treasure. He might be offering it to Connor. He might be pulling it away. Apolline cried out: "Now, nestlings! Now!"

Fire exploded—a perfect ring that stretched all the way to the ceiling, forbidding escape. David and the wolves were surrounded, along with dozens of salamanders. David was knocked back by the blast, thrown to the center of the blazing circle. Connor howled in dismay as his wolves yelped in pain. Salamanders writhed around them, drawing in the fire, dancing through the flames.

Apolline snatched the Collar from Brule and dropped it over her head, ignoring the sizzle as shimmering iron links seared her chest. Slithering to the edge of her concrete platform, she arched backward, tumbling like an acrobat into the hell of the garage's lower level.

Within seconds, every living salamander followed her into the abyss.

David bellowed his frustration, but he couldn't fight his way through the terrified wolves to the confining wall of salamander fire. His throat was clogged with the stench of burned fur. Shifters howled in pain and fear.

He could *reach* himself free of the conflagration. He could even take a wolf or two with him, dragging their dead weight across the astral plane. But there was no way he could save everyone. He'd never get to Connor, at the edge of the fiery pen.

He wanted to stay and fight. He needed to leave and live.

Hating himself for failing, David sheathed Rosefire and clutched at the nearest wolf. Closing his eyes, he fumbled for his steel-grey guide wire to the ether.

Before he could grab hold, a massive explosion knocked him to his knees.

28

N oise.

Then dust.

Then a flood of water—tumbling, roaring, rushing into the depths of the garage.

David shook his head, trying to get his ears to clear. He was kneeling in a blackened circle, waist-deep in roiling brown water. He tried to get his legs under him, but the garage was tilting like a child's top.

Salamanders. He had to get the salamanders. But they were gone now, vanished into the garage's lower level.

Wolves then. He had to help the pack. Furry bodies lay on the floor around him. Some animals were pinned against the garage's uprights, snapping and snarling at the flood that poured against them. Others had transformed back into men, fighting to stand tall, to help their brothers.

A wall of water rose before him, twisting and spinning. David fought to grab a breath, bracing himself for a new deluge. But then he saw that the wall had tentacles, long fleshy streamers that twined with lavender hair and washed over sapphire lips.

"Bourne!" he gasped.

"Montroseson."

"I thought... When you weren't at the farm... When you didn't come to the Mall..."

"I rode the Falling Water," Bourne said, burbling with laughter. "The Falling Water to the Lake of Tides."

David grasped for meaning. The sprite had journeyed from the lake at the farm, tumbling over Great Falls to the north of DC. She'd ridden the current down the Potomac, to the Tidal Basin that curled around Washington's great monuments. "But how did you..." He trailed off. He wasn't even sure what she'd done.

"The Lake of Tides already knew a way into this cave. I asked it to break through faster."

David remembered the stench of mildew at the garage's entrance. During decades of being ignored, the walls had begun to leak. Bourne had accelerated the decay to spectacular effect, urging the Tidal Basin through the weakening concrete.

The sprite shifted, arching through the water like a dolphin. David suddenly found himself face to face with a cluster of tentacles—feet, he realized, and toes. The sprite gripped a dozen spears, one in each winding appendage. "Salamanders, Montroseson? Where are the salamanders?"

David shook his head. "You're too late. They escaped down the ramp." He gestured across the parking structure.

Bourne's face rippled, shading from eggplant to indigo to black. "Water flows downhill," she said. She shifted half a dozen spears to the tubules that registered as fingers.

Before David could respond, a metallic crash made the floor vibrate. As injured wolves whined, Bourne flowed toward the front of the garage to investigate. Returning, she murmured, "The Bureau."

"Go," David said, gesturing toward the breached walls, toward the Tidal Basin and the Potomac and escape. "Before they catch you."

"Salamanders," Bourne replied, rippling in a motion that suggested shaking her head before she melted toward the ramp.

David grabbed one of her trailing spears. "No! The salamanders know this place. They must have built escape tunnels long ago."

"Salamanders..." Bourne repeated, as if she hadn't heard him.

The sound of boots echoed in the garage. A large company stampeded down the ramp. David nodded once more toward the garage's outer wall. "Get back to the Lake of Tides before the Bureau locks you up forever."

Bourne's face rolled toward human, back to imperial, to human again. Finally, she nodded. One by one, her tentacles retracted, and she dropped her spears into the water that still flowed across the garage floor.

"Go," David said one last time.

And Bourne was gone.

29

David pulled his attention from Bourne's escape as an army marched into the chamber. Each imperial's sleeve was emblazoned with the Eastern Empire flag ringed by a spray of golden stars.

A griffin hulked at the back. The mountain spirit flexed her massive fingers as if she'd just torn a steel door to shreds—which, from the sound of things, she had. A trio of ifrits danced in front, glowing with the fire they breathed like air. A centaur stepped forward, issuing a single sharp command for the majority of his company to pursue the salamanders into the darkness.

The Eastern Bureau of Investigation had arrived.

After that, everything was a blur. Medics circulated among the wolves, triaging the wounded and determining who was stable enough to shift back to human form. Connor had already made the transition, accepting a disposable jumpsuit from the authorities before he started a personal evaluation of each of his wolves. Seriously injured shifters—along with half a dozen slashed and bleeding salamanders—were ushered up the ramp on stretchers and hustled into ambulances marked with the flag-and-star logo.

Scouts returned from the lower level of the garage shaking their heads. David was disheartened but not surprised that the salamanders had conducted a subterranean retreat. They'd excavated through the walls of the garage, probably months or even years before tonight's Congress. Apolline, Brule, and the rest were gone, along with the Collar.

Soon enough, the centaur in charge ordered David to be patted down. After that, he was handcuffed to two shifters, one on his right hand, and one on his left. Even if he were inclined to fight his way free, he couldn't draw Rosefire without harming his own allies.

Ignoring the wolves' complaints, the centaur extended the chain, cuffing two more men on the ends. The EBI wasn't taking any chances that David might *reach* out of their custody.

All five men shuffled up the ramp together, along with the other captured combatants. A black bus sat at the exit to the garage. Its windows were reinforced with metal grilles—tarnished silver to deter vampires, shifters, and mere mortals from shattering the glass and escaping.

The prisoners were soon installed on cracked leatherette seats behind a gate of the same metal. David was stuck standing in the aisle between his shifter ballast. He tried to keep his weight on the balls of his feet as the bus lurched into gear, but he banged his hips against the seats more than once as they sped through the city streets.

The rest of the night was lost in a blur of legal procedure. No one read him his rights. Miranda protected mundane defendants, not imperials.

Once David was in the processing room, they caught his wrists in odd-shaped cuffs, designed to keep him from clutching a sword from the ether. They continued to keep him from *reaching* as well, chaining him to a block of marble that must have weighed ten tons. The shifters who'd secured him on the bus gave him dirty looks as they shuffled off to another desk.

He didn't have any personal possessions to hand over; he'd purposely fought without his wallet, keys, or any identifying information. The intake clerk, a cat shifter, seemed surprised that he didn't have a Hecate's Torch. She actually checked her paperwork, purring, "Hecate's Warder..." but he didn't feel obliged to explain.

She recovered enough to record his personal information—name, address, date of birth. Fingerprinting was complicated by his cuffs and chains, but the clerk finally got ten clear prints. Rolling her camera into position, the cat told him to look straight ahead, to turn left, to turn right.

The Empire's night court was specifically designed to arraign supernatural prisoners before any mundanes wandered through asking uncomfortable questions. Therefore, David wasn't surprised to find himself in the courtroom a couple of hours before dawn, cuffed to a waist-high iron block, ten feet in front of the Honorable Judge Robert DuBois, a vampire with iron eyes and thin, angry lips.

The judge ordered a nervous dryad to read the charges against him. The young prosecutor licked her lips and ran twig-like fingers through the tangles of her hair. She had to clear her throat twice before she could make herself heard from counsel's table. Judge DuBois looked distinctly unamused.

Finally, the dryad wheezed through the charges. First degree working of magic in a public place. First degree criminal trespass with disregard for imperial life. Aggravated exposure of imperial life. Felony endangerment of imperial forces during the commission of a crime. Revelation of imperial resources within a specially designated tourist district. Revelation of imperial resources upon United States federal land.

"How do you plead to these charges, Warder David Montrose?"

He was guilty as sin but he looked the vampire directly in the eye and said, "Not guilty, Your Honor."

He ignored the details after that. The judge set bail. His case was assigned a number. He was advised to hire a lawyer. A huge griffin of a bailiff ushered him down the marble stairs, chaining him to an iron rail at the back of a holding cell. As she leaned close to test the bonds, the griffin's turquoise eyeshadow flashed against her matching earrings and necklace. "You'll get your phone call in an hour or two. The desk sergeant is working through the crowd."

He nodded and waited for her to close the barred door to his cell. Now, in the aftermath of adrenaline, his body was reacting to the battle. His left shoulder ached deep in the joint; he must have jammed it against a concrete column or the floor of the garage. His right knee screamed its own protest. His black shirt was stiff, the fabric singed by flames. An ugly bruise rose on his forearm. He took a deep breath, which triggered a fit of coughing, his lungs protesting the smoke and water and exertion they'd endured in the underground chamber.

He could hear salamanders down the hallway, hissing and thrashing against the bars of their cages. A wolf howled in response, a lonesome keening that emptied the marrow from David's bones.

One phone call. Someone to come to the courthouse with enough cash to get him out of there.

Ordinarily, he'd place that call to Connor, but the wolf alpha was mired in his own legal hell. Any self-respecting warder would call his witch, but David didn't have one. Haylee would laugh herself hoarse if he begged her for help. Jane wouldn't have a clue what to do.

He couldn't call Kyle Hopp or Aidan O'Rourke—he didn't have a number for either man. Bourne Morrissey couldn't possibly own a phone, and even if she did, he was pretty sure he'd never see the sprite again.

He'd kill himself before he called Norville Pitt, and there wasn't a chance in hell that he'd ask his father to bail him out.

He couldn't ask George. But he could ask Linda. The witch would berate him, he was certain of that. She'd tell him he was a warder, not a wolf, that Hecate would be his sole judge on Samhain.

She'd scold him. But she'd still come to the courthouse and bail him out.

He recited her number from memory when the desk sergeant finally arrived.

30

David was a waste of good air at the office on Monday. After Linda had bailed him out, she'd taken one sniff of his singed clothes and ordered him to *reach* for home. A quick shower and a gallon of coffee were forced to stand in for a full night's sleep.

All day long, he kept his cell phone on his desk, waiting for Connor to get in touch. He was certain the alpha had been bailed out; the she-wolves had been mobilizing even before Linda got to the courthouse.

The imperial rumor mill was operating at full tilt. The prosecutor had asked for and received maximum bail on every combatant arraigned. Half a dozen shifters were in Empire Memorial, with injuries ranging from smoke inhalation to third-degree burns. The salamanders had already filed formal charges in the Empire's civil courts, claiming trespass, invasion of privacy, and a dozen other trumped-up actions.

So David didn't worry too much when he didn't hear from Connor during the day. But the instant his shift ended, he *reached* to the shadowy garage behind the pack's house. He walked around to the front door of the row house and raised his hand to knock, but the door opened before he could make contact.

Tala stood in the doorway, feet planted firmly in bright white Keds. He ignored the plaid mini skirt she wore over black leggings and the embroidered vest that covered her sleek black T-shirt. More accurately, he noticed them, but he kept his eyes locked firmly on her face.

"You're not welcome here," she said.

The words hit like a physical blow. He'd expected Connor to feel defensive about his choice to bring two dozen wolves to the center of the National Mall, but he hadn't realized Tala would be on edge too. He forced his voice to a soothing register. "I need to talk to Connor."

"He's busy."

He wasn't looking for a hand-written apology. He just needed to make sure his friend was safe. "This is important, Tala."

"Not as important as the pack."

He was strong enough to shove past her, but he wouldn't do that to a friend. He sighed and asked, "Will you give him a message for me?"

The she-wolf actually snarled. "I can't be sure he'll get it."

"What the hell is wrong with you?" David gave into his fatigue and let his temper flare.

"Leave my mate alone." Connor dropped the words like depth charges as he bulldozed past Tala. He pulled the door closed behind him.

The shifter seemed to have lost ten pounds in the last two days. His face was gaunt. An angry red burn stood out on his cheekbone, sure to leave a scar even after it healed. His right wrist was wrapped in a supportive brace as he barred David from entering the house.

"Say whatever you have to say," Connor growled. "And get the hell off my porch."

"Wait a second," David protested, holding up innocent hands.

Whatever he'd expected coming to Seymour House, this wasn't it —no apology, no regret, not even a hint of concern for David's own well-being. "You don't think *I'm* responsible for what happened down there."

Connor's eyes narrowed. "You're the one who brought a flaming sword to the party."

"We were attacked by *salamanders!*" David shouted, only to remember they were arguing on a city street. At least a quick glance confirmed that no mundanes happened to be on the side-walk. He lowered his voice and repeated, "We were attacked by salamanders, Con. The congress knew we were coming. Brule must have been stringing us along."

Connor shook his head. "Brule meant to give us the Collar. He was as surprised as the pack."

"Were we in different garages?" David insisted. "Something was off, Con. The whole garage smelled wrong."

"You're saying you smelled something a wolf didn't?"

"You smelled it too." Urging his friend's sanity to return, David explained: "The gasoline. That garage was abandoned too long ago for spilled fuel to remain. The salamanders planted it. They meant to burn us alive. We never had a chance."

Connor glanced at the door behind him. His voice tightened, and his words came too fast. "My wolves would have had the Collar if they weren't startled by your ward-fire."

"You've got to be joking."

The alpha's voice was desperate now. "I don't joke about the pack. You cost us the battle."

As David spluttered for an answer, the door opened behind Connor. Expecting to see Tala, David pasted a smile on his lips. Maybe she could talk sense into her mate.

But Tala wasn't standing in the doorway.

Instead, David found himself staring at another wolf. In human form, the man was enormous, a full head taller than David, his barrel chest barely encased in a flannel shirt. The tips of his mustache were waxed into miniature spears above his full beard. "It's time, Connor."

"Time?" David asked.

"Who's this?" the giant countered.

"Someone who's just leaving," Connor said. He directed the words to the other wolf, but David saw the expression on his face. He was cornered. Desperate. Pleading.

"Con," David said. "What color is the moon?"

"Let's go," the giant said, closing his fingers on the meat of Connor's arm. "You'll only make it worse, keeping the Chase waiting."

Connor raised his eyebrows, a facial shrug that David was bound to accept. But as the shifter closed the door, he mouthed a single word: *Blue*.

The answer was the most troublesome possibility in their childhood game. The situation was unclear. Everything might be fine. But everything might be on the verge of disaster.

The Chase was the gathering of wolves that witnessed one brute challenging an alpha for supremacy. Connor's hold over the Washington Pack was in jeopardy.

David had to help him. He had to explain. He had to make the pack understand that the salamanders had caused all this chaos, twisting vengeance for their stolen karstag without regard for any imperials caught in their burning net.

But Connor had closed the door, completely shutting him out. The Chase belonged to the wolves. There was nothing David could do to make things right, not now.

He slunk into the shadows and *reached* for home.

31

By Tuesday morning, word had spread throughout the Eastern Empire: Connor was ousted as alpha of the Washington Pack.

One report said he'd shifted on the front porch of the townhouse, then loped into Rock Creek Park. Another said he'd abandoned his car at the entrance to the Den, shifting before dawn and taking refuge in the woods. A third said he'd bought a plane ticket for Portland and was abandoning the Eastern Empire altogether.

The reports all agreed on one thing: Tala had caught an overnight flight to Norway. She'd turned her back on Connor and retreated to her parents' home.

David clenched his fists with frustration. He'd do anything for Connor—that's what friendship meant. But before he could do anything, he had to know what Connor actually wanted. And for now, his friend wasn't speaking to him.

The office was curiously quiet all day. Pitt sent a single email in the middle of the morning, asking for an annotated list of all office supplies kept in the third floor closet. David was happy to escape to the quiet room. He used the afternoon to think about his future.

Linda had warned him to prove himself to Hecate by Samhain. Well, he had three and a half weeks left to accomplish that.

He still believed Jane Madison could be his salvation. Standing in the supply closet, thinking about the pull of her powers on his, he recognized a spark of true warder/witch bond. He'd studied it in school, reading dry academic accounts of famous warding pairs through history. Graduating from the Academy, he'd recited a warder's traits like some sort of twisted Boy Scout oath: he'd vowed to be trustworthy and loyal, honest and brave, reverent to Hecate and her witches in all things true.

He'd started his search for Jane's lineage, but he'd been side-tracked by Aidan O'Rourke. O'Rourke and Kyle and Connor and a dozen other blind alleys.

The weathered old warder had said he'd never heard of Abigail Somerset. But that didn't mean Hecate's Court didn't have records about the New England witch.

If David had mastered one thing at Pitt's behest, it was tracking down court records. The instant he clocked out at the end of his work day, he commandeered a computer in a conveniently empty office near the supply closet. He started with the obvious databases. He checked to see if Abigail had ever registered a warder with the court. Of course, few witches bothered with paperwork in the seventeenth century. If Abigail had been partnered with a warder, there wasn't any official record.

Next, he checked the listings of familiars. She'd come from Salem, a conservative community even before the infamous trials. She'd be inclined to go with a traditional familiar, a black cat if possible. Thinking of Jane's Neko, David pulled up a database of familiars, using filters to select all cats, then all black cats. No familiar, living or dead, was bonded to an Abigail Somerset, Abigail Windmere, or Abigail Carroll.

She could have brought a case against a fellow witch or had one filed against her. For the oldest court documents, only litigants' names were available. There were no detailed records of briefs filed or motions argued before the court. Still, that was enough for David to learn that Abigail had never stood before Hecate's Court.

If only there was a way to reach out to Abigail's possessions... A book she might have owned, an athame she'd handled, a wand she'd used to channel power for a spell.

Closing his eyes, David sifted through the kaleidoscope of sensations in his memory, all the references he'd ever cataloged with countless orphaned items. Any one of them could have belonged to Abigail, linked to the witch's unique signature.

A unique signature like Jane's night jasmine, the alluring scent that even now enveloped his senses. He took a deep breath and allowed himself to relax for the first time in days.

The *tug* came through the astral plane, stronger than any summons he'd felt from Jane yet. He didn't think. He didn't reason. He simply *reached* to the cottage in the Peabridge gardens.

He closed the distance to the front door with a dozen long strides. The nearer he got to Jane, the more he was able to parse the sensations he'd gleaned from their jasmine bond.

She'd worked a fire-dampening spell. He knew that before he hit the porch. He didn't know which spell in particular, or why she'd harnessed her powers that way. But he could have used her magic on Sunday night and spared himself and the Washington Pack a nightmare without Bourne's watery destruction.

Pushing aside an iron pang of regret, he knocked firmly on the cottage door.

"David!" Jane cried.

Her voice was strangled. She let him sweep into the living room, but he had the distinct impression she wanted him gone. In fact, her words were filed to a precise point as she said, "I was just about to finish cooking dinner for my guest."

Guest. That had to be the guy standing just inside the kitchen. He wore jeans and an open-necked dress shirt, along with a tweed jacket. His face was pale beneath curly hair, and he kept glancing from Jane to Neko and, now, to David, his eyes wide with a stunned look of disbelief.

First things first. He had to find out exactly how much magic her *guest* had witnessed. "I'm sorry to interrupt," David said, barely bothering to match tone to words. He strode directly into the kitchen, the better to observe the threat from Jane's mundane companion.

Great. There was *another* person present—a buff giant of a man who stared at Neko with adoring eyes.

Jane hurried to join him beside the scorch-marked stove. "David," she said, with a spirited attempt to sound welcoming. "I don't think you've met Roger, Neko's friend."

He exchanged a somewhat wary handshake with Adonis.

"And this is Jason Templeton." Jane sighed as she gestured toward Mr. Tweed. "Jason, this is David Montrose. He's the, um, mentor I mentioned earlier. The one who's guiding my independent study."

David shot a quick look at her. What *study* was he supposed to supervise? Lies worked better when all the relevant parties were in on the story. Tweed cautiously offered his hand, saying, "David."

"Professor." David shook, but he kept his voice flat. Out of the corner of his eye, he saw a book on the counter. *Elemental Magick.* That explained the fire spell he'd felt. But Jane must have had one hell of a motivation to pour as much energy into the working as he'd felt from his office. He turned to her and said, "Jane, we need to talk."

"Can't it wait?"

"No."

"Look," she said, and her cheeks flushed pink. "This has not been my dream night, okay? First, I almost burned the pear tart because the oven runs hot. Then, I came close to poisoning Jason with peanut soup. As you can see, the oven caught fire while I was preheating the broiler. I don't have time to talk to you, David. Not tonight."

He knew he shouldn't laugh at her. Not when she was clearly upset. But her catalog of so-called catastrophes was so picayune, so *refreshing* after a week of sprites and salamanders and EBI arrests and a werewolf Chase and whatever Pitt was up to... He fought to sound sincere as he followed the lead she'd unwittingly set. "There are just a couple of details we need to work out. Tonight. Some problems have come up with your...independent study, and I would hate for the *administration* to get involved."

She looked so distraught that he settled a protective hand on her elbow. The move was pure instinct—pure warder—but it felt right.

Tweed blanched. Darting a nervous glance at David's face, he said, "Look, Jane. Maybe I *should* head home."

Jane shrugged off David's grasp, clearly annoyed. "But we haven't eaten!"

Neko looked at the lamb chops on the counter. "I wouldn't trust the oven," he said sincerely. "But I've heard lamb tartare is considered a delicacy in some parts of the world."

Tweed looked repulsed, either by the notion of eating raw lamb or the thought of spending another minute in the chaotic cottage. "You probably *should* get someone to check that oven. We'll do this again, though. Some time soon."

"But I baked a pear tart!" Jane protested.

Tweed glanced at it with barely masked horror, as if the dessert might fly from the countertop and attempt to choke him. David wondered exactly how bad the evening had been *before* the oven caught on fire. "I'm sure it's wonderful," Tweed said. "Look, you can bring it into the library tomorrow. I'm sure you could sell slices to go with lattes. It would give a real colonial feel to the library."

"Jason—" Jane protested, but Tweed was edging around David, making his way past Neko and Roger. Jane followed him to the front door, her voice dipping into a soft, apologetic register.

Unwilling to eavesdrop on a witch, even one who tantalized him with the scent of jasmine, David made a show of turning toward Neko and his human companion. The blond sex god was conveniently occupied with pouring himself a full tumbler of vodka from the supply under the sink. "Everything under control here?" David asked.

"It is now," the familiar replied.

"I take it you walked her through the fire-dampening spell?"

"She had all the power she needed. I just helped with focus."

"She seems to have a *lot* of power." David glanced at the front door as Neko nodded. Jane was clutching Tweed's arm. Like any concerned warder anywhere, David demanded, "Who is that guy?"

"She calls him her Imaginary Boyfriend." The familiar feigned coughing up a hairball.

David grimaced, but he didn't have time to reply, because Jane was finally saying goodbye to the loser. Instead, David fished his wallet out of his pocket and forked over a pile of crisp twenties to the obliging familiar. "Get out of here, you two. I'll make sure she's okay."

He was just returning his wallet to his back pocket when Jane entered the kitchen.

"Right." Neko's stage whisper was clearly meant to entertain everyone in the room. "Roger and I will have a 'late supper.' At Bistro Bis. On Capitol Hill." He winked and put his hand on his boyfriend's shoulder.

As the men slipped out the front door, Jane surveyed the kitchen wreckage. David fought for a light tone. "Well, at least you weren't frivolous about using your magic this time."

She actually smiled. "I'd pretty much run out of other options."

"Come on," he said, before he realized he'd made up his mind. "Let's go."

"Where?"

"Out to dinner. Some place safe. Where someone else cooks the food."

She started to protest, but then her shoulders slumped. She looked like a witch who'd completed a Major Working on short rest. She looked like a woman whose carefully planned dinner date had turned into a disaster. "Thank you," she said with palpable gratitude. "I'd like that. Very much."

Sitting in a nearby Italian restaurant, they didn't talk about her ridiculous Imaginary Boyfriend. They didn't talk about witchcraft. They didn't talk about shifters or the EBI or salamanders or his lost Hecate's Torch. Instead, they filled hours with easy conversation about favorite foods and treasured childhood books and perfect dream vacations.

And if he noticed she'd painted her fingernails burgundy— that she'd grown her fingernails long enough to paint them—he told himself that was unimportant. She was his witch. He wasn't supposed to concentrate on mundane things like fingernails.

He walked her to her door long after midnight. She laughed as she thanked him for a wonderful dinner. He told her the pleasure had been all his. He waited until he heard her engage the deadbolt inside.

And then he sat on a bench in the chilled autumn garden, staring at the darkened cottage that housed the Osgood collection and the most intriguing witch he'd ever met.

32

David was still replaying dinner as he went through his morning routine—shower and shave and a fresh cup of coffee, bracing himself before he *reached* for the office.

Haylee James had been a stunning witch, precise with her spellcraft, dramatic with her presentation. She'd worn her Torch like a battlefield medal, displaying it proudly to imperials and mundanes alike. She'd shimmered with *power*, a force only amplified by her close friendship with the Washington Coven Mother, Teresa Alison Sidney.

And when Haylee dismissed him, he'd thought his life was over. His life as a warder, certainly, but his life as a man as well. He'd poured himself into being her protector. He'd twisted his beliefs, his values; he'd done his damnedest to justify her inappropriate demands. He'd compromised on every single aspect of who he was and still she'd left him like a piece of fruit rotting in the sun.

Jane's energy was completely different. She had a greater well of potential than any witch he'd ever met. He could sense her capacity when she worked her spells. He could feel her untapped power pushing against the ether like the pressure of water against eardrums after diving deep into a swimming pool. She'd never known the restrictions of a magicarium, never been taught the limits of her ability. She was like a child playing on a parent's computer, utterly unafraid to push any button.

And because she'd lived outside the strictures of witchcraft, she had a world of other references—Shakespeare and her best friend's bakery, artisan cocktails and old black-and-white movies. She was fresh. She was new. And his helping her might be the very thing to gain Hecate's approval by Samhain.

With new determination, he *reached* for his cubicle, already reminding himself it was Hump Day.

His grip slipped on the steely thread spun out across the astral plane.

Still in his kitchen, he blinked hard, shaking his head to drive away the first inkling of a headache. He hadn't lost an astral thread in years, not since his first days of learning to *reach*. Then, he'd had trouble concentrating; he'd fought to measure the precise tension he needed to place on the line. But for decades now the touch had been automatic, especially when he was traveling to a place as familiar as the court's downtown office building.

He really must be shaken by the events of the past few days. And he hadn't done himself any favors, sitting outside Jane's cottage until three in the morning.

Squaring his shoulders, he *reached* for the office again.

And once more, he found himself reeling in his kitchen. This time, he had to take a few quick steps to keep from staggering into the center island. He felt as if he'd bounced off an invisible wall, a plate glass window stretched across the astral plane.

Swallowing panic, he *reached* for the wooden dock on the lake. He landed on the smooth wood with perfect ease, and he transported back to the kitchen as soon as he felt a breeze rise off the water.

He *reached* for George's house, for the backyard shed his father had built to keep warders' comings and goings safe from neighbors' eyes. The familiar room surged into place with its Queen Anne chairs, decanters of red wine and brandy, and a humidor of his father's favorite Cuban cigars. He bounced back to his kitchen immediately.

Once more, he *reached* for the office, taking the time to picture his cubicle—the precise angle of his computer monitor, the shelf of reference books he still kept in paper, the telephone with electrical tape covering the message light that always pulsed red. Pulling the image close, he sent his body onto the plane.

And he fell to his knees on his cold kitchen floor.

Swallowing the coffee-flavored acid of panic, he grabbed his keys and headed out to his Lexus. He wasn't going to chance *reaching* to some other destination downtown, not if his powers were flickering in some way he didn't understand.

He fought traffic on the interstate, around the Beltway, and down the crowded arterial road into the heart of the city. He discovered he'd missed Early Bird Parking by an hour, but an exorbitant garage rate was the least of his concerns. He shuddered a little as he slid into a parking space. At least this garage was flooded with fluorescent light instead of Tidal Basin water.

Walking the half-block to his office building, he tried to slow his galloping heart. There had to be a simple explanation, an obvious reason he was foolishly overlooking. He concentrated on the cool brass beneath his palms as he pulled open the door to the lobby.

Norville Pitt waited for him in the center of the atrium, pocket protector jutting from his yellow short-sleeve shirt, crumbs speckling the wool of his mud-brown trousers. A wide grin split his face, making him look more frog-like than ever.

"David Montrose," Pitt said, his nasal voice echoing off the marble walls. He slapped a sheaf of papers against David's chest. "Your employment is terminated with cause, pursuant to section seventeen point four slash 3 sub a double-i of the employee hand-book. You are hereby fired, permanently and without recourse, from your position at Hecate's Court."

33

You can't fire me. I quit.

For the hundredth time, David shouted the words inside his head. He knew they were childish. They wouldn't have changed anything, even if he'd bellowed them at the top of his lungs in the sunlit atrium. *Especially* if he'd bellowed them. They certainly wouldn't have wiped the smug grin from Pitt's face or kept people from staring—a pair of senior students scurrying to beat the bell for second period, an ancient warder helping his equally ancient witch to the elevator bank, a wide-eyed cadet whose jaw hung halfway to the floor.

The words wouldn't even be true, because David *couldn't* quit. He couldn't throw himself out of the society of witches and warders forever, not voluntarily.

That's why he'd hurried to the Imperial Library after Pitt's smug declaration. Now, David huddled deep in the belly of the Eastern Empire Night Court. He already knew the warders' library was useless, and he no longer had access to the computerized records of Hecate's Court.

But any member of the Eastern Empire was cleared to use the

trove of books in the courthouse. He just had to find what he
needed.

The library looked like it hadn't been maintained for
centuries. Books were strewn across tables the size of aircraft
carriers—leather-bound parchment mixing with scrolls and a
handful of modern editions. Abandoned notepads were tucked
into some volumes, along with an assortment of discarded pens,
from quill to Rollerball.

A computer lurked in the corner, but its screen was dead. If
there was a secret to bringing the machine to life, it was beyond
David's skill. He'd given up after ten minutes of turning the
machine off and turning it back on, only to hear a wheezing
whirr deep inside the plastic casing.

Sighing, he read through his termination papers one more
time. They were filled with the court's customary legal jargon—
parties of the first part, parties of the second part, and countless
Latin phrases. He'd already memorized the inventory of his
supposed failings, starting with his being accused of felony
endangerment in an Eastern Empire proceeding. Even without
trial or conviction, that single count made him too dangerous to
exist in the society of witches.

Staring at the courthouse library's jumbled bookshelves, he
almost capsized under a wave of hopelessness. The materials
weren't in any order. Handwritten docket sheets were shelved
next to procedural rules for the Council of Giants, an entity that
had been disbanded the year before the Pilgrims landed at
Plymouth Rock. Case reports from the Dryad Circle were inter-
leaved with criminal indictments from the griffins' Court of
Elementals.

He had no way of knowing where to find information about
Hecate's Court. And even if he discovered *those* records, he'd still
have to locate specific information about employment law.

He'd worked for the court long enough to know he shouldn't
bother hiring a lawyer to press his claim. The court had been

created by witches, for witches. They bothered themselves with warders only when absolutely necessary. Sure, the court administered the Academy, but that was only to guarantee ongoing corps of fresh cadets for new witches.

The last time the court had considered an action brought by a warder had been during the Harding administration. A witch had used spellcraft to increase her investment portfolio during the corrupt presidential regime. A warder—not hers—filed an action for conversion when he lost his life savings following the witch's lead. But even that case was dismissed after Harding died in office.

No, the court would not hear David's complaint. But he had to do *something* to thwart Pitt.

As he slammed his hand down on the table in frustration, his attention was drawn to the far side of the underground chamber. While the library was an unqualified mess, the rest of the room seemed to be a perfectly maintained gymnasium. A boxing ring was roped off in one corner, and a number of blue mats covered the floor. An armoire was filled with neatly folded practice uniforms. A variety of weapons hung on the wall. Ominously, a cage hulked near the locker room, its tarnished silver bars spaced close enough to keep even the thinnest vampire at bay.

David's temptation to drown his annoyance in a thorough workout was almost overwhelming. But he didn't dare give in. Because if he didn't find an answer here in the Imperial Library, he might find himself with infinite time for exercise. He might never work in the Eastern Empire again.

Well, if the materials weren't organized, he only had one choice. He had to read through the titles, shelf by shelf, book by book. And he might as well start in the corner farthest from the door.

An hour in, he was ready to give up. He'd found nothing remotely relevant to salvaging his career. But he didn't have anything better to do with his day—not when he'd been disgraced in his profession, with his family, and with his best friend. So he kept on reading.

Two hours in, he wondered if any other imperial had actually used this library in the past decade.

Three hours in, he considered how long it would take someone to find his body if he died down there.

Four hours in, he hit pay-dirt.

Not the books he'd hoped to find—*Imperial Employment for Dummies*, or something along those lines. Instead, he discovered the Boston Coven's tax records.

They were stacked haphazardly on a series of dusty shelves. Unlike the parchment-paged tomes scattered through the rest of the library, these records were all kept on cheap paper. It only took a moment for David to realize they were photocopies of handwritten documents that must be maintained in some mundane library.

At first, he brushed past them because the endless lines of addresses and tax receipts were useless in his quest for reinstatement. But he only got one shelf further along before he realized the tax records might answer a different question. Nothing in life was certain but death and taxes. Well, Abigail Somerset Windmere Carroll was long dead. But if she'd paid taxes, he might be able to trace her descendants. He might be able to prove Jane Madison was a legitimate witch. And Hecate might reward him for his labors.

He started in Salem. The photocopy was in bad shape; someone had obviously had a hard time getting foxed parchment pages to reproduce. "Somerset," he muttered to himself, scanning down columns of names. "Somerset... Somerset... Somerset..."

And there, three lines from the bottom of a page, he found it. *Abigail Somerset, spinster*, the spidery writing said. There was an abbreviated inventory of her farmhouse—one bed, a good milk cow, six laying hens. A splash of water had ruined the opposing page so he couldn't make out the precise number of shillings and pence she'd owed the Massachusetts taxing authorities.

But once he'd found his target, it was easy to follow her through the records. She'd rendered unto Massachusetts the things that were Massachusetts's—namely, hard cold cash every year. And in 1683, there was a curious abbreviation: O.Salem, CNCT.

Old Salem, O'Rourke had told him. Connecticut—the location of Jane's family farm.

The mundane tax records managed to do what Hecate's Court had not, tracing the existence of a colonial woman from one residence to another. Muttering thanks to some long-dead clerk with a passion for complete records—along with whatever imperial had thought to add the tax rolls to the Eastern Empire collection—David scrambled along the shelves, looking for Connecticut records. It took him fifteen minutes amid a choking cloud of dust, but he finally located the book he needed. And there, written in a loopy scrawl that was nearly impossible to decipher, he found her: *Abigail Windmere, widow.*

She'd paid her taxes on the farm for four years, and then she was listed as Abigail Windmere Carroll. He squinted through page after page. Abigail's name disappeared—her husband, Theophilus, was listed as the owner of the farm. But Theophilus gifted the property to his daughter, Priscilla, who owned it until she married Thomas Stark. Thomas, in his time, gifted the farm to *his* daughter, and so the records proceeded, generation after generation until the nineteenth century, when women were finally able to inherit property in their own names.

Ida McGill held the farm in 1917. She passed it to her daughter, Eleanor Marks, in 1940. And Eleanor passed it to her daughter, Sarah Smythe, in 1972.

He had it.

Jane Madison's full lineage. She should be welcomed into the fold of true witches. Hecate should be pleased.

Maybe it was his imagination, but the dusty old library suddenly seemed to fill with the scent of jasmine. He took a deep breath, soothed by the now-familiar aroma. It only took him a moment to realize the scent wasn't coincidence.

Jane was working another spell.

Closing his eyes, he let his warder's consciousness follow the astral path back to her working. He couldn't see her, not quite. But he received a clear impression of Neko standing by her side, leaning close to lend her physical and magical support. There was someone else in the room, a presence he'd sensed before. Melissa White, the baker friend.

Dark shies.

He *felt* her speak the first two words of a spell. It was one of the first a new witch would take on after mastering the Rota in her magicarium. Jane was lighting a candle, delighted and awed by the power that rose within her.

He should go to her. Protect her. Watch her expand the range of her magic. At the very least, he should chastise her for demonstrating her power before a mundane companion.

Climbing to his feet, he touched the astral bond between them, ready to *reach* for Jane, regardless of where she stood in physical space. The link was strong enough for him to follow. He took a calming breath and stretched his consciousness toward her.

Before he could make the leap across space, though, footsteps echoed in the stairwell outside the Old Library. David looked up, surprised that anyone else had bothered to come to the wreck of a room.

John Brule stood in the doorway.

34

B efore David could pull Rosefire into the room, Brule held up his hands in a display of good faith.

"I wouldn't advise that," the salamander said. "You never know what's going to attract the attention of the Night Court's Director of Security. I hear he's a cold-hearted bastard, even for a vampire."

David relinquished his grip on his sword, but he edged around the table, putting the large plane of polished wood between himself and Brule. "What are you doing here?" he demanded.

"You and I should talk. I tried reaching out to your shifter friend, but he's gone off the grid."

A twinge of worry tugged at David's conscience, but he ordered himself to pay attention to the disaster at hand. "What makes you think we have anything to say to each other?"

"I'm afraid you and the alpha misunderstood what happened in the garage."

"We understood *exactly* what happened. You lured us there under false pretenses. And you did your best to kill us when you thought we couldn't fight back."

Brule sighed. "That's not what happened. Not that I have any way of proving myself to you."

David thought about his last conversation with Connor, when the shifter insisted Brule was innocent. David hadn't believed Connor that night, but maybe he owed it to his friend to listen to the salamander now. He asked, "What do *you* think happened down there?"

Brule's lips pursed in a Gallic pout. "I left the door open for you and your shifter friends. I placed the Collar as close to you as I could. I did my best to draw the attention of the nest from your wolves."

"And the gasoline? The fire?"

"Bad luck all the way around. Ms. Fournier used the Congress for her own purposes. I had no idea she intended a fire circle."

The secretive fire-lizards had rituals David had never heard of. Reluctantly, he asked, "What's a fire circle?"

"It's the prerogative of a Salamander Queen. The fire brings a certain...ecstasy. It gives us—*le mot...le mot*—joy. No. Euphoria."

David remembered the lizards writhing in the flames, their faces transformed into something beyond their physical form. "Why give it then?"

The salamander shrugged. "It was a reward. Many among our people opposed our taking the Collar. They said we should kill the wolves who stole our karstag and be done with the entire matter. Ms. Fournier felt differently, and she offered the fire circle out of gratitude to her followers who obeyed."

"You had no idea she'd planned that? No idea wolves would be caught inside the flames?"

Brule stared directly into his eyes. "I had absolutely no idea."

David didn't want to believe the fire-lizard. He didn't want to think that everything had gone wrong in some sort of arcane accident. Apolline just *happened* to reward her followers that night. Caught in a cosmic jest, half a dozen wolves were hospitalized. Connor was toppled as alpha. David was fired from the court.

David had been terminated because of charges brought by the Empire Bureau of Investigation. "Who called the EBI?" he asked.

Brule spread his hands in a gesture of innocence. "I cannot say. Perhaps that was a random patrol."

"Not if they had a griffin on hand to open that door. A griffin and enough agents to subdue two dozen wolves."

Brule's eyes narrowed. "*Peut être.* But there was something else that night. Some water creature. Perhaps *it* drew the Bureau's attention."

David's protest was wordless. So far, no one had asked him about Bourne. He hadn't needed to lie.

Brule went on as if he'd stayed silent. "Don't forget—my people suffered too."

"Not a single salamander was arrested!"

"We lost our only meeting place in the district."

"Except for Apolline's mansion," David said. He fired his words with bitterness, remembering the heat of the salamander queen's firepit against his eyelids.

Brule merely said, "Our meeting place is gone." When David stayed silent, the fire-lizard clicked his tongue once, a gesture of patent dismissal. "I did not come here to argue over which of us has suffered more."

"Why *did* you come here? How the hell did you even know where I was?"

"I tracked you through your Torch," the salamander said simply. "Your insignia is attuned to you. It gives off a...spark."

Reminded of his loss, Davis was suddenly exhausted. He was tired of standing on guard, constantly poised to pull Rosefire from the ether. "What do you want, Brule?"

"I want you to know I'm still your ally. I want you to trust me if we ever meet again. I want to exchange the Collar for the karstag so my people can go back to their own quiet lives."

Quiet lives. Right. Quiet like a forest fire.

But David said, "I suspect the karstag's off the table now. Connor meant to give it back at the new moon, but he's not the Washington alpha anymore."

Brule's left eyebrow twitched in irritation. "Whoever leads the pack won't be a fool. An even exchange, Collar for karstag. That should end this mess."

"Why should any wolf believe you?"

"They won't believe me. They'll believe you."

"And why should *I* believe you?"

"Because I'm giving you this." Before David could react, the salamander reached into his pocket. As Rosefire flickered on the edge of the ether, Brule withdrew his hand, unfolding his fingers to offer up his bare palm.

No. Not bare. Centered on his hand, glimmering blue under the fluorescent lights, was a graceful twist of silver. Hecate's Torch.

Brule placed the Torch on the reading table, then backed off several paces. "Go ahead," he said. "Take it."

The metal emblem called to David. He could taste it at the back of his throat—the rich splash of brandy he'd savored for the first time when the Academy granted him the symbol of his graduation. He wanted it. He longed for it. But he had to ask, "Why are you giving it back?"

Brule shrugged. "Call it a gesture of good will."

The Torch spoke of honor and power, of possibility and potential. It reminded him of all the hope he'd had when he graduated from the Academy. He'd worked warder's magic with his fingers closed around its silver whorls. The Torch had calmed him, centered him, made him the best warder he could be.

He needed it like air.

He spoke through set teeth: "What do you want in exchange?"

"I already told you," Brule said. "Your trust."

David could give that, for now. Until he learned more, until he understood the long game the salamanders played.

The instant his fingers curled around his Torch, he felt whole again, balanced. He swayed like a drunken man, swallowing the rush of brandy down his throat.

"Thank you," he said, his voice gone husky.

For answer, the salamander bowed from the waist. "Until we meet again," he said.

"Until—"

But Brule flickered out the door before David could finish his reply. Even with his Torch as anchor, he couldn't hear the salamander's feet on the stairs outside the Old Library. Apolline's wily ambassador could be going anywhere, doing anything.

But in that moment, steadied by the ballast of his Torch, David couldn't bring himself to care.

35

F or one full day, David merely reveled in the return of his
Torch. He used it as a focal point to extend his consciousness, testing the perimeter of the farm. He plumbed the depths of
the lake, confirming all the work Bourne had done and verifying
that the sprite was no longer on—or even near—the premises.
He shored up all his protective spells on the old logging road at
the south end of the property, and he reinforced the charms on
the gate that faced the main road.

He worked his fighting forms. He practiced warder's magic,
driving into town and fashioning impossible parking spaces for
the Lexus on crowded Main Street. He practiced *reaching* to new
destinations, places he only knew through the descriptions of
other warders. He drilled himself on nurturing magic, the
calming and strengthening spells he could offer a witch. He practiced clearing his mind, becoming a blank slate dedicated to the
service of Hecate.

By Friday afternoon, he was going stir-crazy. He set off to find
Connor, determined to help the shifter make things right with his
pack. He drove to the Den and parked his car on the concrete pad
outside the rough cabin that was the only structure on the prop-

erty. Torch in hand, he explored the landscape, extending his senses in hopes of crossing the former alpha's trail. Three separate times, he sensed that Connor had been nearby, recently enough that a nightingale sang loud inside David's skull. But the wolf knew the land far better than he did. If Connor didn't want to be found, he wouldn't be found.

Defeated, David returned home.

Saturday morning, David woke to a knock at the farmhouse door. A uniformed courier handed over an envelope, requiring him to sign a receipt. He took the package into the kitchen and opened it as his coffee brewed, finding a stack of legal documents. *Empire vs. Warder David Montrose* read the caption, along with an official case number and the name of Judge Robert DuBois.

It was time to find a lawyer. He pulled out his phone and started placing calls. Half the imperials he spoke to got spooked when they learned salamanders were involved. Three more already represented wolves. Both an ifrit and a gargoyle told him the best they could do was argue for him to serve his sentences concurrently.

Finally, he reached Keiko Matsuhara, a fox spirit who agreed to review his arguments. He scanned the court's official documentation and emailed it to the kitsune, trying not to feel defeated before he even heard her legal opinion.

He spent Saturday afternoon doing mundane chores around the house, organizing files in his office, cleaning out the garage, and discarding stale food from the pantry. He understood exactly what he was doing—trying to control his home because he couldn't control anything else in his life.

Near dusk, he took Spot for a run, stretching an easy three miles into five. As he ran, he thought.

Three weeks remained before Samhain. Hecate would never care that he'd helped a sprite, that he'd stood by his imperial shifter friends against the salamander threat, even that he'd protected the borders of his farm against evil. The goddess would judge him on how well he'd served her witches.

On how he'd helped Jane Madison.

Even now, his warder's senses were attuned to her magic, to the scent of jasmine swirling around a green bar of light. Jane was thinking about magic. She was leaning on her familiar for strength.

Night fell, and he considered stretching out his run, adding a loop that would tack on a couple more. Spot was flagging, though, favoring his front right paw. David fed the dog before he stumbled into his shower.

There was no time like the present to act on his new resolve. He chose clothes he thought Jane would like, jeans and a plaid shirt she'd find non-threatening.

He made himself a decent dinner—grilled pork chops and a baked potato with an entire forest of broccoli. Linda would be thrilled he was eating right, for once. He told himself he was building strength for a warder's duties.

Soon, midnight approached.

Jane was still awake.

Determined to acquit himself well before his goddess, David folded his fingers around his Torch and *reached* for the Peabridge cottage. Taking a deep breath, he knocked on the door, only to be met by silence.

Jane was definitely inside. The blanket of jasmine settled over his thoughts told him she was in the basement, surrounded by the Osgood collection with Neko beside her. She hunched over a tray of crystals, all of her concentration devoted to the stones' magical vibrations.

Without a conscious effort on his part, the front door's lock shifted beneath his hand. *Warder's prerogative.*

The living room was just as he remembered it—a pair of hunter green couches around a carefully braided rug. Sure enough, Jane's voice floated up from the basement, too soft for him to make out words, but he could tell she was asking a question. Neko answered quickly, his voice warm and reassuring.

David wasn't ready to see her yet, and he didn't want to interrupt the rapport she'd built with her familiar. Instead, he headed to the kitchen and made himself a cup of chamomile tea. Only then, steaming mug in hand, did he make his way down to the basement.

Jane sat before the largest array of crystals he'd ever seen in a private collection. She'd cut her hair since he'd seen her last. She'd invested in some decent makeup too; he could still see traces of mascara on her lashes despite the late hour.

Shaking his head, he reminded himself that he shouldn't be paying attention to how Jane *looked*. He was interested in her magical ability.

Neko, with his feline hearing, had probably known David was in the house from the instant he worked the lock. He considered it a good sign that the familiar hadn't alerted his mistress. Neko trusted him.

Jane, meanwhile, was awed by the crystals. "What *are* these things?" she whispered.

He had to make her aware of his presence. If he waited any longer, she'd be outraged by his presumption. "Neko," he said, purposely keeping his tone light. "Aren't you obliged to warn her before she touches the Spinster Stone?"

Jane jerked her hand back from the harmless sphere of rose quartz. He saw the instant she recognized his voice. Her shoulders relaxed, and she turned to him with a tart grimace. "Don't you knock anymore?"

"I did. You must not have heard, because you were down in the basement. I let myself in and helped myself to some tea." He saluted her with his mug of chamomile as she glanced up the stairs. He could practically hear her wondering if she'd locked the door before she went to bed. "You did," he said. "You locked it." And then, because it felt like the right time to share the truth, he added, "It's standard practice, though, for a warder to be able to open his own witch's locks. It can come in handy if she's ever in real danger."

She frowned. "I guess witches don't feel the need for privacy."

David shrugged. "Not from their warders, anyway."

He wasn't her warder yet, not in any formal way. But her magic called to his. He knew how to protect her. He knew how to guide her on her path to witchcraft.

As she caught her lip between her teeth, he spoke quickly, determined not to let the conversation grow awkward. "So you want to learn about crystals?"

"I told Neko. I want something to help my grandmother. She collapsed yesterday, when we were out at the museum. The doctors say she has double pneumonia, and she probably cracked a rib, coughing so hard. They held her overnight because she was so dehydrated. They put her on IVs."

He pictured Sarah Smythe, the woman who could eat him under the table at breakfast, who had stood fast on her refusal to worry Jane about witchcraft. But Jane was worried now. She needed reassurance and grounding if she was going to use her powers for anything constructive.

He said, "You've shown some affinity for spells. But working with crystals is completely different. Most witches can't handle both areas. At least not well."

"I think I might manage." She eyed the box of magical stones. "I think my mother has an affinity for crystals."

His mind flashed on Clara serving up tea as he scouted out information. He'd glimpsed the tensions wired through this family of witches. It couldn't have been easy for Jane to call Clara her mother just now.

Respecting her effort, he came to sit beside her. "Let's see what you can do, then." He reached into the box and shifted the layers to get to the bottom. His fingers ranged over the divided compartments, alighting first on one stone, then on another.

"Wait," Jane said. "What were you talking about, a Spinster Stone?"

"I was joking."

She looked skeptical, and he regretted teasing her. Time to make up for that. He plucked a rod of clear quartz from the bottom of the box and settled it in her palm, saying, "Tell me what you feel."

She studied the crystal carefully, holding it up to the light and viewing it from all angles. Frustration grew on her face. "What?" he asked.

"Nothing!" she said, clutching it tightly, "It's a rock."

Neko shifted closer to her, focusing all of his attention on the quartz. Taking a deep breath, Jane opened her fingers. "It's clear," she finally said, her tone flat with reluctance. "It's heavy for its size."

"Very good." She *was* trying. It was difficult to shift perspective from the mundane to the magical. "How does it feel?"

She took a deep breath and closed her eyes. After a long pause, she said, "It doesn't have a feeling. It doesn't have an emotion of its own." He saw the instant she recognized the truth of her words, the exact moment she became aware of the crystal's arcane force. "Instead," she said, "It's like a magnifying glass. It makes other things more intense." She became more confident, her words flowing faster. "Yes! That's it! It enhances other feelings. It makes me more sure of myself right now!"

"Precisely." He smiled as her eyes popped open. "That's clear quartz in your hand. An excellent specimen of it, too. It's an amplifier, a strengthener of your existing thoughts. Try this one."

He dug around in the box again, extracting a smooth disk of rhodosite. He traded stones with her, then watched her fold her fingers and close her eyes. As soon as she extended her senses, her face softened. A gentle smile curled her lips. "Love?" she asked.

"Yes," he said, keeping his voice low so he didn't break her trance. "It's called rhodosite. It eases stress. Heartache."

Her eyes snapped open. So, she wasn't ready to talk about matters of the heart.

He retreated to the box of crystals. If she wanted to heal her grandmother, then aventurine was the trick. He settled the stone in her hand.

The first night he'd met her, he never could have read her emotions. Now, he could see the aventurine's energy move through her body. The vibrations warmed her arm, her chest, her heart and lungs.

Neko leaned in, and David watched her draw from her familiar's power. She did it naturally, gracefully, without any jerk as she made the connection. Like a witch with decades of experience, she used Neko's energy, positioning it to reflect her own as she deepened her bond to the green crystal.

He saw the instant she realized how the stone could help her grandmother. She channeled energy from her own body into the stone, transferring her unbridled love for the woman who had raised her. Offering up her power as easily as any witch he'd ever seen, she dove deeper. Her touch was easy, so light that that he nearly overlooked the sheer volume of energy she was siphoning into the crystal.

"That's enough," he murmured when he realized how much power she'd transferred.

Her magic snagged on his voice. She used his words to pull herself back to consciousness, and the tug between them felt practiced, secure. She opened her eyes and stared at the crystal on her palm. "What is it called?"

"Aventurine. It's a quartz as well. But one that focuses healing." He reached into the wooden box and pulled out a velvet drawstring sack. "Here."

She stared at him as if she'd never seen a bag before, and he realized he'd let her go too deep, pouring too much of herself into the aventurine cure. Neko finally took her hand and tilted it gently, making the stone roll into the bag.

He nodded as the familiar tightened the silk ribbons and tucked the sack into his pocket. David said, "You can give it to your grandmother after you sleep."

"No." She clearly meant to protest, but her voice was a broken whisper. "She's sick. She needs it tonight. I'm family. They'll let me in."

"It's practically morning anyway, and she has mainstream medicine for now. You said they put her on IVs; those will help her even more than this crystal can. When you give it to her, it can start the long work of rebuilding and strengthening against future illness."

She shook her head and tried to climb to her feet, but it took three tries before she was standing. At least she laughed at her lack of coordination. "Neko!" she cried, like a queen suddenly mad with power. "Mix some drinks! The magic wand is in the drawer!"

The familiar looked disconcerted, but David only pursed his lips before he said, "Come on, Jane. It's time for you to get some sleep. Let's get you ready for bed."

She stumbled into the sofa, barely catching herself before she hit the floor. Shooting out a hip in a mockery of seduction, she said, "Is that an invitation, big boy?"

He'd committed a rookie teacher's mistake, letting her go too far with her first crystal working. It certainly didn't help matters that her damned familiar was snickering under his breath. David shook his head and said, "Just doing my job."

At least Neko helped walk Jane to her bedroom. The familiar watched a little too avidly, though, as she produced a key from her pocket. David unlocked the door, and all three of them stumbled over the threshold.

"No!" Jane suddenly exclaimed, flailing around to push a hand against Neko's chest. "You can't come in here!"

David followed her line of sight to the aquarium that crouched against the wall. He was pleased she'd taken his admonition seriously, keeping the neon tetra safe. As if to prove his point, Neko licked his lips, sharp eyes following the fish behind a frond of fern.

David nodded toward Jane and said firmly, "I've got her from here."

The familiar's disappointment was comical, but David didn't have time to laugh. Jane's body was sagging; she was close to passing out. He jutted his chin to get the familiar out of the room before he half-carried Jane to her bed.

She moaned a little as he peeled off the bunny slippers she'd tried to hide on his first night in her cottage. Certain she'd be mortified in the morning, he schooled his face to stillness.

He'd trained for this, learned to care for an exhausted witch. He concentrated on the mechanics of loosening the knot on her bathrobe belt. He helped her into a sitting position and slipped the garment from her shoulders. With professional hands, he twitched her pajamas into place and eased her onto her pillow, settling the top sheet and comforter into place.

There was nothing seductive about his gestures, nothing untoward. He was protecting her. Caring for her. He might never have kissed her outside the gate of the Peabridge gardens.

"Go to sleep," he said, passing his hand over her forehead. As his fingers tangled in unseen jasmine vines, he *pushed* with a little of his warder's strength, urging her to follow his command.

She relaxed against her pillow, but she still found the energy to ask, "David?"

"Hmm?"

"What just happened out there?"

"You used new powers. I let you go deeper than you should have. I felt the strength of your love for your grandmother, and that swayed my judgment. Get some sleep. You'll be fine when you wake up."

Her face smoothed, but she asked again, "David?"

"Hmm?"

"You're different now."

"Different?"

"Than the first night. You scared me then."

He'd never wanted to scare a witch. He groped for an answer. "That first night, I didn't know who you were. I came here as a warder, trying to protect resources that were in danger."

"And then?"

How could he explain everything that had happened? He'd lost his best friend, his job, everything he thought mattered. She didn't need to know that. Not now. Maybe not ever. Still, he found an honest answer. "I met you. I did some research. I became the warder you wanted me to be—you *needed* me to be. So you would listen. And learn."

Her forehead wrinkled in the tiniest of frowns. He passed his hand over her brow one more time, pouring in more of his warder's compulsion. "Sleep, Jane. We'll talk more later. Sleep."

And she did.

36

"Well, what am I *supposed* to think, David?" Linda sighed in frustration as she passed him a cup of coffee. "You call me to bail you out at the Night Court and then you disappear for a week. Didn't you think I'd be worried? That I'd want to know how you're doing?"

Out of habit, he glanced toward the stairs. The last thing he wanted was for George to walk into the kitchen.

"Oh, you're safe," Linda said. "He's getting in one last round of golf before the weather turns."

David gave her a grateful grin. "I'm sorry I was out of touch," he said. "I thought you'd be fed up with my screwing up everything I touch."

"Oh, David..." She took her time arranging snickerdoodles on a plate. "You don't screw up everything. You've made a few spectacularly bad decisions. But you've had more than your share of decisions made for you."

David grimaced as he tilted his head toward his absent father's study. "Does he know Pitt fired me?"

"Of course."

"And what did he say?"

"Nothing. He didn't say anything." She studied the cookies as if they were the most fascinating thing in the world. "Come to dinner tonight," she urged. "Please. For me. James and Tommy will be here."

For just a moment, he almost gave in. But then he shook his head and said, "I can't."

"Can't? Or won't?"

"Can't, this time. Really."

She gave him a wary look. "What's going on now?"

He took a deep breath. This was the real reason he'd come to Linda. He needed her advice more than ever before. "I think I've found a Samhain offer worthy of Hecate."

"What?" she breathed.

"I've found a witch who needs me."

There. He'd finally succeeded in shocking Linda Hudson. She finally asked, "Who?"

"You don't know her."

"I know every crone who's ever joined the Washington Coven."

"She's not a crone. And she's not in the coven."

Linda gaped. "You're talking about Jane Madison."

"You know about her?"

"The entire coven is talking about her."

"How the hell—"

"Norville Pitt," Linda interrupted. "He told Teresa Alison Sidney that the Osgood collection was found. He never mentioned you, though."

"He wouldn't," David said dryly.

"Teresa Alison Sidney is just waiting for the new year before she summons the upstart."

"Jane's not ready for that."

Linda's eyebrows arched. "All witches belong in a coven. You know that."

"Not this one." He waited a moment, to emphasize his next words. "She's stronger than Teresa Alison Sidney."

"Impossible."

David was adamant. "I've felt her work. And now I'm teaching her how to use her powers."

"You're a warder, not a teacher!"

"I can't exactly drop her into the nearest magicarium! This is all new to her—her powers, her familiar, the Osgood collection. Right now I'm the only one she trusts. And if that means I learn how to teach a witch, I'll do it."

Linda's voice grew heated. "Did you decide to become a magister before or after you started playing cops and robbers with your werewolf friend?"

"Shifter," he corrected. "You know that. And you know I couldn't abandon Connor." He folded his fingers into a loose fist, hiding the scar across his palm.

"You're facing six counts in the Eastern Empire Night Court! You're loyal to a fault."

"Impossible." He said the word exactly the way she had, placing equal emphasis on each of the syllables.

She stared at him as if he spoke a foreign language. He met her gaze without flinching.

He wasn't a child any longer. He wasn't trying to hide a broken window after a baseball went astray. He wasn't hoping to lie his way out of mowing the lawn.

He was a man now. A warder. And he needed Linda's help because she was the best witch he'd ever known. Not the strongest. Not the most politically connected. But simply the best follower of Hecate he could imagine.

He knew he had her when she pushed the plate of cookies across the table. "You're going to present yourself to Hecate on Samhain, offering your warder's bond with an unknown witch, without benefit of coven or magicarium?"

"If you say you'll help me." He got the words out. But then he could only hold his breath, waiting.

Finally, she sighed. "What do you need me to do?"

"Tell me what it feels like to work with crystals," he said. "I know the basics—which stones are good for what, how to store your power in a matrix, how to magnify it in the crystal. But what stones are best to learn with? What order should she use? And how can I keep her from exhausting herself every time she works on something new?"

Linda laughed. "You don't ask for much, do you?" She got up to grab the carafe of coffee. "It looks like we're both going to need another cup."

37

Now that David had spoken to Linda, everything fell into place.

He came to Jane's home every evening, giving her just enough time after work to change out of the ridiculous colonial costume her library employer required. As he prepared dinner to give her the ballast she needed for serious magic work, Jane gushed about her day. In short order, he'd become intimately familiar with the Peabridge's collection of early colonial almanacs, Jason Templeton, the library's surveys of farm boundaries, Jason Templeton, the circulation desk's policies about lending the reference collection, Jason Templeton, and Jason, Jason, Jason.

David supposed it was a positive sign that Jane trusted him enough to share her infatuation with the professor. But he barely managed to bite his tongue when she launched into yet another explanation of the research she'd completed for the guy. Professor Templeton seemed to have perfected the art of conning gullible librarians into doing his work.

Not that David would say that to Jane. He was pushing boundaries enough, teaching her about witchcraft. As her warder

—could he really call himself that?—he had no say in her private life. Absolutely none.

That's what he reminded himself as he caught flashes of laughter in her hazel eyes. He shouldn't even notice that she'd set aside her eyeglasses, that she was wearing contacts now. He shouldn't think about the way her cheekbones angled as she bowed her head to concentrate on crystals.

He should only have worried about her studies. Jane took easily to natrolite, with its powers of psychic protection. Her powers melded seamlessly around bloodstone's purification, its grounding of negative energy. And if she had to work a little harder with chalcedony, that was no great surprise. The stone stimulated maternal instinct. By her own admission, she hadn't had a strong role model in that arena—at least not from her *actual* mother.

They took a break on Saturday. Jane said she had to attend the Harvest Gala, some sort of fundraiser for an opera organization her grandmother supported. She returned to her studies more than a little distracted.

Once or twice each session, she completely lost her concentration. She forgot which emotion she was supposed to channel through which stones. She fumbled connections she'd previously made. But with a nudge from Neko, she always got back on track.

Until Wednesday.

She'd been in her hoop skirts when he arrived that night, and she took so long to change that he almost sent Neko in to help. The entire time she ate her dinner—cheese, crackers, and an apple, because she didn't have anything else in the house—she cast a longing eye toward the fish-decorated pitcher on her counter.

"That's for mojitos!" Neko helpfully pointed out, when he caught David following her gaze.

"Not tonight, it isn't," he answered, keeping his voice even.

He wanted to stretch their session that night and introduce

her to half a dozen new crystals. He was already feeling anxious that they'd miss their weekend training. Jane was heading up to Connecticut for some family reunion.

Family. The descendants of Abigail Somerset.

He wanted to go with her. He wanted to see the farm that had been in her family for generations. All those witches had avoided formal education, membership in a coven, and traditional trappings of any kind, but there had to be remnants of power throughout the property.

David hadn't been invited, though. Jane was taking that damned professor instead. What did Neko call him? Her Imaginary Boyfriend. Well, given Jane's level of distraction, she was clearly planning on moving the exploitative jerk from the "Imaginary" category to "Real."

David didn't care who Jane took to bed. Really. He didn't. He just wanted her to focus on their last night of training before her road trip.

But trouble began as soon as he set a chunk of pink fluorite in the center of the coffee table. The stone was known to provide a strong focal point for arcane meditation. As soon as Jane grew accustomed to the crystal's feel, he'd add a candle and ask her to work the simple kindling spell she'd already mastered. She'd be astonished by the brilliant light she created.

Her first attempt ended when she got a cramp in her foot. She stood up to walk it off, laughing nervously before settling back on the hunter green couch.

Her second attempt was derailed when her phone buzzed with a message. "Sorry," she said. "I thought I'd turned that off." But she stared at the device longingly, and it took her even longer to return to the coffee table.

She'd barely started her third attempt when she jumped up from the overstuffed cushions. "It's cold in here," she said. "Are you cold? Neko? Don't you want me to turn up the heat?"

"Jane, you're just not concentrating."

"I'm trying!"

"No, you're not." He shifted the fluorite closer to her.

She glared at the stone. "Maybe my strength isn't really with crystals."

"Your mother's seems to be," he said in a perfectly reasonable tone.

Neko had the good sense to cringe. Sure enough, Jane's words dripped with acid. "And if *Clara* had bothered to train me, then maybe all this witchcraft stuff wouldn't be so hard to pick up now. Maybe I'd be ready for a teacher, if a decent one could be found around here."

Neko winced and sidled toward the kitchen. "Perhaps if I made you both a cup of tea..."

David snapped, "We don't need tea. What we need is a bit less self-pity and a lot more concentration."

"It seems to me that at least one of us needs a nap," Neko said archly. "Awfully cranky tonight, aren't we?" He retreated into the kitchen before either of them could ask who was supposed to be tired.

Jane leaned back, exhaling sharply before she closed her eyes. He could see the weariness in her face, in every line of her body. He wondered if he *was* pushing her too hard. He'd never trained a witch before. And he had to admit he had his own agenda: he wanted Jane confident enough in her powers by Samhain that Hecate *had* to recognize the worthiness of his service.

"Neko," Jane called into the kitchen, her voice creaking with fatigue. "A cup of tea *would* be wonderful."

As David heard the kettle hit the side of the sink, he felt guilty for pushing Jane so hard, but he tried to explain how their sessions were really to her own advantage. "I'm not supposed to be your teacher. I'm here to protect you. To keep you safe."

She didn't even open her eyes. "Fine, then. Don't teach me anymore."

That attitude was never going to impress Hecate. But he

fought his own fatigue and pressed her, nevertheless. "You don't understand."

"Explain it to me, then." She struggled to sit upright. "Tell me what I'm missing. Why is this so important? There are about a hundred other things I'd rather be doing, you know. I was supposed to be at yoga tonight with Melissa. And I should be packing for the weekend. I leave Friday morning."

Leaving with Jason Templeton. That's what her reluctance was really all about. He didn't bother to soften his disapproving tone. "I know."

"And what's that supposed to mean? Are you saying I shouldn't go to my family reunion?"

"I don't have anything against your family." He laid his answer out precisely, giving just the faintest emphasis to the last word.

Before Jane could challenge him on that pronouncement, Neko slunk in from the kitchen, carrying a tea tray laden with the largest cream pitcher David had ever seen. The familiar poured for all of them, giving himself a single dash of tea in a mug otherwise filled with cream. After taking a delicate sip of his concoction, Neko pursed his lips and asked, "Are we having fun yet?"

"I'll be having fun Friday afternoon," Jane said. "When I'm in Connecticut." She crossed her arms over her chest like a defiant teen.

David sighed in exasperation, returning his mug to the table. "You know, we don't have to do this, Jane. You can just hand over all the books downstairs. Let the Washington Coven take charge, and you won't have to worry about them any more. The crystals, too. The coven would be thrilled to have the entire collection."

Neko slammed his own mug down. "Stunning advice," he hissed.

David kept his gaze on Jane as he answered the familiar with mock patience. "It's not 'advice', Neko. It's merely a statement of fact. The coven hasn't interfered so far because I've convinced them a valid witch has possession of the materials downstairs."

Well, that was almost true. He'd told Linda as much, certain she'd carry the message back to Teresa Alison Sidney.

His shaving the truth made him defensive, and he leaked a little more aggression into his tone. "But they're definitely getting curious about the situation. They want to meet Jane, and I can't put them off forever."

"Dammit, David! I never asked you to!" She looked surprised by her own outburst. "All I want is to be left alone until after my family reunion. Is that so much? The books were missing for decades. Can't I take one more weekend, for myself?"

He knew he was pushing too hard because Samhain loomed less than a fortnight away. His entire future rode on convincing Hecate he was worthy. But Jane was a witch, and he was—at least until Samhain—a warder, so he sighed and said, "You can take one more weekend."

She gloated behind her mug of tea. As she swallowed, though, she cast a quick look at Neko, who was still glaring daggers across the table. With dawning concern, she asked, "David?"

"What?" He didn't bother to disguise his annoyance—with himself, with her, with the entire situation.

"If I did give back the books, what would happen to Neko?"

For the first time since Jane discovered the Osgood collection, David felt sorry for the familiar. He'd had no say when Hannah Osgood broke their bond and linked him to the objects in the basement. When David finally answered, his voice was soft. "He goes with the materials. He's part of the collection."

"He's not *my* familiar?"

He couldn't believe she didn't know that. Neko had made the situation clear to David the first time they spoke. But David had known enough to ask the right questions. Jane hadn't understood a thing about what happened that day.

David said, "He's yours as long as you have the collection. But if you reject the collection, he'll go with it to the next witch who has the power to transform him."

Jane looked at Neko, but the familiar wouldn't meet her eyes. After a long pause, she sighed. "Fine," she said. "I'll make a serious effort with my witchcraft after I get back from the Farm. But I really don't have any choice about this weekend. I promised Gran."

"And Jason," Neko added.

David couldn't read the familiar's tone—whether he was truly trying to be helpful, or if he was turning a little blade for spite. But he felt his own spine grow stiff with dislike.

"What?" Jane shouted at him. "What can you possibly have against Jason Templeton?"

David eyed her coolly. "Do you really want an answer to that question?

"Yes! I am sick and tired of your coming in here and posturing every time his name comes up. This isn't some kind of contest between the two of you. Jason Templeton has nothing to do with you, Scott!"

The fact that she called him by another man's name struck like a physical blow. He had no idea who *Scott* was, but from Jane's shattered expression the man had hurt her badly. She was clearly mortified by her mistake, or maybe by her entire tirade.

He wanted to say something. He wanted to tell her he wasn't like Scott, or Jason either, for that matter. He wanted to assure her he was only there to serve her, to be her bonded warder come Samhain and beyond, if only Hecate found him worthy. But the silence grew between them, metastasizing into something ugly and broken.

In the end, Neko spoke first. "Well now. Isn't this uncomfortable?"

"Shut up, Neko," Jane said. Her chagrined command gave David the opportunity to school his face to impassivity before she turned to him. "Seriously," she said. "Jason has nothing to do with you. He is completely separate from your world. From witchcraft. From warding."

"My job is to keep you safe," he said flatly.

"And how can Jason possibly be a threat? Do you think he's going to arrive at the Farm with a stake, or a silver bullet or, or, I don't know, whatever kills witches?"

"Of course not." He had to remove emotion from his reply, scrubbing away any hint of feeling lest she shut him out forever.

"Is he a threat to my powers? Do you think he'll suddenly decide to burn the books downstairs? Steal my crystals? Stab Neko?"

"I have no reason to think that he will." He sounded like a robot, even to himself.

"So maybe he'll sell the Osgood collection to the highest bidder on some sort of magic black market?"

"No."

She was trembling as she climbed to her feet and gestured toward the door. "Then I think we're through with this conversation."

He didn't want to be through. He wanted to tell her about Hecate, about Samhain, about all the ways he could and should and would serve her.

But that wasn't fair. Jane wasn't some wind-up toy he could take out of a box and march off the edge of a table. She was a free and independent witch—even if she was pining after her *Imaginary Boyfriend* or still longing for Scott, whoever the hell that was.

David didn't have a right to use her for his own Samhain scheme.

He put his mug on the table and brushed his hands down the front of his pants, as if he'd collected cookie crumbs by mistake. He looked at Neko, wondering if there was any way to make the familiar understand, to help redeem this absolute disaster. But the creature stared back without blinking, his eyes as cold and distant as a cat's.

"Very well," David said. "No more training."

She waited a beat before she made an attempt at clarification: "Until I get back from the Farm."

"No." He'd ruined everything, and this was the only honorable thing to do. "No more training from me at all."

He held out his hand, because that seemed polite. She stared at it, not offering her own.

"You're kidding, right?" she said. "You want me to think about what you've told me tonight. You want me to realize I need you, and then get back to witch school like a good little student. Right?"

He wanted all those things, more than he could say. But he didn't have the right to ask them of her.

She tried again. "So, you want me to apologize? Is that it? I'm sorry, and I want you to be my teacher again?"

He heard the emotion scrabbling in her voice. He was hurting her, even when he tried to do what was right. He had to stop. Now. "Not at all," he said. "I want you to be content in your life. I want you to know who you are and what you are. I want you to be balanced, so you can find all your natural power and strength. Jane, I want you to be happy."

"And your walking out of here tonight is going to make me happy?"

"In the short term," he said. His throat was so dry he couldn't swallow.

"And in the long term?"

"In the long term, the coven will take care of you. They'll place you in a magicarium. Maybe find you a proper tutor, someone used to teaching witches. You don't need to be afraid; they'll be fair. They won't test you until you say you're ready."

He had to make it seem reasonable. Sane. Normal. Because every word he said was the truth. It's what he should have told her from the moment they met—would have told her if he hadn't been focused on his own Samhain scheme. But she asked, "And if I can't learn from the coven's teacher? If I'm never ready?"

"They'll take back the books."

"And Neko?"

He nodded, not daring to look at the familiar. "And Neko."

Her throat worked. He had to get out of there, now, before he registered that he was voluntarily walking away from warding forever. From the safety of the doorway, he said, "Enjoy the Farm, Jane. But be careful. And apply yourself when you come back here. Work *with* your teacher."

He *reached* for home the instant he shut the door.

38

The ache was still there in the morning, clawing at his sleep-starved brain like a rat in a maze. He would never prove himself to Hecate by Samhain. In less than two weeks, he'd be cast out as a warder forever.

Breaking the magical bond was his fault—he'd pushed Jane too hard, too far. But Norville Pitt had stolen away the safety net that was available to every other warder in the Empire. Pitt had made it impossible for David to work at the court.

The toad must have decided to destroy David three years ago, that first week, after that first memo where David pointed out the accidental double billing for the Atlanta centerstone.

And the worst part was, Pitt could do it again. He could eviscerate any other warder who came under his control.

What would happen when Kyle Hopp washed out? Even if the kid actually graduated from the Academy, he wasn't likely to match with a witch, not for any meaningful period of time. He'd end up working for the court for the rest of his life. That should be an honorable course, a valid way to serve the goddess.

But Pitt would eat Kyle alive.

No warder should be subjected to that.

David owed it to Hecate herself to bring Pitt down.

He opened his computer and started his last warding mission ever: Destroying Norville Pitt.

39

As the sun rose over Parkersville's Main Street, David stood beside a public trashcan, balancing a computer thumb drive on the palm of his hand.

He'd spent the night creating dozens of false documents. The first one had been the most difficult. He'd called up a blank Request for Protection form, the template he'd kept on his home computer to complete long hours of overtime. He'd hesitated for almost an hour before typing Pitt's name into the appropriate blank. It had taken him another fifteen minutes to add a description of the artifact requiring protection—a magnificent specimen of chrysolite that Pitt kept locked in a display case in his office.

The yellow-green crystal was known to bolster fame and self-importance. It made Pitt an easy target. Having finally chosen his weapon, David lost no time recording the stone's identifying characteristics, its provenance, and its supposed last known location.

He only hesitated when he got to the last blank. This was it. His chance to bring Pitt down for good.

David was lying. He knew that. He wasn't being noble. He wasn't being heroic.

But Pitt had lied every single day he worked for the court. He'd hectored David, hobbling him and keeping him from offering true service to every witch in the Eastern Empire. If Pitt wasn't stopped now, he'd destroy the court and everything it stood for.

David tapped a single key, falsifying a date stamp.

The rest of the forms were easier. He planted false correspondence, showing Pitt's willingness to procure arcane treasures for a shadowy Russian counterpart. He created the illusion that Pitt had taken bribes to channel a contract for the construction of the Charlotte Coven's recent safehold.

He couldn't plant his documents inside the court's computer system. He'd been locked out of that the moment Pitt fired him. But he could send his manufactured evidence to every one of the judges on the court. It was easy enough to create a fake email account.

He'd completed his work on the thumb drive; there wasn't a hint of what he'd done on his home computer or anywhere in the cloud. Even if the files were ultimately denounced as fraudulent —and there was no way that could be determined—they couldn't be linked to David in any way.

Checking to make sure no one lurked in the shadows on Main Street, David twisted the thumb drive into pieces. The plastic shell went in the trashcan in front of Parkersville Fire Station Number One. The metal sheath was buried beneath a pile of pink spoons in the can in front of Ice Dreams. The flooded, scratched, and torqued memory chip went into the recycling bin at Town Hall.

Next, David drove down to Upper Marlboro, in Maryland's Prince George County. He'd never set foot in the town before, for business or for pleasure. No one could connect him with the place.

It took three tries to find what he was looking for, but he finally succeeded in the county courthouse. A pair of public telephones hung on the wall in a dimly lit corridor, long-neglected holdovers from the days when reporters filed breaking news from the county seat.

He dug change out of his pocket and dialed a number from memory. A wheezy treble answered on the first ring. "Help Desk!"

"How's your Snake form going, Kyle?"

"Mr.—"

David cut him off before he could say too much. "I need your help. When do you get off work today?"

"Five o'clock." The kid answered without hesitation.

"Can you meet me at the DC Courthouse? Say, five thirty?"

"I'll be there."

"Excellent. And Kyle? Make sure you aren't followed."

He hung up, before the cadet could make a mistake.

40

D avid sat on a bench in the plaza in front of the DC courthouse, as far from the street lamps as possible. His shoulders were hunched, and his hands dangled between his knees.

He knew he should feel guilty about what he'd done to Pitt. He'd acted dishonorably. He'd lied.

But every time he tried to muster regret, he thought about how Pitt had purposely destroyed David's life. About what the toad might do in the future. Pitt was a menace that had to be put down, even if that cost David what was left of his career.

Freed from a warder's honorable obligations, David was finally able to settle other scores. It was time to resolve things with the salamanders once and for all.

As twilight deepened, David watched the stream of people leaving the building. Litigants crowed about their cases. Court employees headed home at the end of their long workdays.

But a handful of people walked *into* the building. A few were mundanes, people with business before the DC night court. In addition, David quickly spotted a vampire—risking immolation with the sun barely below the horizon—and a pair of kitsune leaning close to compare notes as they climbed the steps, their fox tails barely disguised in a series of intricate braids.

It was 5:45 before Kyle appeared, his face flushed with worry. Aidan O'Rourke strode behind the cadet, his head freshly shaved.

"I'm sorry, sir," Kyle gasped. "I didn't realize he was following me until I got off the subway. I took the stairs instead of the elevator at the office so no one would see me leave. I don't know how he guessed—"

David cut him off. "You took the stairs instead of the elevator at the office." He turned to the old warder warily. "O'Rourke," he said.

"Montrose." The man gave away nothing with those two syllables.

"What are you doing here?"

"If *I* followed him, someone else could have." He paused, just long enough for David to nod in acknowledgment, and then he confirmed, "We're clean."

"You don't want any part of this," David warned.

"And that one does?" O'Rourke nodded toward Kyle, who was following their conversation as if it were a tennis match.

"He can always claim I forced him. No one would believe I forced you to do anything."

O'Rourke's face was carved into dark planes by the overhead lights. "You brought me food and drink. I pay my debts."

"If the court ever finds out you're helping me—"

"That's one advantage of being burned. No one gives a damn who I help." He glanced toward the courthouse entrance. "What are we waiting for?"

David wasn't going to get a better invitation than that. He led the way up the stairs.

They made it through security without any hassle. David turned down the long corridors, past the courtrooms, through the warren of offices that hummed with business during the day. The stairwell he chose was darker than he recalled. At the bottom, he set his palm against the iron lock, taking time to expand his warders' senses around the tumblers. A few twists and a solid click... The door squealed in protest as he pulled it open.

The light switch was where he remembered. The tables, too, with their disarray of books. David stepped back to let Kyle and O'Rourke survey the mess.

"Gosh!" Kyle gasped, sounding more like Jimmy Olsen than ever.

David pointed to the computer terminal in the corner. "That's why you're here."

The kid crossed the room as if drawn by a magnet. "I've only seen a monitor like this in movies! And a *tower*! This has to be at least fifteen years old. Maybe more!"

"Can you turn it on?"

Kyle didn't answer. Instead, he lowered his hand to a toggle switch, the same on/off button David had tried multiple times before. The kid's lips moved, and David realized he was offering up a prayer—to Hecate or maybe to some god who cared about computers. Kyle pressed the switch and nothing happened.

David's belly tightened. Kyle merely fell to his knees. For a moment, David thought he was upping the ante on his prayers. Then he realized the cadet was fiddling with a nest of wires behind the machine. He fastened several connections, sat back on his heels to study the results, then exchanged two links.

His hand was steady on the toggle when he tried again. The screen bloomed to life with a wavy image of a sword impaling a scroll of parchment.

"Yes!" Kyle shouted, pumping his fist in the air.

"Excellent," David said. "Now I'm looking for any reference to salamanders in the court records. I'm trying to locate the address of Apolline Fournier. I already know about her home on S Street. I'm hoping to find something different."

Kyle nodded his comprehension. Already typing on the ancient, gritty keyboard, he reached behind himself for a chair.

O'Rourke shook his head in disbelief at the kid's handiwork. "And he calls himself a warder."

"He calls himself a cadet," David corrected under his breath. He was just grateful for the student's computer obsession.

"At least there's something for a *real* warder to do down here." O'Rourke nodded toward the wall of weapons on the far side of the room. "Up for a round or two while Junior works his magic?"

David didn't want to spar with O'Rourke. Unlike the first time they'd fought, David now knew O'Rourke had been friends with his father. Failing in front of the shunned warder now would feel an awful lot like failing in front of George.

But Linda had said O'Rourke knew his mother too. And Karen Callahan Montrose had never dreamed her son could fail.

Adrenaline sparked through David's fingertips. He'd rather grapple with the old warder than watch Kyle type in countless queries. He'd just have to remember his mother's faith in him.

"Name your weapon," O'Rourke said.

David's gaze skipped over the gym equipment, ignoring the balance beam, the parallel bars, the stacks of iron plates for the Universal gym. He needed something to bleed off some of his nervous energy.

Hooks on the wall held a wide range of tools suitable for maiming and massacring. Foils, epées, and rapiers hung between a gallery of greatest hits from the Middle Ages—broadswords and maces and lances and staffs. A pair of katanas gleamed as they guarded a collection of murderous-looking daggers.

David had more than enough experience with long blades. He wasn't entirely sure he wanted to be on the receiving end of whatever O'Rourke could do with a staff. He crossed the room and tested the edge of a dirk. It was sharp—no blunting for the imperials who practiced there.

He lifted the blade from the hooks that captured its wrist-guard. It was properly balanced, well-made. He tossed a matching knife to O'Rourke.

The warder made his own test of the weapon, nodding as his thumb crossed the edge. He rotated his wrist, rolling the pommel across his lifeline. When he looked up at David, his face was split by a devilish grin.

"First man to three touches?"

David nodded his acceptance. He expected O'Rourke to lunge before David could adopt a defensive stance. The warder, however, took his time, tracing out a cautious circle. All the while he tested his blade, learning its weight, calculating proper angles.

David made the first attack. Closing the distance to his rival in three liquid strides, he swept the dirk from his side. The motion was easy. The blade was a fraction of Rosefire's weight, and he didn't have to account for the energy drain of ward-fire.

The dirk clanged on the floor, spinning across the wooden planks until it came to a stop against the boxing ring.

He didn't feel the ache in his wrist until the metallic echoes stopped. By then, O'Rourke had danced out of reach, following the dropped blade and fetching up against the ropes. The sole of the old warder's shoe had left a clear mark across David's forearm.

"Point one: Don't keep your grip loose, even if the weapon's light," the warder said.

David cast a chagrined look across the room, checking to see if Kyle had witnessed his disgrace. Fortunately, the cadet was typing furiously on the computer keyboard, fingers pounding hard enough that David worried the plastic might crack.

Looking back at O'Rourke, he saw that the warder had slipped between the boxing ropes. He stood in the middle of ring, bouncing lightly on the balls of his feet. He nodded toward David's blade.

David didn't have a choice. He inclined his chin to acknowledge the lost point. Then he retrieved his dirk and stepped inside the ring.

This time O'Rourke didn't hesitate. He lunged before David could even raise his knife. David felt the ropes behind his back yield to his weight as he arched away from O'Rourke's swift thrust.

His feet slipped from beneath him, and he sat down hard, his fingers tight on his dagger's grip. He wasn't going to make the same mistake twice.

But he managed to make a different one. He tried to swing the blade wide, to set up a defensive perimeter of steel that O'Rourke could never penetrate. The warder merely waited until he'd completed one broad arc, and then he planted his own dirk at the junction of David's arm and shoulder.

"Point two: Small spaces call for small moves," O'Rourke said.

David muttered a curse under his breath, but he lowered his head, accepting O'Rourke's second point.

The warder closed again before David could brace himself. Taking his last lesson to heart, David collapsed into the corner, letting the ropes protect him on either side. He stabbed up with his knife, ignoring everything he'd ever learned with Rosefire, any technique designed to take advantage of a sword's superior reach and weight.

O'Rourke staggered back, forced to take a defensive stance for the first time. David immediately pressed his advantage, powering across the ring. He chopped with his blade—short, aggressive motions that kept the warder from finding his balance. He gripped his weapon tightly, determined to foil any wayward kick, any explosive thrust of the other man's blade. Foot by foot, he forced O'Rourke back until the warder was pressed against the ropes, leaning away, bent nearly double.

David raised his arm, ready to stab the other man's neck. Before he could close the gap, though, O'Rourke's left fist shot out, catching David squarely on the solar plexus. Gasping on hands and knees, David felt the icy point of O'Rourke's dirk against his nape.

"Point three: Don't rely too much on any blade."

"Where the hell did you learn to fight?" David wheezed.

"Not in any Academy gym," O'Rourke said, reaching down to help David to his feet. "That's the problem with Hecate's Court, with all the training they think we need. It's all well and good when we're waiting on witches. But the real world doesn't give a damn for all our rites and rituals. Half the warders in the empire have never used their weapons for more than setting a circle and calling the Guardians. All those flaming swords lead to an overdeveloped sense of security."

David finally managed to straighten. "I think I'm glad I didn't choose a mace."

O'Rourke grinned. "A staff is the real danger. It's the backswing—"

"Mr. Montrose!" Kyle shouted. "I think I've got it!"

David let O'Rourke take both weapons before he limped across the room. The image on Kyle's computer screen rippled, but David couldn't tell if that was a problem with the monitor or his own inability to draw a full breath.

"These records are really a mess, Mr. Montrose," Kyle said, his voice full of apology. "Some are saved on the C drive, and some are on the I drive, and I even found a few in the sysop files. Whoever made them didn't care a lot about spelling either. But I think this is what you're looking for."

David squinted and forced his mind to parse the words on the wriggling screen: "Defendant styles herself the Salamander Queen. Defendant has residences in and about Washington DC, including 1931 S Street NW, Washington DC 20009. She also maintains a lair in Rock Creek Park, on the Pinehurst Branch north of the Rolling Meadow Bridge. Therefore, this court holds personal jurisdiction over Defendant for this case and all other matters arising in Washington DC."

Rock Creek Park. The heavily wooded enclave cut through the heart of DC. A parkway carved out passage for cars, and scores of expensive homes backed onto the woodland. Nevertheless, the park held hundreds of acres of undeveloped space, with the titular creek itself winding for miles through undisturbed forest.

It was dark.

Dank.

Secluded.

It was the perfect habitat for a murderous, thieving salamander. He'd found Apolline Fournier.

S taring out at the Den, David waved a hand over a standing rib-roast, driving off another fly. At least it was October, not the height of summer heat. And the moon was high, five days past full, which seemed to deter at least some insects from swarming.

Not that wolves were picky about what landed on their dinner.

David had bought the largest hunk of beef he could find at Safeway. His aching wrist had protested carrying the thing from his car, but *reaching* from the parking pad to the rustic cabin had seemed like an admission of weakness. His chest still ached from O'Rourke's sucker punch. He was tired of sitting, but his back had registered a protest after he'd paced the porch for an hour or two.

At least he'd had time to think about the past couple of days.

Everything had been a blur since his fight with Jane. No. Not "fight." "Fight" required people to say what they were thinking. He'd let Jane think he was angry about Templeton, as if that pretentious twit was worth arguing over. He had no doubt Templeton would break her heart, probably the same way *Scott* had—whoever the hell Scott was. He still didn't know.

No. His break with Jane was because of Hecate, because he'd thought he could impress the goddess by training the newfound witch. He'd been certain his connection to Jane was growing, solidifying, becoming something he could count on even when he wasn't giving it conscious thought.

But she obviously didn't feel the same thing, not if she was willing to ditch their training for a wild weekend with Templeton. He'd failed Jane. And now he'd never convince Hecate to accept his warder's vow.

That was his only explanation for what he'd done to Pitt: He'd wanted to hurt someone as badly as he'd been hurt. And if he could keep a ruthless, power-mad martinet from ruining another warder's life, then it was worth it.

After Samhain he was through being a warder forever. He had nothing left to lose.

And that made him a very dangerous man.

A shadow flickered on the edge of the clearing. He would have missed it if he hadn't been staring at the same array of light and shadow for the past four hours.

He caught his breath, reluctant to move even that much. Widening his eyes to keep from blinking, he concentrated on projecting an image of safety, calm, and peace.

The wolf ventured from the forest's skirts.

It was Connor.

He saw that in a glance. But the shifter's coat was muddy, as if he'd been forced to lie in shallow pools. His tail was pocked with burrs. Each individual rib was visible as he shuffled three steps closer. He whined as he snuffled toward the meat.

"Go on," David said. "You won't catch *me* eating any of it."

Connor's lips curled back over his teeth, and he sprinted to the porch. Pinning his prize with filthy paws, he ripped off huge gobbets of meat. swallowing them whole. In shockingly little time, he was crunching the bones, slurping marrow with abandon.

David had watched Connor catch prey before—mice in his parents' attic, a rabbit here at the Den. But he'd never seen him devour a meal. He'd never seen the power of a ravenous wolf allowed to feed at will.

Connor only jumped down from the porch when the bones were reduced to snow-white splinters. He rolled in the grass, rocking from side to side, his distended belly gleaming in the moonlight. He snarled as he rubbed his face against the ground, lost in some sort of lupine ecstasy.

Finally flipping onto all fours, he shook his entire body, flinging off bits of grass and fallen leaves. He arched his back, making his ruff stand on end. His legs stiffened, tendons standing out from muscle. He stretched his neck, down, then up, and he transformed into a man.

David waited until the transition was complete before he reached into the shadows by the cabin door. He tossed down a set of black sweats, certain Connor would hate the shapeless clothes. Oh well. Shifters couldn't be choosers.

"Would it hurt you to keep a chair on the porch?" he asked, after Connor had pulled his arms and legs through the garments.

"Keeps the riffraff out." Connor grunted as sat next to David. He kicked at the pile of bones, spreading them over the dark patch where the roast had rested for the evening. "Thanks for that."

"Looks like you needed it."

"I've been down here almost three weeks. Squirrels don't have a lot of meat on them, and I didn't want to risk taking down a deer. The way my luck's going, someone would ignore the *No Trespassing* signs, find the remains, and report a wolf on the loose." He ran a hand through his hair, grimacing when he came up with twigs. "What have I missed back home?"

"I checked with Empire Memorial before I drove down," David said. He paused, giving Connor a chance to brace for bad news. "Three of your men didn't make it. Noah, Steven, and Zeke."

Connor threw back his head and howled. The raw, raging sound was torn from a human throat, but it still raised the hair on the back of David's neck. He clenched his fists to keep from covering his ears.

Only after Connor's echoes had died away did David dare speak again. "Last time, we did it your way. This time, we're doing it mine. This is how we're going after Apolline."

42

David and Connor crouched on the bank of Rock Creek, peering into the gloom beneath the canopy of trees. They were deep in the park, far from any of the roads that crisscrossed the tract of land. Early morning sunlight sifted through the growth above them. Half the branches had already lost their leaves.

The creek took a bend in front of a massive pile of fallen logs. A casual observer would assume the obstruction was from a long-past winter storm, the trees fallen victim to wet snow and heavy winds.

But David made out more ominous signs. Strategically placed wedges kept the entire structure from slipping downstream. A mud-covered passage led from a haphazard doorway to the creek. From David's current vantage point, it looked as if the land dropped off steeply beneath the tree trunks, a slick ramp diving down to some sort of underground chamber.

Connor raised his head, sniffing at a breeze that drifted downstream. His lips curled back in a silent snarl. They'd found the salamanders' lair.

David's belly tightened in anticipation. O'Rourke had been

right in the Imperial Old Library. Warders didn't fight battles. They performed rituals with their witches.

Well, David wasn't a warder anymore. He'd seen to that, taking down Pitt. Whatever vestige of the Academy's blessing he'd retained after his fiasco with Haylee was well and truly gone.

He might as well go out in a blaze of glory.

He just hoped it wasn't a literal blaze. He'd had enough of Apolline's fires to last a lifetime. And who knew how many salamanders she had down there with her?

He and Connor had argued for the past twenty-four hours. The shifter wanted to scout out the enemy. He wanted to know exactly how many fire-lizards they were up against. He wanted to be certain Apolline had the Collar with her.

But David had argued none of that mattered. The element of surprise was their most valuable asset. They'd have to fight however many salamanders were there; it didn't matter if there were two or twenty. If Apolline didn't have the Collar, they'd make her tell where she'd hidden it.

They were a warder without a witch and a wolf without a pack. They didn't have the luxury of planning.

David took a deep breath. Held it for a count of five. By habit, he offered up the briefest of appeals to Hecate before raising his hand and counting down with silent fingers: Five, four, three, two—

A creature appeared in the mouth of the den, bobbing low before emerging on the riverbank.

No, not a creature. A man.

John Brule.

A swirl of wind circled upstream. Brule stiffened and looked down the riverbank, losing no time pinning first Connor, then David with his onyx eyes. He took a step away from the burrow.

"Monsieur Hold," he called softly, pitching his voice so it barely reached them. "Monsieur Montrose. Well met, at last." He extended his right hand, ready to shake.

David took his own hand from his pocket, where his Torch hummed, bright and strong. Brule had returned it to him. Brule was greeting them now, outside the safety of his den. Brule was still their ally.

But before David could shake, his mind exploded in a nightmare of jasmine and rage.

43

"Neko!" Jane cried before David could travel through the ether. She repeated her familiar's name even more urgently: "Neko!"

Hearing the blind rage that fed her command, he reached into his pocket with his left hand. He closed his fingers around his Torch, trying to gauge whether Jane was in physical danger.

As he narrowed his concentration, Brule closed the distance between them. The salamander's silver hair flared around his face, a sunlit halo that emphasized the whiteness of his teeth. His smiling lips curled in his meticulously trimmed beard, and he said, "I'm glad you came, *mon ami.*"

His fingers were cold as they closed around David's. Connor stepped to his side, and the salamander extended an equal greeting to the wolf.

Channeling through his Torch, David focused on the energies surging inside his brain. Neko materialized beside Jane, the familiar's emerald bar leaning into Jane's jasmine. She was still broadcasting wordless, mindless rage, but Neko's signature was more complex. He was amused and somewhat surprised. And underneath that sly joviality, there was a streak of something else: Disgust.

David gathered the strands of his warder's powers. He'd *reach* for Jane from this riverbank. She was more important than any dispute with the salamanders. Besides, Brule was the only fire-lizard who knew that he and Connor had arrived. He could go to Jane and guarantee her safety, then come back to this final confrontation for the Collar.

Before he could voice the first of his excuses to Connor and Brule, Jane seared his mind with a burst of power. He'd never felt any witch summon that amount of energy. The bolt she'd just released was hotter than the flames that had scorched his face in Apolline's mansion.

Another blast, this one brighter than the salamander queen's fire circle.

A third, and he was blinded, his senses overwhelmed by the sheer power of Jane's unfettered rage.

"*Neko?*" he sent, the instant he was able.

"*A little busy here,*" came the familiar's reply.

Connor was moving toward him, concern puckering his brow. Brule stood behind the shifter, his head cocked at an angle as if he fought to hear the conversation inside David's head.

Another blast from Jane. Another. Another.

Finally, her incandescent rage was burning off. He could sense thoughts beneath her emotions, hear the words she chanted to herself with every bolt of fire. *Jason.* And then, a sigh wreathed in despair: *I'm such an idiot.* Another blast of magic. *Jason.* A final bolt. *Such an absolute idiot.*

"*Neko,*" David sent again.

"*She's fine,*" the familiar answered. "*Or at least she will be.*"

"*I'm coming.*"

"*Don't.*"

"*She needs me.*"

"*Not now.*" The familiar's refusal was firm.

David hadn't realized he'd closed his eyes to enhance his concentration, narrowing his focus on the distant familiar. But when he heard a grunt followed by a loud splash, his eyes snapped open.

Brule and Connor grappled in the riverbed. The salamander's fingers were wrapped around Connor's neck; he was holding the shifter's head underwater.

Connor arched his back, heels scrabbling for a purchase against the creek's slippery floor. Hissing all the while, Brule shifted his weight, planting a knee in the other man's belly. Connor rolled to his right, obviously trying to smash the salamander against a rocky outcropping. He lost his purchase and tumbled back into the water.

This was all a trap—Brule's hail-fellow routine, his easy handshake. The salamander had baited them by returning David's Torch, reinforcing the promise of an alliance. He'd greeted them alone outside the lair, offering the guise of friendship.

But the instant David was distracted by Jane, Brule had pressed his attack. He now used his considerable weight to pin Connor beneath the surface of the swift-flowing stream.

David had to act. He could not let Connor die. Not here. Not today.

He pulled Rosefire from the ether, automatically igniting ward-fire. He didn't care who saw the burning sword. The Eastern Empire already had him on six counts of exposing magic. Who cared if they added a thousand more?

Besides, the salamanders had built their lair far from human paths. No mundane eyes would see Connor trapped beneath the surface of the stream. No human would cry out at Brule pinning the shifter, holding him down until he no longer had the strength to struggle.

David waded into the creek. The water was colder than he expected, slicing through his jeans like shards of glass. He ignored the pain, pushing himself past the shock before Connor drowned.

One step. Brule kicked the shifter hard, connecting a boot to Connor's temple.

Two. The salamander pressed on Connor's yielding chest, shoving the limp body deeper beneath the water.

Three. David called out Brule's name, shifting his weight to swing his sword.

The fire-lizard looked up, as if by reflex. He darted a hand toward his leather boot and came up with a narrow blade, a throwing knife. David barely saw sunlight glint on steel before he dropped to his knees, dodging the attack. Icy water surged against his chest, stealing his breath.

Brule exploded out of the stream bed, scrambling up the bank toward the pile of debris that marked the lair. David lost precious seconds banishing his sword so he had two free hands. He hefted Connor out of the water, dragging the shifter's dead weight toward the riverbank.

He propped Connor against the trailing roots of a willow tree. The shifter's face was deathly pale; his lips were blue inside his matted beard.

The water, was flowing fast enough to pull the shifter downstream. David closed his arms around his friend's chest and tugged him higher onto the bank. The effort forced a gout of water from Connor's lips. He groaned and turned to vomit up more of Rock Creek.

David clambered up the muddy bank, pulling Rosefire back from the ether. Brule had almost reached the salamanders' lair, would have slithered inside already if he weren't weighed down by sodden clothes and slippery boots.

"Brule!" David shouted, arresting the fire-lizard's progress.

The salamander whirled and threw something at his feet. A burst of light exploded and mud flew up.

But Brule had miscalculated. The earth was too wet for fire. A dozen tiny flames hissed and died before they could work any damage.

David poured energy into Rosefire, raising a full arm-span of ward-fire from the sword's edge. He lunged as he swung his blazing weapon, using both hands to keep the motion steady.

Steel-colored flames sizzled as they bit into the salamander's side.

Brule hissed, thrashing to escape. David pressed his advantage, sheathing Rosefire in the traitor's body.

Brule's eyes opened wide. His head jolted back. His fingers scrabbled at his gaping wound, as if he could cauterize it and keep his bright green blood from flowing.

David pulled Rosefire free and glanced back toward the willow. Connor had crawled up the bank. He crouched on all fours, shoulders heaving as he coughed up half the creek. His feet were still perilously close to the water. He'd freeze if he slipped back into the stream. But at least he was breathing.

As David turned back to Brule, the salamander pulled himself toward the entrance to the lair. Emerald flames dripped from his side, great gouts of imperial blood sizzling on damp leaf litter. Brule fell to his knees two steps shy of the threshold. Stretching out his hands, he dragged himself up the muddy slope, shuddering with effort as he tipped over the edge into darkness.

David shimmied up the bank, determined to see this battle through to the end. He could just make out Brule's feet in the gloom beyond the doorstep. Gripping Rosefire tightly, he drew his ward-fire back to a mere flicker and plunged into the lair.

Brule was sprawled before him, mouth stretched in a rictus of agony, obsidian eyes rolled back in his head. Verdant fire licked at his side, but David could already see the flames were fading.

The salamander was dead.

Before David could turn back to help Connor in the creek bed, he caught the glint of eyes in the darkness. Automatically, he swept Rosefire in a massive arc. Ward-fire illuminated bodies, at least two dozen, salamanders all.

And every last one was writhing toward him, fire pouring from savage claws.

44

David poured his energy into ward-fire.

Flames leaped from Rosefire's edges, a dancing steel-grey curtain. David gripped the sword with both hands, planting his feet and raising the blade above his head. He pledged his strength to Hecate, swore that he would honor her, serve her till the day he died, regardless of the court's approval, separate and apart from any service he gave to any witch. He offered himself to the goddess forever, if only she would save him now.

Burning steel teeth tore into the rotten tree trunks above him.

The flames started as ward-fire, blossoming with grey in their hearts. As they spread, they sparked little tongues of green. The sword was kindling the salamanders' ichor, slime they'd left upon the lair they'd used for years.

As David poured more energy into his sword, its flames surged higher, burning off the surface coating of green on the ceiling. Only the steel-colored flames survived, drowning out every vestige of grass-green. Silvery smoke roiled against the roof, billowing back toward the advancing salamanders.

David drove deeper into the cave.

A dozen steps in, a salamander surged through the wall of smoke. David braced for impact. Before the fire-lizard could reach him, a massive branch fell from the ceiling. The wood was completely alight, steel-grey fire consuming what had once been a mammoth oaken trunk.

David despaired. Salamanders reveled in fire. They'd danced in ecstasy in the garage beneath the National Mall. They'd writhed through Apolline's fire circle. Now he'd given them the only thing they needed to prevail. He'd sealed his fate with fire.

But the attacking salamander screamed as steely flames burst against his skin.

Another lizard burst through the smoke, only to trip over his writhing fellow. Three more stumbled toward David, but they misjudged the distance, hitting Rosefire's biting edge instead. Another burning tree trunk crashed to the floor.

David blinked hard, peering through grey smoke. The fire-lizards had been arrayed in a half-circle around the back of the den. They'd stood like a phalanx, protecting their queen. Now they'd broken ranks, panicked by the burning ceiling.

Squinting in the murk, David could just make out a darker circle against the mud-slick floor. Ignoring the burned and burning fire-lizards, David threw himself toward the hole.

A last pair of salamanders hissed defiance, fighting the silvery conflagration to reach him. Golden crowns were emblazoned on their leather jackets. These men were Apolline's private guards, and they would stop at nothing to save their queen.

As they rushed David, he flashed a command to Rosefire. The guards careened into a wall of ward-fire and were immediately blinded, instantly destroyed by steel-grey flame.

As their bodies crisped, David reached for the dagger in the nearest lizard's hand. The salamander's fingers were scorched bone, wrapped around the obsidian knife. But to David, the volcanic blade was cool to the touch. He could not be harmed by ward-fire of his own making.

Before other guards could take their place, David sheathed his sword in the ether. He slipped the bodyguard's dagger behind his belt, nestling it against the small of his back. He raised one last blinding wall of ward-fire, thrusting it toward the well-caught ceiling, and he slid down the passage to whatever waited below.

45

Apolline Fournier sat on a throne fashioned out of the same obsidian as David's hidden knife.

Her shoulders were thrown back, emphasizing the long lines of her leather coat. Her jet black hair was sleek and manicured, not a strand out of place. A circle of crimson fire burned around her feet, tiny flames licking her boots, constantly burning but somehow never consuming the leather.

The Collar was draped around her neck.

"Warder Montrose," she said, a kiss of a French accent flavoring her words. "*Bienvenue.*"

"Apolline," he said.

She flinched, as if she smelled something rotten. He remembered Brule's refusal to reference his queen without an honorific.

Overhead, David could still make out the crackle of ward-fire, punctuated by the crash of tree limbs falling to the cavern floor. The screams of salamanders were gone. His conflagration had destroyed the last of the Apolline's guards.

"You've taken John out of commission?" she asked. The flames around her feet darkened as she spoke, as if the question cost her something dear.

He inclined his head. He would have preferred to answer by pulling Rosefire in from the ether, but there wasn't room to maneuver the sword in this tiny chamber.

Apolline accepted his silent admission with her own curt nod. "And my guards?"

"Burned or fleeing." Another branch fell above.

The salamander queen absorbed that news without changing expression. "I expected you to come with the *loup-garou*."

"He's a shifter. Not a werewolf. And he's standing guard outside." No reason for her to know Connor shivered on the shore of the creek. At least David hoped he was still *alive* to shiver.

"He sent you in to do the dirty work."

He didn't rise to the bait. "Give me the Collar, Apolline."

"The werewolves stole my karstag."

"You would have gotten it back on the night of the Hunter's Moon."

"So your *loup* said." Apolline pouted in Gallic dismissal. "But the moon came and went, and we saw no karstag."

"Connor was ousted after your fire circle. The new alpha chose not to return your knife."

He couldn't tell if she already knew Connor was out. In the end it didn't matter.

Connor had offered to broker an honest deal. Apolline could have had her karstag if she'd waited a few weeks. She'd even held David's Torch as security.

But she'd chosen to stir up chaos instead. Like an arsonist setting fire to a country church, she reveled in her ability to destroy. Salamanders were true to their nature, just as shifters were true to theirs. Warders, too.

"I'll ask you once more," David said. "By the Guardians of Fire, give me the Collar."

She laughed as if she'd never heard of the Elementals. "Why don't we try... *Comment dit-on?* Double or nothing."

"I'm not a gambling man."

"You'll want to wager for this." She reached into her corset and extracted a small brass key.

Another branch crashed upstairs, this one loud enough to sound like an entire tree trunk coming down. Soot drifted from above, and David fought to keep from choking.

Apolline clearly wanted him to ask what the key was for. He refused to give her that satisfaction—just as he would not wipe ash from his face or labor to draw a full breath in the chamber's close air.

Crimson flames surged to her knees before she smothered her disappointment. With a moue of resignation, she forfeited the round. "The key is for a post office box, in the Kalorama station. You and your lapdog visited my home near there, *n'est-ce pas*?"

He smothered his rage at the memory. "We met Brule there. We worked a fair trade."

Her lips puckered, as if she were annoyed. Or maybe she didn't care at all. "There are documents in the box. Proof that John Brule set up the...*aventure* beneath the Mall. The EBI would drop all charges against you and the *loups* if they read those papers."

His heart soared at the possibility of vindication, but he had to ask, "Why would you keep that?"

Her lips quirked in a wicked smile. "What would your cub say? To keep John on a...short leash."

David wouldn't waste time feeling sorry for Brule. The double-crossing salamander had chosen his mistress a lifetime ago. He must have known the cost of his service.

Apolline affirmed: "John knew I could give this key to anyone, anytime. Revenge if he betrayed me."

As she spoke, the fire climbed to her waist. She thrived on her power, reveled in her cruelty to an ally who had done nothing but serve her well. Her eyes gleamed like lava in the darkness.

David shed the last of his concern that the salamanders had been unfairly denied the return of their karstag. Apolline was anarchy personified. Even if she had her knife, Apolline would likely keep the Collar. Keep the Collar or find some other pretext to wreak havoc on the Washington Pack.

When David didn't respond, Apolline slowly clicked her tongue. "I grow weary of this game," she said. "My key and my Collar—I'll give them both to you."

He tensed, knowing this was the true heart of their negotiation. "And what do you want in exchange?"

"You."

"Me?" The single syllable threatened to choke him.

"With Brule gone, I need a new lieutenant. You're the perfect man for the job."

David started to laugh in disbelief. Apolline flouted the Empire's rules and regulations. She set fire to anything resembling decency among all imperial society. She maintained a blackmail file on the man she claimed to value.

But his laugh caught hard in his throat.

He'd already toppled rules without regard for consequences. He'd just ignited a supernatural fire in the heart of DC's largest public park. He'd trained a witch, when he had no business acting as a magister. He'd framed Pitt.

Apolline Fournier had every reason to think he'd serve her.

The salamander queen's laugh rippled through the tiny room, crawling down his chest like a finger tracing his sternum. "Think of the power you and I could share together. We salamanders have secrets you warders have never seen. Even the petty Bureau tyrants can't find all our lairs. No prosecution for acting according to your true nature... No penalty for being your real self..."

Brule had betrayed him.

Apolline had lit a fire circle at his feet.

The salamanders were the worst imperials he'd ever seen,

pure viciousness untempered by any form of respect. He looked into Apolline's dead eyes and said, "Never."

She howled in outrage, a soprano ululation that echoed like a battle cry. At the same time she cast off her human shell, transforming into an unbound imperial. Her skin darkened to jet traced with crimson hieroglyphs. Her face elongated into a snout, and she opened her mouth to reveal a long, forked tongue. As her clothes burned away, she unfurled sinuous limbs, multi-jointed arms and legs that ended in burning claws. The Collar still swung from her smoking neck.

"Dance, Warder," she hissed as the last of her human jaw melted away. "Dance!"

The throne burst beneath her, its volcanic glass shattering in the untamed heat of the salamander's rage. David shielded his eyes from obsidian shards, reflexively falling to the floor to avoid the shrapnel.

The air was too hot to breathe. His shirt was smoking, its cotton scorching his back. He reached behind to pull the garment from his waistband, desperate to tug it over his head. His fingers brushed against the bodyguard's dagger he'd shoved into his belt.

He clutched the blade, tightening his grip despite his sweat-slicked palm. He heard O'Rourke whisper in his memory: "Point one: Don't keep your grip loose, even if the weapon's lighter."

Forcing himself to his knees, he gained all the height he needed in the narrow chamber. O'Rourke growled inside his head: "Point two: Small spaces call for small moves."

His hair began to kindle. The knife was too hot. It seared against his palm.

He dropped the dagger then brought his open hand up, sharp and hard. As he crushed the salamander queen's larynx with the base of his palm, he heard O'Rourke's last lesson: "Point three: Don't rely too much on any blade."

Apolline rasped for breath, a hideous chitinous sound that

grated against his ears. One blow wasn't enough. He had to pick up the knife. He had to scorch his palm.

Clenching his teeth against the scalding pain, he buried the obsidian blade inside her chest.

The knife was too short to reach Apolline's heart. He couldn't kill the salamander queen. She pointed her claws at his face and rained crimson fire on his head.

Thrashing against the agony, he leaned into his weapon with all his weight. The knife was caught on something—leathery skin or splintering bone or sheer, ornery stubbornness. "Sweet Hecate!" David cried. "Goddess give me strength!"

Power surged from the Torch nestled in his pocket. Magical energy coursed through his body. Cool grey washed over his flesh, soothing his burns, healing his blistered wounds. He was sheathed in power, armored, protected.

As Hecate healed his body, she cleared his mind. He was washed clean, balanced in a place of perfect peace, ideal calm. He'd felt that way before—stable and centered, confident in all his power as a warrior for his goddess. He'd touched perfection when he completed his meditation of Snake Form, when he'd taught Kyle Hopp how to fight.

He offered up his conscious thoughts as a sacred gift to Hecate. He let each twitch of his muscles pull him deeper into his body. A pulse of violet light drifted into birdsong. The trilling sound melted into the flavor of vanilla. The sweetness coating his throat swirled into the sharp scent of juniper.

His senses merged. He felt the knife; he *was* the knife.

He guided the salamanders' obsidian blade through the warders' ancient fire form of fighting. The knife shifted a fraction of an inch, digging deeper.

Another flash of perfect unity—seeing, hearing, tasting, smelling, feeling the perfection of battle. The blade shifted again.

One more blast of wholeness, all of his senses melted into one solitary state of being.

The obsidian point pierced Apolline's heart.

The salamander queen's animal face crumpled. She threw back her head to hiss in anguish. For a heartbeat, fire flared green around her, bright as an emerald's soul, and then it faded away to nothing.

Plunged into absolute darkness, David fumbled in the ashes where Apolline had stood. His first find was easy—the Collar's heat drew his fingers. His annealed fingers closed around the iron links, protected from burning by Hecate's magic.

His second dive into the pile of ashes was harder. The brass key was so small... So delicate... It might have melted in Apolline's final conflagration. It might be destroyed forever.

But no. The key remained, trapped in the shattered base of the queen's abandoned throne. He thrust it into his pocket before he lost it in the dark, letting it settle beside his Torch.

Staggering to his feet, David was panting, desperate for a single breath that didn't stink of smoke. He turned around, trying to remember the direction of the tunnel back to the surface of the earth. He couldn't see. He couldn't breathe. He fumbled for his Torch, thinking to call on Hecate one last time. Before he could form the words, though, a single shaft of light cut through the darkness.

He blinked, thinking his eyes were failing, but then he made out the shadow of a hand.

"David?"

Connor's voice was hoarse and cracked and sweeter than any other sound in the world.

"Here!" he managed, stumbling forward.

The shifter's fingers closed around his own, guiding him out of the salamanders' hell.

46

David stood in the garden of the Peabridge Library, shivering as a blood-colored sunset glinted on the cottage windows. His brain knew it wasn't on fire, but his heart took a moment to catch up.

He'd already weathered a dozen rounds of panic since climbing out of the hole in the middle of Rock Creek Park. Only now, at the end of the longest day of his life, was it becoming reflexive to shut down the memories, to remind his body that he was alive, that all was well.

Hecate had rescued him. Against all odds, he *was* alive.

Connor had guided him to safety. He'd blinked in the shifting sunshine under the trees, wondering if he'd hallucinated everything that had happened underground. The salamanders' lair had completely collapsed, consumed by ward-fire. The creek flowed fast and clear in its usual bed as if it had never been diverted.

Despite their exhaustion, he and Connor had searched for the remains of more than two dozen salamanders to hide all evidence of their supernatural battle. Bodies should have fetched up against banks. Corpses should have been trapped in the curves of the stream. But it soon became clear there was nothing to find. Ward-fire—or Hecate—had scoured all evidence clean.

The only thing left was a hole in the ground, the chamber where Apolline had died. Looking up from the newly channeled stream, David and Connor could scarcely discern the gap in the forest floor. They dragged a few branches over the place, enough to keep the shaft from attracting casual hikers.

After that, David had used the last of his energy to wrap his arm around Connor's shoulders. Taking as much support as he gave, he *reached* for the farmhouse, pulling the shifter with him across the astral plane. He couldn't remember staggering into the house, up the stairs, and into his own bed, where he'd awakened several hours later.

He'd limped downstairs to find Connor asleep on the living room floor, his back pressed up against Spot. The lab had looked up when David entered the room, his tail hitting the floor in slow even sweeps. David nodded and headed back upstairs for a shower and clean clothes.

Now, as he stared at Jane's home, the door swung open. Neko waited on the threshold, a shadow barely distinguishable from the living room inside. As David entered, the familiar sniffed delicately, as if he could still make out the scent of smoke. Neko, however, graciously declined to comment.

"You got her home?" David asked.

The familiar cocked his head as if David had just told a joke. "She got herself home. She's good at that sort of thing."

"What happened up there?"

"How much could you follow?"

"I caught Jason's name. And a lot of self-flagellation. I gather the Imaginary Boyfriend left something to be desired?"

"The Imaginary Boyfriend was someone else's Actual Husband."

David winced. He'd known the guy was off from the moment

they'd met. But he'd never wanted those bragging rights. Not where Jane was involved. "She didn't deserve that," he said.

"No one does."

David looked around the darkened cottage. "She's asleep now?"

"I think so. She's in the basement."

"What's she doing down there?" David took three whole steps before Neko got a hand on his sleeve.

"Not using her powers," the familiar assured him. "She's working through some things. About Jason. About Scott. About a certain familiar who might not have restrained himself when he came home to an unlocked door and a very tempting superannuated tetra."

"You ate Stupid Fish?" David asked in disbelief. "I warned her about that, but I never actually thought…"

Neko dropped his head, as if he felt actual remorse.

"Wait," David said. "Who is *Scott*?"

"An old boyfriend. An old fiancé actually. She hasn't told me a lot more than that."

"He must have been a controlling SOB."

"Why do you say that?"

"She called me Scott when I was pressuring her to work on the crystals."

Neko smirked. "She did, didn't she? Well you *were* a little… domineering. I guess that's not surprising. You must be under a lot of pressure to present yourself to Hecate on Samhain."

"I'm not presenting myself to Hecate."

"Of course you are!"

"I'd need a witch to ward."

"You've got one. She'll get tired of living in the basement. I give her three days. Four at the most." Neko spoke with all the confidence of an experienced familiar.

"She'll never accept me as her warder," David said.

"She already has." At David's wordless expression of disbelief,

Neko said, "She has! It never occurred to her to choose anyone else."

Of course it hadn't. Jane hadn't been trained in a magicarium. She didn't belong to a coven. She didn't have the first idea of how to be a witch.

Neko stared at him as if he were mad. "Come on!" he said. "You felt her when she was all the way up in Connecticut."

"I'd feel her anywhere," David said, before he realized how much he was admitting. He crammed his hands into his pockets. His thumb brushed against his Torch. The metal was warm to his touch.

"There," Neko said, with a familiar's absolute certainty of facts he couldn't possibly know. "You're still a warder. Hecate clearly thinks so."

Hecate, who primed his Torch. Hecate, who'd answered his prayers in Apolline's chamber of horrors. Hecate, who sanctioned the entire idea of a warder who stood outside of the Academy, outside of reason and expectation, outside of order.

Hecate, who hadn't abandoned him, even after he'd built his lies about Pitt.

"There's only a week till Samhain," Neko said. "You can still change your mind."

Only a week. Seven more days of living a life out of balance. If only Hecate willed it so.

He nodded toward the basement. "Let me know if she needs anything?"

"Of course. We'll see you on Samhain, if not before. *After* your ritual."

The familiar sounded so certain, David couldn't imagine there was anything else to say. He let himself out the front door and *reached* for home.

47

L ife without a day job kept David busy.

On Monday, he took Apolline's key to her post office and collected the documents she'd held against Brule. Everything was in order, and he delivered them directly to the Empire Bureau of Investigation.

On Tuesday, he helped Connor move into a condo in the trendy NoMa neighborhood. The shifter would be deprived of his possessions, his beehives, and the companionship of his pack, but at least his one-bedroom came with windows on two sides, for better viewing of the moon.

On Wednesday, he tracked down a pair of gnomes to fill in the riverside hole in Rock Creek Park. It cost him two pieces of new-minted gold, but he considered the coins well spent.

On Thursday, he visited Linda for breakfast and told her he was prepared to offer himself to Hecate, presenting his bond to Jane as proof of his worthiness. She blinked away tears and told him she was proud of him. Immediately after that, she asked if he'd come to dinner with his father, but he declined. Of course.

On Friday, Saturday, and Sunday, he prepared for his ritual. He fasted, purifying his body in service to his goddess. He drank nothing but pure rainwater collected in a silver basin on the night of a full moon. He bathed at moonrise and moonset, embracing the rhythm of the natural world, taking care to scrub away the last possible scent of his fiery ordeal beneath the earth.

For the entire week, he worried about Norville Pitt. He should have heard about the court's action by now, steps they'd taken to handle their wayward official. Kyle should have filled him in even if no one else did. The cadet knew enough about the bad blood between David and Pitt.

But there was absolute silence from the court. Maybe they were taking time to review all of David's concocted files. Maybe they were making inquiries, tracking down other—possibly real —offenses.

Perhaps he never should have planted the documents. If he'd been patient, Pitt surely would have exposed his true self, the way he had during David's first week on the job. The double billing for the Atlanta centerstone had really happened; David hadn't created it out of whole cloth. Pitt would eventually have been caught making more mistakes.

But how many years would that have taken? How many careers would have been destroyed in the meantime? Would Kyle have suffered? Other well-intentioned warders?

David had done what he had to do. And Hecate herself could not be too upset. The goddess had come to him in the salamanders' lair. She'd given him the strength to pierce Apolline's heart. She'd guided his hands to the Collar and the key.

Sunday evening, David dressed in khakis and a soft flannel shirt. He'd come to think of the clothes as "Jane" clothes, one of the outfits he'd worn as he taught her about crystals, as she learned that she could trust him. He fed Spot an early dinner, then made his way down to the lake just before sunset, carrying a woven basket of supplies.

The last glints of daylight melted across the glassy water, reflecting the oak tree and the osprey nest in its rose-colored sheen. He paused at the end of the beach, the toes of his shoes almost touching the water.

He wanted to make some offering, some gesture of appreciation to the sprite who had stood by him against Apolline. But Bourne was long gone now. The lake already felt different—less conscious, less aware. It had gone back to being a passive provider of life to fish and fowl, grass and reed.

The sun was barely visible over the horizon, a rind of orange glowing above the trees. The boundaries between the astral world and the mundane were thinnest now, stretched between day and night, between wakefulness and sleep, between known and unknown. Hurrying, because he dared not lose the crux of transitional power, he stripped off his clothes.

The evening air was cold against his flesh, but he'd learned at the Academy to overlook physical discomfort. He turned his concentration to the basket he'd brought down from the house.

Taking care, he lifted out a small handmade broom. It was made of birch twigs, bound with willow withes to a staff of ash. It had been a gift from Linda, the day he'd first been bonded to Haylee. It was time to consecrate the broom to better service.

With the confidence of familiarity, he walked to a point halfway up the beach. As he lowered the broom to the sand, a clear chime sounded in his head, the sound of the shortest bar on a xylophone being struck with a metal mallet. He swept from left to right, slow, even strokes that revealed a length of sun-bleached driftwood. Returning to the basket, he took out a candle made of jet-black wax. He set it in a hollow of the embedded wood, taking care that it was perfectly level.

After the candle was set, he walked a perfect arc ninety degrees to the south. A splash of lemon arced across his tongue, sour and bright. Once again, he swept the sand, revealing a stretch of gnarled driftwood. He produced another candle from the basket, burgundy this time, and balanced it on the bleached wood plinth.

Another curving walk. The taste of caramel, creamy and rich. More sand swept, a third driftwood marker, a deep violet candle placed.

He ended at the north. The prickle of sun-dried hay scratched against his face, down his arms, and across the backs of his thighs. He swept sand from the driftwood and placed the candle, burnt orange against white.

When the four cardinal points were set, he took the last thing from the basket—his Hecate's Torch, strung on a band of shimmering black silk. He settled the ribbon around his neck, taking care to nestle the emblem over his heart. The metal was already the same temperature as his body.

Taking a deep breath, he found the precise center of the circle he'd created. He planted his feet in the sand and reached into the ether. It was comforting to find Rosefire waiting for him. He folded his fingers around the grip and pulled the sword through.

Sword in hand, Torch on heart, he turned to the eastern corner where he'd started his rite. Pointing at the candle's wick, he intoned, "If Hecate wills it, may the Guardians of Air light my way."

He was a warder, not a witch. He didn't have the power to work spells, to master the primary elements of the universe. His role was to nurture and protect, and maybe, just maybe, to teach.

But Hecate could lend him her strength. The witches' sacred goddess could intercede on his behalf as she had in Apolline's lair. Focusing on the silver emblem that lay upon his chest, he caught his breath and waited to see if Hecate still looked on him with favor.

The wick kindled.

As power rose through that quadrant of his circle, he turned to the south. Once again, he pointed and spoke, "If Hecate wills it, may the Guardians of Fire light my way." The candle leaped to life and the southern arc was secure.

He repeated the process in the west and north. When he was

through, he was centered in a circle of steely light. The shimmering haze softened his view of the beach, the dock, and the lake.

Drawing a deep breath, he sank to his knees in the precise center of the space, resting Rosefire on the smooth-swept sand before him. Only after he was settled, balanced in body and mind, did he extend his arms to either side. Palms up, head bowed, he offered his plea to Hecate.

A witch would have an incantation tried and true. He had nothing but the desire of his heart, the words he'd been thinking for days, for weeks, ever since Linda first proposed the notion of making a Samhain offering.

"Hear me, Hecate, though I am not worthy. I come before you as a warder, a man sworn to serve you, to act always as you will. In the past, I offered my sword in protection of your daughter, and I was found wanting." He pictured Haylee, her shrewd eyes and cruel lips. "I beg forgiveness for my failures. I kneel before you, a hopeful penitent."

He waited, in case Hecate chose to give him a sign. She could reject his plea without cause, forcing him to set aside his quest before he'd even begun.

But the candles continued to burn strong at the cardinal points. As near as he could tell, the air remained still outside his sheltering arc. No sand blew. No waves broke upon the beach.

Taking heart that he wasn't dismissed out of hand, he braced himself to make his true request. He raised his head, then lifted Rosefire from the sand. He extended the blade before him, balanced on his open palms. The weight of the sword tugged at his wrists, pulling at his shoulders. But he braced himself and offered all he had to give.

"Look on me with favor, Goddess. Let me raise this sword in your honor. Let me protect the vulnerable and guide the lost. Let me teach the unknowing. I beg you, honored Hecate, to allow me the grace that is solely yours to grant. Blessed Goddess, bind me to a witch this Samhain night. Allow me to serve your daughter, Jane Madison, daughter of Sarah, daughter of Abigail, of no known Coven."

As he completed his prayer, he pictured Jane as he'd seen her the night they met, her auburn hair sparking in the soft light of the cottage, her hazel eyes blazing with defiance. He remembered her sitting across from him at La Chaumiere, pushing to understand the shape of the new world she'd joined, the meaning of a sisterhood of witches. He felt the force of her fire-banishing spell, searing across the ether, and the sheer power as she bound healing strength to the first aventurine crystal she'd ever encountered.

She laughed. She wept. She was a witch enrobed in the all the power of her kind, strong and terrible and proud.

For an endless moment, there was nothing.

Then he was crushed by the goddess.

Magic flooded him, suffusing his body and capsizing his mind. For decades, he'd discerned individual strands of power—sights and scents, sounds and tastes and touch. Hecate was all those and more: A perfect light woven of all the colors of the rainbow, a symphony composed of every sound he'd ever heard, a banquet of flavors filling his nose, wrapping his tongue, enrobing his throat. She covered his body; she *became* his flesh.

He was the goddess, and she was him, perfectly empty, perfectly full. She tested every crevice in his heart, every fold of his brain. She held him in an empty void, perfect and endless and unchanging. He could not measure time. He'd lost the anchor of his worldly body in space.

One moment, he was lost. Suspended. Gone.

The next, he was drawing breath—a jasmine-filled gasp that flooded his lungs and suffused his being.

Hecate spoke through that heavy cloud of sweetness. Her words formed in the air around him, vibrating through every bone in his body. "I hear you, child. Your heart is pure and your desire sound. Go forth, warder, and protect your witch. Be bound to Jane Madison, daughter of Sarah, daughter of Abigail, of no known Coven, until such time as she desires to walk alone. Serve her and guide her and teach her in all my ways. So mote it be."

The goddess's declaration ended in a flash of sound, a crash of light, a brilliant, chaotic overwhelming of every sense he had, of every sense he could imagine. The earth trembled and the air shook, and his carefully constructed circle buckled and swayed and came crashing down around him in a perfect rain of power that soaked into the sand. The candles leaped skyward, transforming into torches, their wicks annihilating their perfect columns of wax. Sand rose up to the heavens, only to drift back to earth, covering the driftwood markers as if they'd never been exposed.

David was a naked man, kneeling on a beach, holding a sword that threatened to pull his arms from his sockets.

He staggered to his feet. Water lapped against the beach, soft ripples sinking into the sand. A fish jumped, somewhere out on the open water. A quartet of bats flew overhead, swooping high above the lake for a buffet of mosquitos and gnats.

He'd done it. He'd offered all he had to give to the only goddess he'd ever served, and she'd found him worthy. He was bonded with Jane Madison.

With a grateful sigh, he banished Rosefire to its astral sheath. Despite the trembling in his arms, he felt invigorated, wholly alive in a way he hadn't been for years, maybe forever. He took one step, then another and another, still feeling the remnants of power through the soles of his feet.

He didn't need to retrieve his candles; they'd been consumed by his rite. There was only the basket, with his broom and his clothes. He stepped into his trousers and pulled on his shirt, each gesture feeling like a tiny offering to Hecate, a show of gratitude for the energy that suffused his body. He slipped on his shoes and headed back to the house.

The woods were more alive than he'd ever known before. Maybe this was what it was like for Bourne, this hyper-awareness of every animal that crossed his path, every plant that spread roots beneath his feet. He could see them all in the darkness, limned with an ethereal glow. He could hear them, down to the whisper of breeze against the ridges of a fallen pine cone, swirling and echoing in the night. So much life, so much power— it was nearly more than his warder brain could process.

That was the only explanation for why he didn't see the man lurking on his porch until he stood on the bottom step.

48

N orville Pitt was framed by the door. His eyeglasses caught the moonlight, smudged fingerprints obscuring his eyes like pools of stagnant water. On this Samhain night, he wore what passed for casual attire—a plasticized track suit of dingy beige, with rusty racing stripes bleeding down his legs. His forehead shone as he stepped forward, moving to the edge of the porch.

David had known this moment would come. Truth be told, he'd longed for it. He'd wanted to stare into Pitt's eyes when the man realized his career was sunk. He'd wanted to hear that wheezing intake of breath as first one email then another and another and another came to light, quoted by the court, forwarded by the witches Pitt only claimed to serve. He'd wanted to watch Pitt die just a little, shriveling up in anguished rage as he realized he was through terrorizing the clerk's office.

But he hadn't anticipated Pitt looming over him in the moonlight. Rather than crane his neck, David took two measured steps back. It felt awkward to clutch the basket, but he wasn't going to give the toad the satisfaction of summoning his sword, or taking any other action that reflected the slightest hint of concern.

Truth be told, though, he *was* concerned. Because Pitt should have been here a full week earlier. He should have come during daylight, frantic, broken. Something was very, very wrong.

Pitt reached into the pocket of his crinkling track suit and pulled out a thumb drive. David barely cut off an astonished gasp. There was no way the man had reconstructed the device David had destroyed, no way he had mended the bent memory chip, restoring it to its metal bed and plastic shell.

With an awkward twist of his wrist, Pitt flipped the drive to David, who caught it automatically. "What's this?" David asked, not bothering to study the anonymous bit of plastic.

"A little light reading material," Pitt said. "Oh. Wait. I think you've read this crap before."

"I don't know what you're talking about," David said. But he had to admit his words were not convincing. They sounded frayed. Torn. As if all the power and glory of Hecate by the lake had evaporated into the cool night air.

"Ah, ah, ah!" Pitt scolded, wagging his finger as if he were disciplining a dog that had soiled the rug. "Hecate doesn't take much to liars. Especially on the very night of Samhain."

Cold sweat slicked David's palms. He buried the thumb drive in his basket. "What do you want, Pitt?"

"I *want* you to stand before the court and tell them you were responsible for sending that pack of utter lies. I *want* you stripped of your Torch and your sword. I *want* you drummed out of the warder corps forever."

David's throat was too dry for him to swallow. He could hear Spot barking inside the house. He knew he should call out a command, get the dog to stop, but he was afraid he wouldn't be able to voice even that single syllable.

"But none of that is going to happen," Pitt said. "Not yet."

"I don't know what lies you're talking about," David finally managed. "I haven't sent anything to the court. My computer is clean—a fact I'll happily show to anyone who cares to look."

"Now David, I am truly disappointed in you. All these months —*years*—you've worked for me, and you still don't understand the importance of details. I didn't *say* you had files on your computer. You're not a total idiot. I'm certain you created a new account, that you saved your data somewhere in the cloud. Maybe on a drive like the one you just placed in your pocket."

Pitt couldn't know. David had left no trace. Not on his computer. Not anywhere.

He stayed silent, rather than give anything away.

Pitt laughed. "If you could see your face now... I don't need a thumb drive with evidence. I collected all the proof I needed as you typed your vicious lies. I captured every single keystroke, transmitted directly from your keyboard. You really should work on the typos, son. They're hell on your overall productivity."

Pitt was bluffing. Telling his own lies. Pitt tracked his keystrokes at the office, but he'd never had access to the farmhouse. There was no way he could know what David had typed in the privacy of his own home.

But as David started to deny everything, his boss planted his feet, linking his fingers behind his back like a schoolboy quoting from some ancient text. "Memorandum dated March 27, for the purchase of a silver athame intended for use by the Washington Coven in rites conducted by Teresa Alison Sidney—"

David had typed the words himself. He'd made up the purchase, cited the Washington Coven Mother in his attempt to bring down Pitt. Nevertheless, he spluttered, "Those emails have already been sent. The judges already know—"

"It didn't take a genius to block the court's incoming emails from unknown sources. Enhancements to judicial efficiency— you should appreciate that. Your eager beaver Hopp was only too happy to implement the change."

Kyle, used against him. David was doomed. Lost. Destroyed.

"What do you want?" he asked, each word sharper against his throat than the business edge of Rosefire.

Pitt gloated. "Nothing, for now. I'm not going to do anything tonight. I'm going to wait until the time is right, and then I'll use my information. Until then, you can keep doing whatever you want to do. Pledge your right arm in the service of a witch, if you can find one foolish or desperate enough to accept you. But be fully aware that some day, when you least expect it, when all seems well and you're coasting along like you don't have a single care in the world... I'll be waiting. I'll be waiting, and I'll be ready —to share every word of your disgusting lies to Hecate's Court. And there's nothing you can do to stop me."

Pitt threw back his head and laughed, once again distorting pure beams of moonlight on his eyeglasses. David resisted the urge to leap up the stairs, to close his fingers around the man's neck and rid himself of all his problems once and for all. Before he could think of a reply, impotent words to raise in defense, Pitt disappeared, *reaching* somewhere only he could know.

David should admit his failings to the court now. Subject himself to their justice. Beg for mercy and hope that somehow, in maybe a decade or two, he'd be allowed to clean toilets in the basement of the office building.

But when he finally climbed the steps of the farmhouse, he caught a whiff of the jasmine scent that had enveloped him on the beach. Hecate had stood by him in his ritual. She was a goddess; she knew all he'd ever done, all he'd ever thought of doing. She'd accepted him as her warder, despite his lying about Pitt.

He bowed his head, fighting to push down a swirl of emotions —anger with himself, shame for what he'd done, anxious, desperate hope. "Give me some sign, Hecate. Show me your will. Tell me if you'll accept my service, knowing all you know."

He caught his breath, waiting for an omen. And then he had it—a wash of jasmine against the back of his throat, headier and sweeter than he'd ever sensed before. *Jane*, his brain chimed.

And Hecate's energy rose within him—her light and her song and her glorious terrible power. "Serve my daughter," he heard, each word echoing through the caverns of his mind. "Serve Jane Madison."

He *reached* for the cottage in the Peabridge Library garden.

49

H e stood on the stairs that led to the basement, listening to Jane chatter. "I promised Gran," she said. "The day Evelyn told me I'd be living here in the cottage, Gran called at work and made me promise not to lick any toads."

"What sort of fool would lick a toad?" Neko sounded scandalized.

"My point exactly. I promised, without considering the consequences. Drinking a potion poured over the skin of a toad might violate the spirit of my promise."

The familiar had to be pushing her toward the elixir of joy, one of those ancient potions that had probably never worked but had found its way into the oldest magic books. Rainwater, bluebird wing, apple blossoms, all poured over the back of a garden toad...

Neko sounded surprised. "You've got to be kidding."

"Nope." Jane replied, and he could picture the stubborn tilt of her chin. "I'll talk to Gran. Take back my promise. But not tonight."

"Would she ever know? I mean, I don't think the elixir of joy is what she had in mind when she called."

Bingo. David had correctly remembered the ancient text.

Jane said, "A promise is a promise. We've always trusted each other. Besides, I'm pretty sure she *would* know. When I was a kid, she could always tell when I was lying."

The simple statement pricked David's conscience. Jane wouldn't take kindly to discovering he was eavesdropping on her conversation. Averting potential disaster, he moved down the last three steps, entering the basement before he said, "Now that sounds like a witchy power, if ever there was one."

She startled visibly, but he saw the moment she recognized his voice. As she turned to greet him, a faint smile played about her lips. "I don't think I invited you in."

David inclined his head up the stairs. "Warder's rights, remember? In any case, you shouldn't leave your front door unlocked, if you don't want visitors. Especially on Halloween. Who can say how many ghosts and goblins might take up residence here?"

At the same time, he shot a silent message toward Neko. *"Help a warder out? Give me a minute to talk to Jane. Alone."*

The familiar shook his head, a tiny flicker of disagreement. *"She's terrified you'll punish her for working spells at the Farm."*

"By Hecate, I'll never do anything to hurt her."

The familiar was no fool. He correctly read David's sincerity, all the devotion he'd ever sworn to Hecate transferred to the witch who stood between them. Neko stood and stretched with deceptive casualness. Pointing toward the disputed lock upstairs, he said, "I'll go check on it."

"You don't have to," Jane said.

So she didn't want to be alone with him. Probably didn't want to be alone with any man, after the fiasco at the farm. David sent another mental nudge toward Neko.

"No," the familiar said to his witch, but his eyes stayed on David. "But I need to, um, get a drink of water." And he was gone, before Jane could beg him to stay.

David's witch wasn't a coward. She took a deep breath and turned to face him directly. "So," she said.

"So," he repeated.

"Just how much trouble am I in, for Connecticut?"

He studied her face for several heartbeats. "If you'd stuck around till I arrived? You'd still be unable to use your powers. I would have locked your witchcraft down so tightly, you wouldn't be able to watch *The Wizard of Oz.*"

"But now?" she asked warily.

"Now, I've had a chance to calm down. Neko explained everything to me." Neko had explained. And Pitt had reminded him of the stupid things anyone could do, even when they had good intentions.

And Hecate had spoken. Most of all, Hecate had spoken, confirming that he was exactly where he was supposed to be, doing exactly what he'd trained to do.

"Everything?" Jane blushed, and he knew she was ashamed of how she'd let herself be fooled by that lying, pretentious jackass of a professor.

"Enough," he said.

"I suppose you're here to gloat over the mess I made of things."

"Mess? It seems to me that everything worked out pretty well."

She shrugged. "If you don't count lying, cheating, and deception."

He didn't. He couldn't. But he asked, "Who did you lie to?"

"Harold? Jason. Mr. Potter." Suddenly, she looked stricken. "You! Oh my God, you too. That's why you kissed me that night. That's why you changed your clothes, why you became something you weren't. You were caught up in the love spell too! Be free, dammit! Just leave me alone!"

She froze, like she was listening for a distant sound. Her

hands extended toward the ceiling, fingers pointed as if she were summoning Hecate directly.

He'd kissed her because he'd been a fool, a schoolboy lost without the anchor of his Torch. He'd started wearing clothes that he knew wouldn't intimidate her, wouldn't make her think of every man who'd ever held a position of power over her. If not for her obvious distress, this would all be a funny misunderstanding.

Okay, it *was* funny, distressed witch or not. He let some of his amusement sift into his voice. "Jane, I don't have any idea what you're talking about."

She crossed to the cracked leather couch and collapsed against its cushions. "That first spell I did, the grimoire spell. It worked, but it made too many men fall in love with me."

She actually thought her little love spell had reached them all. Him. Mr. Potter, whoever that was. Her disastrous excuse for a boyfriend. The poor janitor at the library. She believed her working had ensorcelled them all for days, weeks...

He crossed his arms and shook his head. "You don't get it, do you?"

"Get what?"

Her stubborn question woke a bubble of laughter inside his chest. "The way spells work."

"I think I have a pretty good idea. You've been a good guide to all this witchcraft stuff, and Neko helped a lot too."

She was so damned earnest. He could respect that. He could pity her, too. She'd been trying to make her way through a strange new world, and neither he nor the familiar upstairs had turned out to be a very good guide. In fact, he admitted as much: "Well, neither of us taught you enough about the grimoire spell."

She ground her teeth. "No time like the present, then. What about it? Did I change the balance of the universe as we know it? Have I set the world of Faerie upside down, releasing petty spirit vengeance on all the world?"

"Nothing quite as dramatic as that," he said, trying not to

laugh as he sat beside her. First things first. He had to reassure her she wasn't the monster she'd become in her own mind. He took a deep breath and met her eyes. "The grimoire spell only worked on the first man you saw after you worked it."

"The first man..." She trailed off, clearly thinking back to the night she'd worked that initial spell. "Neko!"

"No." He shook his head in brief annoyance. Even now he wasn't making things clear. "Neko doesn't count. For purposes of magic, he's a part of you."

She blushed again. It seemed to take an effort, but she said, "You, then."

"No. Warders are immune to their witch's workings."

"Then the first man was...Harold."

"Precisely."

"But the others? Jason, finally realizing I was alive? Mr. Zimmer, ordering coffee? Mr. Potter, talking to me at Gran's, and at the Gala, and making his donation to the Peabridge?"

This was important. He had to make her understand her innocence. "Just Harold," he insisted. "The spell bonds to the first man. The others weren't caught up in your magic."

He watched her process what he said. She clearly wanted to argue, wanted to fight. But she finally asked, "But why? Why would everything change now, all at once?"

David gestured smoothly. "Look at yourself." She glanced at her jeans. She raised her fingers to her hair. "You're the one who's different, Jane."

"I'm not! I'm the same person I've always been!"

"Are you, really?" He tried to keep his voice soothing, knowing instinctively that she'd reject his next words: "You've cut your hair. You grew out your nails. You put on makeup every morning and touched it up during the day. You started wearing contact lenses."

It felt odd to say those words to her. Intimate. But she was his witch, and she needed his reassurance. When she started to get up from the couch, clearly uncomfortable, he reached out and grabbed her wrist. "We men are really dumb creatures, you know. We can be led anywhere by our...senses."

He'd started to say something else, but she wasn't ready for that. She already seemed dangerously close to dying of mortification.

"Jane," he said, and he removed his fingers from her wrist, only to cup her jaw with his palm. "You've grown. You've changed. You like yourself more, and people can see that. *Men* can see that. You have confidence. You're at ease—and that draws us like flies to honey."

His fingers tingled where they touched her skin. He was nearly overwhelmed by the scent of jasmine, by the heady essence of this woman he'd sworn to protect.

He watched her accept what he was saying. Her shoulders straightened. A light kindled deep in her hazel eyes. She measured out a reply and made the decision to challenge him. "And you? If self-love and independence are symbolized by wardrobe shifts, what are you doing in those clothes?"

He glanced down and shrugged. He could tell her about Hecate. He could explain about his rite on the beach, about the goddess binding them together with the power of Samhain.

But that was too much. More than she could needed to hear tonight. So he answered her with other words, honest ones, but less supernatural. "I've grown, too. I'm not the same warder who was fired by my last witch. If I'm going to succeed as a warder, as *your* warder, I'm going to succeed on my ability to guide you, to protect you. No one will care if I wear stiff, formal clothes or magical robes inscribed with symbols." Her skepticism felt like a physical veil between them. He fought for more words, different words, words that would convince her. "I like myself this way."

She actually laughed out loud. "That, I understand."

He joined her in laughter then, all the tension between them drifting away. She *did* understand—on some essential level. As their laughter trailed off, he looked around the basement. "I like what you've done to the place."

"Really?"

She wanted his approval. She needed it. She needed him.

He got up to study the nearest bookshelf, walked to the next one, and eventually traced his way around the entire room. He nodded when he found the spice chest, and he took note of the tackle box full of crystals. He made a mental inventory of the little cauldrons and other witchy supplies stored on their respective shelves. "A place for everything," he pronounced at last. "And everything in its place."

She beamed her appreciation. "It just feels...right like this. I hadn't realized how much the disorganization was bothering me."

"So now it seems like you're truly ready to study. Ready to learn."

A frown wrinkled her forehead, and she caught her lip between her teeth before she asked, "What about the coven? What are the chances they'll challenge me for all this? For Hannah Osgood's collection?"

David shrugged. "High." Higher, now that he'd made an enemy of Norville Pitt. And if Teresa Alison Sidney ever found out he'd dragged her name into his fabricated documents... He kept his voice even. "They'll say you aren't skilled. You aren't trained. You don't know what to do with everything you have."

He watched indignation bloom across her face.

Before she could protest, he said, "They'll *say* that. But they probably won't succeed. For one thing, they could never come up with a list of everything that's here. They'd have to, to convince Hecate's Court that the books belong to them."

She nodded, but her voice became very small. "But they'll definitely try?"

"They'll definitely try," he confirmed, because his bonded witch deserved his telling her the truth. "But that will take a long time. In the meantime, you can learn more about using your powers."

She caught her breath, and yearning splashed across her face. "You'll teach me?" she asked.

He wanted to. He wanted to do anything she desired. But he had to say, "Jane, I told you before, I'm not supposed to be a teacher. I'm a warder."

"Then, you'll...ward me? Be my guide? Keep me safe?"

He looked at her for a long time. His life had been insane from the first moment he'd been pulled into this cottage. He'd been thrown from one battle to the next, from Pitt to salamanders to shifters to a tender new witch who needed him to stand fast. He'd doubted himself. He'd doubted the entire magical world of the Eastern Empire.

But Hecate had spoken. The goddess had bound them together, and that was more than he could ever have hoped when he'd first pounded on the cottage door in the middle of a driving storm.

"Please," Jane said. "As warder to witch. Say you'll help me."

He nodded gravely. "As warder to witch."

She reached out to embrace him, and he tensed. He couldn't help himself. He was the one who had introduced confusion into their relationship. He was the one who had kissed her when he was off balance, when his Torch was gone, when he'd forgotten what he was trained to do and who he was supposed to be.

But she turned her face away, settling safely, platonically, in his arms. As he allowed himself to relax, he felt her gain strength. She took a deep breath and seemed to set aside her own past. She was embarking on a new journey, same as he was.

Pulling back, she said, "We should celebrate." He saw the moment she remembered his rules, his regulations—more important now than ever, if he was truly to keep her safe from the power she could wield. Especially tonight, on Samhain. "Not with alcohol," she amended. "How about a cup of tea?"

He followed her upstairs to the kitchen. Neko had made himself useful, putting on the kettle and setting out a teapot along with mugs and his monstrous pitcher of cream.

The familiar looked up as they entered the room. He studied his witch, weighing, measuring, calculating every last gram of her emotions.

And then he turned a long look on David, asking a thousand silent questions. David couldn't give him answers, not in words, not even in specific thoughts. But he gathered up his recollection of Hecate's presence on the beach—the glory and the power of the goddess directing him here, binding him to his Samhain witch. He opened his mind enough to share that pure presence with Neko, hoping the familiar would understand.

At last, Neko seemed to agree his witch was safe. With a flashing grin, he asked, "Trick or treat?"

"Treat," David and Jane said at the same time.

It wasn't going to be easy. Pitt still held David's mistake in abeyance; the man could present his evidence at any time. The Eastern Empire would be unsettled by the salamanders' destruction in the lair beneath Rock Creek Park. The shifters had to settle under a new alpha, and Connor was left to find his own way in the world, a solitary brute.

But David had sworn to protect his witch in a magic circle on a moonlit beach, and the only goddess he'd ever served had accepted his oath of loyalty.

None of it would be easy.

But it would definitely be a treat.

GIRL'S GUIDE TO WITCHCRAFT

Did you enjoy David's story? Did it leave you wondering what Jane was doing while David fought the salamanders? Well, you're in luck!

You can read Jane's version of the events in *The Library, the Witch, and the Warder*. Her book is called *Girl's Guide to Witchcraft*, and it's the first volume in the Washington Witches Series (part of the Magical Washington universe).

Girl's Guide to Witchcraft is available in print and as an ebook.

MORE MAGICAL WASHINGTON

David and Jane are working well together now, but there are more magical adventures afoot in Washington DC. Check out these other books in the Magical Washington universe!

∽

Fright Court

Sarah Anderson found her dream job: Clerk of Court for the District of Columbia Night Court. But after she's attacked by a supernatural defendant, she's forced to take self-defense lessons from her boss, the enigmatic vampire James Morton. When a deceptively easy-going reporter starts to ask questions, Sarah wonders just what answers she's supposed to give. Will Sarah be able to create order in the court?

Stake Me Out to the Ball Game

Ava Buchanan is a vampire with a toothache! Desperate for

distraction she heads to a baseball game. At the stadium, she finds herself seated next to the perfect man, Dennis Maugham. There's just one catch: Dennis is human. Can Ava gain her heart's desire while continuing to hide her supernatural existence?

ABOUT THE AUTHOR

Mindy Klasky learned to read when her parents shoved a book in her hands and told her she could travel anywhere in the world through stories. She never forgot that advice. Mindy's travels took her through multiple careers—from litigator to librarian to full-time writer. Mindy's travels have also taken her through various literary genres, including cozy paranormal, hot contemporary romance, and traditional fantasy. She is a *USA Today* bestselling author, and she has received the Career Achievement Award from the Washington Romance Writers.

In her spare time, Mindy knits, quilts, and tries to tame her endless to-be-read shelf. Her husband and cats do their best to fill the left-over minutes.

ABOUT BOOK VIEW CAFÉ

Book View Café Publishing Cooperative (BVC) is an author-owned cooperative of over fifty professional writers, publishing in a variety of genres including fantasy, romance, mystery, and science fiction.

BVC authors include *New York Times* and *USA Today* bestsellers along with winners and nominees of many prestigious publishing awards.

Since its debut in 2008, BVC has gained a reputation for producing high-quality ebooks. BVC's ebooks are DRM-free and are distributed around the world. The cooperative is now bringing that same quality to its print editions.

Sign up for BVC's newsletter to find out about sales, promotions, and new books!

www.bookviewcafe.com